PRAISE FOR THE COSTUME SHOP MYSTERIES

"[A] quirky cast of characters, a fascinating setting, a fast-paced plot, and yummy recipes . . . [A] thoroughly appealing whodunit that will keep you guessing all-night long."
—Kate Carlisle, *New York Times* bestselling author of the Fixer-Upper Mysteries and the Bibliophile Mysteries

"Both madcap and moving, *A Disguise to Die For* has the right amount of humor, poignancy, and danger for a most irresistible whodunit. Highly recommended!"
—Naomi Hirahara, Edgar® Award–winning author of the Officer Ellie Rush Mysteries

"A fresh, funny voice, irresistible characters—and oh, the costumes! No disguising the fact that Diane Vallere's new cozy is a winner."
—Lucy Burdette, national bestselling author of the Key West Food Critic Mysteries

"An unpredictable mystery that serves to both entertain and spark creativity in readers, who may don a costume just for the joy of it."
—Kings River Life Magazine

"The book has depth and the plot is solid. The dialogue between the characters is fluid and the story is fast paced. The murderer(s) is hidden among a myriad of potential suspects and isn't easily figured out . . . Fantastic."
—Sleuth Cafe

Dressed
to Confess

DIANE VALLERE

BERKLEY PRIME CRIME
New York

BERKLEY PRIME CRIME
Published by Berkley
An imprint of Penguin Random House LLC
375 Hudson Street, New York, New York 10014

ISBN: 9780425278307

First Edition: August 2017

Printed in the United States of America
1   3   5   7   9   10   8   6   4   2

Cover art by Mick McGinty
Cover design by Sarah Oberrender
Book design by Kelly Lipovich

To anyone who has ever loved a teddy bear,
because you understand.

Acknowledgments

The acknowledgments for my first Costume Shop Mystery were very official and, to be honest, didn't feel like me. And since one of my goals for 2017 is to be authentic, I'm using this space as a do-over.

My lifelong love of costumes can be traced back to a black cat costume that my mom made me in—what was it—kindergarten? From that moment, I've defined my own identity through those of others: gypsy, hobo, Indian princess, witch, clown, alien, and more. I've suited up as pop stars and B-movie stars, Disney villain and Hitchcock victim, cowgirl, hippie, and more—and not always for Halloween. Every "look" inspired an element of confidence that I otherwise lacked until the elements of costume became part of my style.

I'd like to thank: my parents for buying me a wig for my eighth birthday and not thinking it strange when I wore my dance recital costume to dinner. Josh Hickman for accepting that caftans and go-go boots both have their place in everyday life. Deborah Nadoolman Landis for putting together the most fantastic exhibit of movie costumes that I've seen in my life, and the organizers of Malice Domestic for giving me a four-day event where I can dress like a newspaper boy, policewoman, safari hunter, and flapper. And to the good people who attended Left Coast Crime in Phoenix and acted like my clown tie was high fashion.

Bonus mention to Josh, who seemed to enjoy the conspiracy aspect of this book and also taste-tested the spicy acorn treats featured in the appendix. Thanks to Yumiko Hoshiyama for the gracious use of her name, Gigi Pandian, who handed an early draft of this manuscript back to me and pushed me to make it better, and Kendel Lynn, who makes this whole crazy publishing journey a little more sane with her friendship. To the community of Sisters in Crime, who adopted me when I was little more than a writer with a first draft, and elected me their president around fifteen books later. I hope I make you proud.

Thank you to my editor, Katherine Pelz and the team at Penguin Random House, and to my agent, Jessica Faust, who first heard a story about a teddy bear in a Halloween costume and, instead of saying, "Seek professional help," said, "That's an idea for a series." My life (and that of Bear Vallere) has never been the same.

Chapter 1

PARTY PLANNER EBONY Welles stood in the center of Marvin Gardens. Around her feet, additional properties from Monopoly were scattered, along with stacks of over-sized salmon-colored Chance and ochre Community Chest cards. She had one hand on her hip, while the other held an old orange walkie-talkie up to her mouth. "There ain't gonna be no Ouija board and there ain't gonna be no séance," she said. "I don't care if you can conjure up the spirit of Isaac Hayes. I don't want no ghosts at my festival. You got that, old man?"

The walkie-talkie crackled. "Roger that. Over and out."

On most days Ebony was the spitting image of Pam Grier, a fact made all the more noticeable thanks to her authentic '70s wardrobe. Two weeks ago she'd had her Afro chemically straightened, and now her hair hung in feathered waves away from her face à la *Charlie's Angels*, which did little to soften her annoyed expression.

She dropped her arm and looked at me. "Girl, you would not believe how difficult it is to run a game-themed festival. I've bought up every vintage board game in town and half the ones in Moxie too. I've taken to reading back issues of *Martha Stewart* magazines and even have a call in to some foundation director I read about in *Southern Living*. It's a wonder I haven't redone my bathroom in Scrabble tiles."

"You'll be fine. The park looks great and nobody can run with a theme like you can."

"Tell that to the mayor. He's been breathing down my neck since Monday. I was about to up and quit after the trouble with Trivial Pursuit and now I gotta deal with catfighting dancers and conspiracy theorists."

"'Conspiracy theorists'?" I asked slowly. There were two resident conspiracy theorists in our small town: my dad and his friend Don Digby. Seemed the roots of Ebony's ire were starting to show.

"Your dad and Don Digby talked their way into getting a booth and now who knows what they're cooking up over there."

"A booth for what? The festival theme is board games. Our store couldn't get our own booth. Bobbie gave me a corner of hers to share. I thought my dad knew that."

She shook her head back and forth and rolled her eyes. "Those two are nothing but trouble when they get together." Her walkie-talkie squawked before she had a chance to continue. She raised it up to her head. A tinny voice said, "Ebony, the divas are at it again. We need you at the main stage."

She pressed the talk button. "I'm sending Margo Tamblyn," she said into the speaker. To me, she said, "Ebony can't be everywhere at once." When stressed, Ebony had a habit of talking about herself in the third person. Frankly, based on all of the fires she was putting out, I was surprised it took her this long.

"You sure you don't want me to handle my dad and Don?"

"Girl, compared to the Domino Divas, those two are pussycats. You got your work cut out for you. Good luck," she said. She turned away, crossing over the rest of the Monopoly property pieces that lay scattered across the grounds of the Proper City Park.

Ebony was in charge of planning the annual Sagebrush Festival. It took place for two weeks each year around Walpurgisnacht—the end of April into the beginning of May—otherwise known as the calendar opposite of Halloween. In a small town where we celebrated events with costume parties, holidays were celebrated for more than just one day. According to history, Walpurgisnacht was an ancient ceremony to welcome spring and drive away evil spirits. According to the mayor's press release, it was a community-building, family-friendly event in a public area.

What the mayor's press release didn't mention was that over the years, our festival had turned into his biggest cash cow, bringing in money he used to fund his obsession with incorporating the city. Residents proposed themes for the festival, which were voted on at a town hall meeting. This year's theme was family game night, which explained the large Monopoly properties on the ground. The theme had garnered a significant portion of the votes, but not unanimously, thanks to Don, a self-appointed watchdog for the board game industry.

The hot arid sun of the desert, our own special blessing/curse, combined with the general lack of rainfall, made it impossible to maintain a green park like other cities had. Patches of yellow grass grew here and there, but mostly the public area was comprised of light brown dirt that had been leveled off and tamped down over the years by feet passing through for picnics, cookouts, and the occasional Frisbee game. The festival became the main attraction for anybody who wanted a change of pace from the Las Vegas casinos forty miles to our east.

This morning, it was close to eighty degrees, though the lack of humidity made it tolerable. I was dressed in an old tennis outfit that had arrived at our costume shop with other items left in lost and found at the local country club. The tunic top and skirt were white trimmed with aqua. A small appliqué of intersecting tennis rackets was stitched onto the front, and matching aqua bloomers were under the skirt. I tended to dress in items from Disguise DeLimit, my family's costume shop, for two reasons: it made me a walking ad for our store, and, frankly, the clothes they sold at the mall were boring compared to how I'd grown up.

Ebony headed toward a red and white striped tent and I went the opposite direction toward the main stage. Located at the east end of the PCP—or Proper City Park for those who never learned to speak in initials—the stage faced a row of open tables and booths, including the one assigned to Disguise DeLimit. We'd been commissioned to create costumes for the festival volunteers and the headlining act in exchange for a prime position in the park.

There'd been a time when the Domino Divas were our town's dance troupe. From their first Watusi in the '60s, they built a reputation on elaborate choreography and matching outfits and wigs, and they left behind a case of trophies, blue ribbons, and a collection of domino masks in the front lobby of Proper City High School where they'd been enrolled. The colorful satin masks were the only thing that kept them from looking identical during performances. Each of the women had her own color, like the bad guys in *Reservoir Dogs* except without the "Mr." The masks had done more than hide their identity; it had provided one. In their heyday, the Domino Divas epitomized Proper City in competitions across Nevada, and then to the West Coast. Considering we were a town of people who loved to dress up in costume, we couldn't have picked better representatives.

The real interest in the return of the Domino Divas lie not with their fifty-year-old routine but in the scandal that surrounded them. A robbery at the Proper City Savings and Loan had coincided with their last performance in 1968. The only thing stolen was a block of gold originally owned by Pete Proper, the prospector for whom our town was named. Rumors connected the Domino Divas to the theft, leading them to dissolve the act and go their separate directions. The gold was never found.

The Domino Divas—or Double Ds as people sometimes called them—had agreed to dust off their masks in order to headline the festival. In addition to the costumes for the volunteers, I'd made the dancers black and white dresses that were inspired by domino game pieces. The costumes were white with black felt dots glued on with fabric glue. Felt wasn't the most forgiving—or sturdy—fabric, but considering the dancers were in their late sixties, I didn't expect them to have the kind of moves that required Lycra.

Five identically dressed women milled about on the stage. Each wore a black T-shirt with DIVAS written across the chest in sparkly rhinestones. Two wore short black pixie wigs and two had their hair pulled back, one in a ponytail at the nape of her neck, the other in a bun that looked like a doorknob on top of her head. When they were suited up in matching wigs and their domino masks, I had a hard time keeping track of which was which, but today, I had no trouble identifying Jayne Lemming, the self-appointed choreographer of the Domino Divas. A yoga teacher by day, she lived in stretchy spandex: colorful ensembles that coordinated with her sneakers. She had dark brown hair with chunky blond highlights and surgically enhanced cheekbones and lips. She held up a small compact and adjusted the curls on either side of her face. Her domino mask dangled around her neck like a pink satin surgeon's mask. She clicked the compact shut. "Let's get started," Jayne said.

The woman with the doorknob bun crossed her arms in front of her T-shirt. "We can't start. Ronnie isn't here yet."

"We have two choices. Start without her or cancel the whole thing."

"Wasn't Ronnie the one who talked us into this?" Ponytail said. "Maybe somebody should have said something then." A red domino mask was perched on top of her head like a pair of sunglasses pushed up when someone went indoors.

Jayne turned around and shielded her eyes, scanning the festival grounds for signs of the missing member of their group. A few seconds later, she dropped her arm, turned, and followed the other women to the center of the stage. I was about to suggest that they split up and search the common areas when a woman in a domino costume ran toward us.

"Here she comes now," I said. Jayne and the others turned to look. The approaching woman was dressed to perform, her short black wig and blue domino mask already in place. She stopped a few feet from the stage and held her arms out to keep anybody from getting too close. She pointed at her throat and moved her hands back and forth, one over the other, in a *no* gesture. Either that or she was trying to hand jive.

"Ronnie?" I asked.

She nodded but didn't speak. She moved away from the group to a corner and bent down in a toe touch.

Ponytail and Doorknob pulled on their black wigs, slid their masks over their faces, and took their places on stage. This was it, the final rehearsal before their first performance. I didn't know how they couldn't know their routine by now. I'd spent the past week setting up my corner of my friend Bobbie Kay's booth and *I* knew the routine. Bobbie owned a nonprofit that sold teddy bears as fund-raisers, and I was fairly sure the teddy bears knew the routine by now too.

"Put on your mask, Jayne," one of the now-anonymous dancers said.

"I'll put it on for the performance," Jayne said. She slid her finger around in a circle over a small iPod and music trickled out of speakers that were hung on either side of the stage. She took her place in the middle of the group, three dancers on one side and two on the other, and they started.

Considering this was their last rehearsal before show-time this afternoon, it was painful to watch. Twice the blue domino turned the wrong way, bumping into Jayne, who pushed her away and then spun her around. I turned my back on them before it could happen a third time and set up a display on my table. One by one, I pulled domino masks out of their plastic wrap and lined them up. Instead of tagging each individually, I'd printed up a sign to sit in the middle: PLAY DOMINOS! DOMINO DIVAS, THAT IS. $5 EACH. FESTIVAL SPECIAL: 5 FOR $20!

"Margo!" called a familiar voice. Bobbie Kay, my best friend since we were four, ran toward me. Bobbie was dressed in her usual daily uniform: white polo shirt, khaki pants, and Tretorn sneakers. Her brown bobbed hair swung around her face as she ran. She carried a large, lumpy bag slung over one shoulder. "They're here!"

Back in high school, Bobbie had shot to the head of our class thanks to a natural inclination for business. What most people didn't know was that she'd managed an accelerated pace of diet pills and dangerous levels of caffeine to fuel her as she became the state of Nevada's very own Young Entrepreneur of the Year. A physical meltdown had led her to walk away from it all and seek treatment. When she'd recovered, she turned down several paid internships at Fortune 500 companies and started Money Changes Everything, where she handmade teddy bears and sold them to raise money for worthy causes. Thanks to Bobbie, practically everybody in Proper had a teddy bear.

Had I run across the stretch of the PCP with a Santa Claus–type bag over my shoulder, I'd be more than a little out of breath when I stopped. Bobbie, however, was not. I guess that's the benefit of running ten miles every morning and existing on a diet of kale, quinoa, and almonds. My exercise routine involved yoga approximately once a month—every six weeks if I was really lazy—and my diet involved regular servings of fried rice, homemade smoothies, and the occasional bowl of Fruity Pebbles for dinner.

Bobbie set the bag on the table and pulled the drawstring open. When she tipped it, small, six-inch-tall teddy bears spilled out onto the table. All told, there were probably a hundred of them.

"Mayor Young wanted me to come up with something I could give away for the festival. I have two hundred yards of ribbon that says 'Sagebrush Festival: Game On!' Can you help me get them ready?"

"Sure," I said. I picked up a teddy bear and tipped my head to one side and then the other while I assessed him. "What if I made tiny little domino costumes for the bears? Like the ones I made for the Double Ds? Modified, of course. And not for all of them, but maybe for ten or twenty?"

"That would be perfect!"

A six-foot-tall teddy bear approached us. Earlier in the week, Bobbie had had the idea for me to bring the lone teddy bear costume that we had in our inventory, and she had convinced Don to pose for teddy bear selfies to help her raise money. In addition to being my dad's closest friend and fellow troublemaker, Don was a retired nurse with a penchant for poker games and the blues. He was about five foot eight, short for a man but slightly taller than I was. His wire-rimmed glasses added an intellectual slant to his appearance, which gave him an air of credibility when he spouted off about interplanetary life and the various UFO cover-ups that the government perpetuated.

He reached his paws up and removed the head, setting it on the table, and then looked behind him at the stage. "I didn't think I'd ever see them back together on stage," he said.

"The divas?" I asked.

He nodded. "The last time they performed together was a long time ago. I wonder what made them say yes." He watched as the dancers stumbled through more of their routine before it came to an end. They took their bows and then pas de bourrée'd themselves off the stage.

As we stood watching, Jayne stormed over to Ronnie. "You need to get it together," she said. "This isn't 'The Ronnie Show.' It's the Domino Divas. Nobody cares about your reputation fifty years ago."

Ronnie turned to leave and Jayne grabbed her arm and spun her back around. Seconds later, Jayne smacked her across the face.

Chapter 2

RONNIE'S HAND FLEW to her cheek. I expected her to retaliate with a return slap or some nasty insults, but she remained quiet. Don turned away from them. "Ronnie Cass always knew how to bring out the best in people," he said, shaking his head back and forth. He put the teddy bear head back on and walked away.

Mayor Wharton Young appeared on the opposite side of the stage. A thin man pushing seventy who carried extra weight around his belly, he favored short-sleeved dress shirts, seersucker pants, and rocker-bottom shoes that gave him an extra couple of inches of height. His pants were held up with a pair of suspenders, which he apparently didn't trust because he also wore a belt. He climbed the stairs and approached the dancers.

"Ladies, ladies, let's keep the peace. If I may offer some constructive criticism, I think we can loosen things up a bit. These people won't mind a little sizzle in the routine.

You girls still have a little sizzle in you, don't you?" He swatted Jayne on the tush.

Jayne's face was flushed with anger over her altercation with Ronnie, and the mayor's inappropriate tap gave her a release. She whirled around, her hands in fists. "Keep your hands off me or I'll slap you too," she said.

The mayor stepped backward and held his hands up in surrender. "Calm down, Jayne. I wouldn't want you to get the wrong idea. This little show of yours is just that: a little show. But don't forget, we have a contract. If you don't fulfill your agreement, you're through. And I don't just mean the festival."

I'd gotten so caught up in the exchange between Jayne and the mayor that I'd lost track of Ronnie. When I looked around, I spotted her halfway through the festival grounds heading toward a silver Airstream trailer parked across the street. She hadn't cared much about mingling, that was sure. And there was no love lost between her and the rest of the group. But worse than that, I had a suspicious feeling that there was more to her antisocial behavior than the slap.

Mayor Young approached me. "Margo Tamblyn. Jerry's daughter, right? From the costume shop? What are you doing here?"

"One of the divas was missing," I said. "Ebony asked me to handle this for her while she put out another fire."

"That wasn't her call to make. I have too much publicity riding on this festival to let it be destroyed by a fifty-year-old catfight. Where is Ebony?"

"The last time I saw her, she was by Monopoly," I said, conveniently failing to mention that her other fire pertained to my dad.

"*Proper*opoly, not Monopoly," the mayor corrected. "Our publicist advised us to brand the festival this year. It's one of the reasons I agreed to the Domino Divas being our headlining act. They're the closest thing we have to celebrities."

"I'll take care of them," I said.

"You'd better. I gave them everything they asked for, including their own trailer." He pointed toward the silver Airstream. "They have no right to pull this kind of behavior, even if they do call themselves divas."

I excused myself and jogged across the park. I approached the trailer. Before I could knock, I heard voices arguing from inside. I beat my hand on the door and tried the knob. It was locked.

"Ronnie? Are you in there?" I yelled to the door.

Footsteps sounded inside. Metal lock mechanisms grated against each other and then the door opened. The scent of musk wafted out of the trailer. Ronnie appeared, wearing a man's white dress shirt and little else. Her chemically straightened and highlighted brown hair fell just past her shoulders. One side was tucked behind her ear and the other swung around the side of her face, obstructing her cheekbone and half of her eyebrow. Her face was evenly made up, but the skin on her neck and clavicle showed signs of UVA damage through an assortment of freckles and sunspots. "Hold on," she said. She shut the door in my face. I heard muffled voices, and then the door opened again. This time she had a red silk robe knotted over the shirt.

"Are you alone?" I asked, trying to look past her into the trailer. "I thought I heard someone."

"My daughter asked me to watch her cat," she said,

clearly lying. She stepped out front and pulled the trailer door shut behind her. "What do you want?"

"Mayor Young is concerned about the infighting between the divas. He needs some kind of reassurance that whatever is going on, you won't bring it to the festival. You might want to work things out when they get here."

"Why are they coming here?"

"This is the divas' trailer, isn't it?"

"This is my trailer. I don't think the rest of them were smart enough to ask for perks."

"Please, Ronnie, try to set aside your differences, at least publicly. You don't want to ruin the festival for the whole community."

"Jayne Lemming is the problem, not me. She thinks she's perfect just because her doctor husband gives her a nip and tuck every fifteen thousand miles." She glared over my head toward the festival. "But don't worry. I'll be on my best behavior tonight." She stepped inside the trailer and shut the door in my face.

One crisis partially managed, I trudged back across the street toward the striped booth that my dad and Don occupied. The tent opening had been tied shut, which only raised my concern. Who knew what kind of trouble those two could cook up in secret? I untied the flaps and went inside.

The two men sat at a crude wooden table. My dad wore his usual shirt, tie, and blazer. Don wore the brown bear costume. An open bag of sunflower seeds sat on the table between them. The head of the bear rested on the end of the table. In front of the two men were several three-ring binders that had pages marked with colorful sticky tabs.

"What's all this?" I asked.

"Our contribution to the festival," my dad said.

Don chimed in. "Come on, Margo, you can't pretend that you've never noticed how many board games are just training ground for the military: Stratego, Risk, Project CIA . . . It's up to us to expose the truth."

"The mayor agreed to this?"

"Mayor Young agreed to us having a booth where we coordinated a massive game of conspiracy," Don said. He picked up a blue cardboard rectangle and held it next to his head. "Conspiracy, the game. It came out in 1984. George Orwell would have loved that." They both laughed.

"I think when Mayor Young finds out what you're really doing, he's going to kick you out."

"With everything else going on, he won't even notice us." Don pulled the binder closer to him with the bear paws. "We need a screening process, though. What do you think, a questionnaire? A quiz?"

"You're screening people before they can play your game?"

Don set down the binder and lowered his voice. "The game playing is a front. We're secretly launching a subversive newspaper. We have to make sure it gets into the right hands or else we might have a problem."

He tried to flip the pages, but the paws made him unsuccessful. He pushed the binder toward my dad. "What should be our first story? Kennedy assassination. Martin Luther King, Jr. Or maybe we tackle the faked moon landing. I have a source that will swear that Stanley Kubrick directed the footage of Neil Armstrong."

"I don't see why we can't do them all," my dad said. "This is a chance for us to teach the citizens of Proper

City the truth about what the government has been telling them for years."

"You're a costume shop owner," I said to my dad and then turned to Don. "And you're a nurse. What do you two know about running a newspaper?"

"Do you have any idea what kind of conspiracies take place inside the medical industry?" Don said. He turned to my dad. "Maybe we should start with that. 'Sexy Nurses: Conspiracy or Costume?'" He turned back to me and tapped his finger to his temple. "That one uses both of our experience."

I looked at the stack of board games behind them, which included the games they'd mentioned plus a couple versions of Battleship. "No good can come from this. Dad, you should be helping me with the store."

My move back to Proper had benefited my dad in more ways than one. After his heart attack—and follow-up heart attack—eleven months ago, he'd been willing to sell the store so he wouldn't be chained to the business. It had taken me most of my life in Proper City and then seven years away from it to realize that running a costume shop was just about the perfect job for me. I'd taken over the store, and my dad had made it his mission to follow up on every interesting costume lead in the country. In those eleven months, we'd acquired alien costumes from Area 51, cow costumes from New Jersey, Bavarian waitress costumes from the Midwest, and pink flamingo costumes from Florida. When he returned from those trips, he was happier than I'd ever seen him.

He leaned back in his chair and folded his hands in his lap. "In the year since you've been back, my scouting trips have boosted our inventory by thirty percent. I'll still handle the booth here while you take care of the store. Didn't you ask for my help?"

"With the booth, yes. Distributing a subversive newspaper at the annual Sagebrush Festival, no. And, Don, you don't have time for this. Didn't you agree to wear the teddy bear costume and work with Bobbie?"

"Who says I can't do both?" Don said.

My dad spoke up again. "We can't ignore this, Margo. These army games are training soldiers from early childhood. And Jenga. It's a metaphor for toppling governments and the unstable infrastructure of the world we live in."

"Margo," Don said with exaggerated patience, "we're going to expose their secondary agenda, maybe show a connection between the board game companies and the defense department."

My dad reached behind him and picked up a folded piece of newsprint. He handed it to me. Across the top in an Old English font were the words *Spicy Acorn*. Underneath was a recipe for stuffing.

"I don't get it," I said.

They looked at each other and laughed. "Perfect!" Don said. "If Margo doesn't get it, then Wharton Young won't either."

"Margo, have I taught you nothing? Aside from the art of costumes and the importance of changing the litter for Soot every day?"

I looked at the newspaper again. "Spicy Acorn . . . Spicy Acorn . . . Spicy Acorn . . . nope. Not getting it."

"It's an anagram." He picked up a pen and a piece of paper, wrote *SPICY ACORN* and below it wrote *CONSPIRACY*. One by one he crossed out the letters until they were all x-ed through. "Every issue will have a recipe for acorns. That's our cover. It's genius!"

"We told the mayor we'd be handing out commemorative memorabilia for the festival. Increased value to his constituents," Don said. "You have to know how to speak their language if you want politicians to listen to you."

I set the newspaper on the table and kissed my dad on top of his head. "Okay, you're geniuses. But I thought there were three lone gunmen. Where's Frohike?"

"Margo, this is serious. Somebody has to expose the secrets of the world."

"And nothing needs exposing like a rousing game of Monopoly."

The two men looked at each other and Don did a head smack. "Monopoly! Why didn't we think of that? We're training our children to be ruthless capitalists! There has to be a way to work that into our column on societal influences."

I left the two nuts—I mean spicy acorns—and wandered around the festival grounds. Instinctively, I scanned the staff behind the Hoshiyama Kobe Steak House booth for Tak, son of the owners, though I knew I wouldn't see him. Tak had been my sometimes-companion on Saturday nights until recently, when he'd started interviewing for jobs out of state. During the planning of the festival, he'd been in charge of zoning. It was his responsibility to sort through the applications for booths and then assign them based on the needs of the tenants, which, come to think of it, might explain how the *Spicy Acorn* booth got the green light. He'd left town more than a week ago for a string of interviews a headhunter had set up for him.

Food vendors who had spent their morning setting up

their equipment now put it to work, sending out scents of breakfast potatoes from Eggcetera, grilled scallops from Catch-22, and fried rice from Hoshiyama. I fought the urge to sample one of everything and lost, spending the next half hour at a picnic table with other weak-willed volunteers.

After bussing my spot, I gave up my seat to the next person and then spent an hour helping dress the greeters in their costumes. I'd gone with a playing card motif. Face cards had been scanned in, blown up, and printed at the local print shop. I'd mounted each poster-sized image on thick precut oak tag and attached the front to the back with shoulder straps like a sandwich board. I'd affixed thick black grosgrain ribbon about halfway down the underside of the costume front and back and now tied the ends together. The ribbons kept the rigid pieces from shifting while the volunteers walked. Like everything else at the festival, the cards showed the Domino Divas logo on the back with the words SAGEBRUSH FESTIVAL underneath.

Ebony arrived as I tied the final volunteer into her costume.

The flaps to the booth flipped open and Ebony came in. "Margo, Ebony needs to speak to you. What happened today at rehearsal?"

"Nothing," I said. I pointed out front. I thought back to Ronnie slapping Jayne. "Well, not nothing, but it's under control."

"Then why is Mayor Young throwing a fit about those divas?"

"Another fit? What happened now?"

"It's time for them to go onstage and the blue one is missing."

"She promised me she'd be on her best behavior. What is with her?"

"I don't know, but if she doesn't turn up in the next five minutes, the mayor is going to go ballistic."

"I'm on it," I said.

I found five divas backstage, nervous energy building as their performance time grew closer. They were dressed in their black and white costumes I'd made, their black wigs, and their colorful masks. Three stood in a cluster. A fourth had her palms on the wall while she stretched her calves as if she was about to run a sprint. The fifth stood by a full-length mirror tugging the hem of her stiff black and white domino dress. I felt a tap on my shoulder and turned around.

Mayor Young stood in front of me. "Where is the sixth one?"

"I don't know."

"I suggest you find out. We can't hold this thing up for much longer."

I turned back around and faced the remaining dancers. The cluster looked at me.

"Who's missing?" I asked.

"Who do you think?"

I looked at the women and inventoried their mask colors. "Have any of you heard from her since this afternoon?" I asked.

"You saw her take off after the performance. She just wants attention. She thinks she's the whole act, but she's not," Jayne said. "If she doesn't show, we're done." She snatched the wig off of her head and tossed it onto her duffel bag. "We should have known not to trust Ronnie again. Look what happened the last time we performed."

She wrapped her robe around her and knotted the belt tightly, and then turned around and stormed down the back stairs. A few seconds later, the scent of cigarette smoke wafted through the air.

"Is there something else going on here that you need to tell me?" Mayor Young asked. "Because there's a whole town waiting to see a performance by the Domino Divas. No—not a town. This is bigger than Proper City. There are fans from out of state out there. A couple of Las Vegas talent scouts too. If there's been something brewing between the divas that caused this delay, I will hold them personally accountable for the loss of income from the festival and for any negative press that colors the mayoral office. That crowd out there expects a performance by the original Domino Divas and they'd better get it. Or else."

"Which means there are only two options: postpone the show or find Ronnie."

"There is one other option: find a replacement act."

"The crowd is expecting the divas. We have to find Ronnie."

My words fell on deaf ears. Jayne returned, smelling vaguely of an ashtray. I walked to the front to see the audience. Row upon row of folding metal chairs had been set up for the occasion. Twice as many as earlier. Not only were they filled, there were people standing as well. The nostalgia craze was sweeping the nation, and the mayor's office had been promoting the upcoming Domino Divas performance for weeks. If the dancers didn't deliver, they'd never hear the end of it.

"Did anybody call her?"

"I left her three messages," said one of the dancers.

"I texted her twice," said another.

"Did anybody check her trailer?" I asked. They looked at each other and shook their heads. "Wait here. I'll be right back."

I left the park and waited for the light to change before crossing the street. Something about what Jayne had said struck me as odd. Before I could figure it out, the signal went green. Something blue lay on the sidewalk in front of me. A car drove past, creating a breeze that caused the blue item to skip along the sidewalk and then roll under the trailer. By the time I got closer, I recognized that it was a domino mask. I was about to squat down to retrieve it when the door to the trailer slapped against the latch. It hadn't been closed properly.

I tapped on the aluminum door and called out Ronnie's name. When she didn't answer, I pulled the door toward me and peeked my head inside. And that's where I found Ronnie Cass partially dressed in her black and white domino game piece costume, slumped in a folding chair. A stream of fresh blood trickled down the side of her head from under her black pixie wig.

Chapter 3

I TURNED AROUND and hung my head out the door of the trailer. "Help!" I yelled. "Somebody, help! Call the police! Call an ambulance! Help!" A few people at the festival looked in my direction. I waved my arms and yelled again. One woman waved back. It was clear that she couldn't hear me.

I went back into the trailer. Maybe Ronnie wasn't dead—maybe she'd tripped and fallen and knocked herself out and then pulled herself up into the chair? As unlikely as it was, I couldn't accept the alternative. I reached for her wrists to check her pulse. Her body tipped forward and the black wig fell from her head. Her light brown hair was matted with caked blood.

I looked up and around the interior of the trailer. There had to be a phone. I looked over surfaces covered in silk robes, feather boas, pantyhose, and nightgowns, until I spotted a cell phone on the counter. I stepped past Ronnie's body to grab it and called 911.

"This is Margo Tamblyn. A woman is dead. Send the police."

"Stay on the line," the operator said. I heard her fingers tapping on the keyboard. "Tell me what happened."

"I'm in a trailer parked on the corner of Main Line and Rapunzel Road. One of the Domino Divas—they're the dance troupe that's supposed to be performing at the Sagebrush Festival right now—is dead. Please send the police—"

"How do you know she's dead?" she asked.

"There's no pulse. And she has a head wound. And there's a lot of blood." I felt myself go light-headed and looked away from Ronnie. I reached out for the countertop to steady myself and something jabbed the palm of my hand. "Ouch!" I said. I shook my hand and a small sewing needle with red thread dropped from the fleshy part of my palm to the floor.

"What happened?" the operator asked.

A tiny dot of blood appeared on my palm and I rubbed it against the hip of my tennis outfit. "Nothing. Please send help. Hurry!"

Click click click went her fingers. "Stay right where you are. The police are on their way."

The trailer smelled of musk and copper, an unpleasant combination that spoke of Ronnie's life and death. I had to get fresh air. I turned around and went out the door, gulping deep breaths, trying to calm my racing heart. The small prick in my palm itched. I scratched at it as I stumbled onto the street, and then leaned against the white brick building on the corner and closed my eyes. Images of Ronnie filled my mind. I opened my eyes. Something didn't seem right with the memory.

I took a deep breath and held it as I reentered the

trailer. Ronnie remained in the chair. An empty glass sat on the table next to her. Amber pill vials were scattered about on the table and the floor. She was slumped forward, thanks to me checking for a pulse. Her wig now lay on the floor by her feet. Inexpensive glossy black synthetic hair fanned out against the striated rubber floor. Cabinets were open, exposing shelves of more prescription bottles. I closed my eyes and tried to picture what had happened. She'd been getting ready for her performance when someone had come into the trailer and hit her over the head and killed her. Had she taken prescription drugs prior to performing? Had she been fully dressed in costume when her attacker arrived? If so, it would have been hard for someone to know which diva she was. Had she been the intended victim, or had someone made a mistake?

The blow to the head had been fatal. If there had been a mistake, it had been one of identity, not of intent. Whoever had struck her had done so with the goal of taking a life.

The trailer was a mess, which made it hard to know if there had been a struggle, if someone had searched for something, or if Ronnie was a slob. Glasses sat inside the small sink. A boa lay in a pool of shocking pink feathers. A teddy bear from Money Changes Everything sat on the kitchen table, the red stitching along the base of his head loose, with tufts of gray stuffing poking out.

Sirens grew close. Car doors opened and shut. I backed away from Ronnie toward the door and ran right into Detective Nancy Nichols.

"Ms. Tamblyn, I need you to leave the scene. Please wait outside," she said.

"But—"

"I'll take your statement in a moment."

Nancy Nichols was a no-nonsense officer of the law who had been reassigned to Proper City shortly before I returned to town. She was built like a pro volleyball player and had either been blessed with the sun-kissed blond hair and the even tan to go with it or she'd embraced the look with the help of professionals. I'd first met her when a client of Disguise DeLimit had been murdered at his own birthday party and Ebony had been the number one suspect. I wanted to dislike Nancy for a lot of reasons, but she'd shown me compassion when I'd needed it and that made things muddy. At the moment, I accepted that I'd wanted to find Ronnie's dead body about as much as Detective Nichols had wanted me to, so I stepped out of the trailer and waited for her to join me so we could wrap this up.

Two uniformed officers stood on the sidewalk. I scanned the street. "Did one of you pick up the blue mask that was out here?" I asked.

"What mask?"

"It's a domino mask." They looked at each other and then at me, apparently not familiar with the term. "It's a half mask, the kind that comes to the tip of the nose and covers the cheeks." I held my hands up to either side of my eyes, thumbs down and fingers up, showing them what I meant. "That's what the Domino Divas wore to perform—that's where they got their name. When I crossed the street, I saw a blue one on the sidewalk. It might be a clue."

The men looked at the sidewalk. There was nothing on it. "You sure?"

"Maybe it blew under the trailer." When neither officer made a move to look, I squatted to look. Even though there were aqua bloomers under my tennis outfit, I was too modest to bend over. I straightened up.

"You sure it wasn't a leaf?" the taller of the officers said.

"I know what I saw," I said.

Detective Nichols returned to the sidewalk and instructed the two officers to secure the scene. She turned to me. "Ms. Tamblyn, what brought you to this trailer?"

"The Domino Divas are—were—scheduled to perform at the festival tonight. Ronnie didn't show for the performance. The mayor wasn't happy, and I've been helping Ebony manage them, so I came here looking for her."

"Why the trailer? What made you think she'd be here?"

"This is her trailer. Ronnie didn't seem to want to socialize with the others after rehearsal, so I thought—it just made sense."

Detective Nichols made a note on her tablet. "What made you go inside?"

"The door wasn't closed properly. I tapped on the door and called out to Ronnie. When there was no answer, I looked inside."

"And what did you see?"

"She was slumped in the chair. There were pill vials on the counter and table. I didn't know if she had passed out or worse. I checked her pulse—her wig fell off when I grabbed her wrist—but it wasn't there. The pulse, not the wig. The wig is on the floor next to the pink boa." I pictured the wig, fanned out against the floor.

"Are you trained in CPR or emergency treatment?" the detective asked.

"No, but—"

"Then you should have left her trailer and called for help."

"I did call for help. I hung out the door and yelled as loud as I could but everybody is at the festival and they couldn't hear me and it's dark out here. It can't be much past seven. Why is it so dark out here?" We both looked up at the closest streetlight. The bulb was out. "I went back inside and called you from her phone."

"Where's your phone?"

"In my booth at the festival."

Detective Nichols hooked her stylus to her tablet and tucked it under her arm. "Tell me again how you knew Ronnie would be here?"

"I came here this afternoon." I dropped my voice. "She and Jayne Lemming had a fight during the rehearsal. Mayor Young wanted to make sure they wouldn't air their dirty laundry at the festival."

Detective Nichols stayed silent and watched me. I felt awkward and self-conscious under her stare.

"What does the mayor have to do with this?"

"Mayor Wharton Young has been all over this performance. He even hired a publicist to maximize exposure for Proper City. He's the one who negotiated the Domino Diva contract with Ronnie."

Nancy turned her tablet on again and made a few more notes. "So you came here to check on her," she said. "Did you see anything else?"

"I saw her mask on the sidewalk. A blue domino

mask. A car drove past and the draft sent it under the trailer."

"Keep going."

"The trailer is a mess inside, so I can't say if there was a struggle. But—" I chewed my lip, nagged by the wig. "She has a head wound, right? So why isn't there any blood on her wig?"

Detective Nichols studied my face. "What makes you think there isn't?"

"It's a cheap synthetic wig. We sell them at Disguise DeLimit. If she'd been wearing the wig when she was struck, the blood would have gotten onto the fibers and clumped the strands together, like a glob of peanut butter. But it's not like that. When it fell off, it landed on the floor and the hair fanned out."

She tapped the end of her stylus. "Do me a favor and don't repeat that part to anybody else."

"Why?"

She didn't answer. Instead she turned toward the two officers who'd arrived with her. "Did either of you see a blue mask?"

"No," they said in unison.

Nancy scanned the sidewalk, walked over to the trailer, and bent at the waist to look underneath. "No mask," she said.

She straightened up and then powered off her tablet again. This time she folded the case shut over it, as if to indicate she didn't think I'd say anything else of value. She didn't make a note about the blue mask, the wig, or the possibly inferior housekeeping habits of Ronnie.

"I might have some follow-up questions. In the meantime, you're free to go. I think, in light of what happened, somebody should tell the mayor the divas won't be performing."

"Will that somebody be you?" I asked.

"You deliver the message and have him contact me if he doesn't believe you. Give him this." She handed me a card with her name, e-mail, and several phone numbers on it.

The walk back to the park was a slow, somber one. For a week I'd watched six women who had maintained a zest for life rehearse their show. But now one of those women was dead. Compared to the rest of the divas, Ronnie's attitude had been sour. She'd been late for rehearsals, complained about the routine, and criticized her costume. Had that attitude motivated someone to take her life?

And the wig. Detective Nichols didn't have to answer my question, because I'd answered it for myself. This hadn't been a case of mistaken identity because Ronnie hadn't been wearing her wig when she'd been struck. Whoever killed her had done so first and then put her wig on her head to hide the wound. I'd only seen the gash because her wig had fallen off when I'd checked her pulse. That told me the injury was fresh. Detective Nichols telling me to keep quiet about it—that told me that it was a significant observation.

I reached the stage. Mayor Young was at the back of the crowd talking to a thin blond man in a green floral short-sleeved dress shirt with green tie, green pants, and white shoes. The mayor saw me, said something to the man, and came my direction.

"Where is she?" he demanded.

"She's not coming." I dropped my voice to a whisper. "Can I talk to you in private?"

"What do you mean, she's not coming?" he asked in an equally quiet—but more urgent—whisper. "We have a crowd of over a hundred people here. There's press out there from six major newspapers. Joel pulled strings to get the tabloids here." He turned around and looked at the man in the flowered shirt, waved, and gave him a thin smile, and then turned back to me. "Does that no-good tart have any idea how much we're spending to publicize her act?"

I put my hand on the mayor's arm and stepped backward, pulling him a few feet away from the nearest audience members. When it seemed as though we had a pocket of privacy, I broke the news. "Ronnie is dead. Murdered. Detective Nichols is with her now. It would be wrong for the divas to perform without her." I held out the card that Detective Nichols had given me. "The detective said you should call her if you don't believe me."

"Murdered?" he asked. "At the festival?"

"In her trailer."

He closed his eyes and stood very still. I was touched. Until now, he'd been so focused on the logistics of the festival and the importance of expanding Proper City's allure that he'd seemed to lack the qualities attributed to normal human beings. But now, he was noticeably shaken by the news. I looked over his shoulder and beckoned the blond man toward us.

"The man in the green pants, he's the publicist, right? I'll have him notify everybody that the festival has been postponed and—"

Mayor Young's eyes popped open. "You'll do nothing

of the sort. The trailer was parked on Rapunzel Road, right? That's what I agreed to. That's not part of the PCP, which means it did not happen on festival property. The Sagebrush Festival can continue as planned."

"But there was a murder!" I said. Several people looked at me, eyes wide.

"Those dancers have done enough damage to our town's reputation. They are in breach of contract and everything I agreed to is null and void. I gave them a chance to rewrite history, but this is too much. They are over in more ways than one."

He stormed off, leaving me alone with a crowd of over a hundred, at least six members of the press, and a tabloid reporter, all waiting to see what, exactly, had gotten him so steamed.

Chapter 4

AS I WAFFLED between getting on stage and announcing what had happened and looking for a quick place to hide from the potentially angry crowd, the man in the green floral and stripes approached me.

"Something happened. Good? Bad? I need to know. I can spin it either way. Give it to me straight and I'll get to work."

"Who are you?" I asked.

"JV Publicity. What's the news?"

"'J-V'? Like junior varsity?"

"Joel Vanderpoel. It's a long Dutch last name that nobody remembers so I shortened it." He held up his fingers in a peace sign. "Peace, Roman numeral five, or scissors." He tipped his hand and moved his fingers in a *snip-snip* motion. "Whatever makes you remember me. Now, what's the skinny on the divas?"

Joel V. seemed as good a candidate as any to tell the crowd the news. He was on the city payroll and, as far as

I was concerned, publicity included damage control. No doubt he'd be better at it than I would be.

"The divas have to cancel their performance. One of them was"—at the last minute, I decided the details could fall to Detective Nichols—"is dead. That's why she's not here. There's been some tension among the troupe for the past few days, and I think it's best that you tell them first and then make an announcement to the crowd."

"Better idea. You tell the divas. I need thirty seconds to spin this. Go."

He didn't give me a push, but he might as well have. It was clear that I was to do part one of the dirty work if I expected him to do the rest.

I found the remaining five women behind the stage. Green Mask and Yellow Mask were on the ground, legs stretched out in front of them. They faced each other, feet to feet, and stretched in tandem: one leaning backward while the other leaned forward. Switch. Purple and Orange stood off to the side, talking on their cell phones. Pink Mask paced back and forth. When she saw me, she balled her fists up and approached me.

"Where is she?" she asked.

"Jayne?" I asked, trying to remember who was which color. With her short black wig, heavy application of stage makeup, and scrunched up forehead and eyebrows, she looked like Tinker Bell after a day with Cleopatra's stylist.

She pulled her mask down. "She is dead to me. Officially. I told her if she messed this up, I would never speak to her again."

I reached out to her, more to shock her into silence

than anything else. I didn't know how to tell her what had to be said, but there wasn't time to mince words. "Ronnie *is* dead," I said.

"That's what I said. She's dead to me, she's dead to the divas. She never cared about us, only herself. And after what she put us through to make this happen, it's over. I've given her too many chances to turn things around."

"No, Jayne, listen to *me*." I reached out and took her other hand in mine. She tried to pull away, but I tightened my grip and forced her to look at my face. "Ronnie was murdered. In her trailer. That's why she isn't here."

Whether or not Jayne was predisposed to believe me would never be known, because at that very moment, Joel V. took the stage. "Good evening," he said, his voice came out amplified by a microphone. "You are a lovely and patient crowd, and on behalf of the City of Proper, we thank you for that. For being both lovely and for being patient. I know you're waiting to see the Domino Divas. I regret to inform you that they will not be making their scheduled appearance on stage this evening."

Green and Yellow stopped stretching and looked up at Jayne. She looked at me. I looked at the stage.

"To make up for this unforeseen blip in our kickoff festivities, I'd like to offer everyone here a twenty-five-dollar food and beverage credit to the festival."

A ripple ran through the crowd, though, without seeing them, it was hard to gauge if it was annoyance, excitement, or something else. I didn't realize that I was still holding Jayne's wrists. I released my grip. She stumbled backward. One hand flew to her forehead. "You're telling the truth. She's dead. She's—she's dead? Ronnie's dead?" Her eyes grew wide and tears filled them, spilling down her heavily pancaked cheeks. Droplets of makeup— foundation, blush, mascara—swirled together and landed on the domino costume, leaving a stained spot of a cloudy mauve shade on the white fabric. She swayed again and then fell to the ground.

I rushed to where she'd fallen and put my arm under her head. "Jayne," I said repeatedly.

Green and Yellow ran over. Green unscrewed the top of a nearby plastic water bottle with the Domino Divas logo on it. She threw the contents on Jayne's face. Before I could admonish her for her insensitive actions, Jayne sputtered, shook her head a few times, squeezed her eyes shut and then open, and sat up. Additional streaks of makeup spidered down her cheeks.

Jayne looked at the woman. "Thank you," she said. She pushed herself up to a sitting position and then stood. I followed suit. She wiped her face with the back of her sleeve, smearing what was left of her makeup. "Ladies, it's time for a team meeting. Let's go." She left the tent and the rest of the divas followed.

I stood by myself backstage. What had just happened? Joel V. had bought the crowd's forgiveness with a snack bar credit and had announced—something. I'd missed the second half of his statement when Jayne collapsed. She'd been so overwhelmed by the news of Ronnie's murder that she appeared to faint, at least until she came back to consciousness and led the divas away like the leader of their cult. For a woman on the verge of passing out, she'd pulled herself together rather quickly.

I moved closer to the curtain that separated the backstage from the front and peeked out from between the heavy velvet drapery. The crowd had thinned to the point of empty. A few people stayed behind, resting on the benches, talking among themselves, but by and large their attention had moved on.

Joel's strategy had worked. Nobody seemed overly concerned that the show had been canceled even though that's the precise reason they'd been seated in front of the stage. But for as successful as Joel V. had been, he couldn't change the irrefutable fact that a member of the headlining act had been murdered. Tonight, festival patrons could remain ignorant and enjoy themselves until the booths packed up. Tomorrow, they'd learn the truth of the matter and wonder at the inappropriateness of allowing them to spend their money on game-themed trinkets when a tragedy had taken place so close.

I exited from backstage and crossed the small patch of grass between the stage and Bobbie's booth. Regardless of what had happened, I knew I could count on Bobbie to be levelheaded and calm. It was only after I reached her booth that I realized my hands and knees were shaking from everything that had happened since finding Ronnie's body. I found a white plastic folding chair next to one of the bookcases lined with bears and fell into it—the chair, not the bookcase.

"Bobbie?" I called. "Are you here?" I tipped my head backward and stared at the seams that made up the tent ceiling. "You would not believe what happened today," I said. Deep inside the tent, behind the bookcases, I heard Bobbie curse.

Bobbie Kay was not known to curse.

I found her kneeling on the ground by a shelf of teddy

bears. Two of the bears had their heads torn off. Bobbie looked up at me. She had a bear head in each hand, like Shaquille O'Neal palming a pair of basketballs. "There's only one type of person who tears the heads off of teddy bears: an evil one. I'm going to report this. Somebody is going down."

"Bobbie, wait."

"For what? There's a crazy person running around the festival. Who knows what else they'll do? Trash the snack bar or vandalize the restaurant booths?"

"Or commit murder," I said.

"I don't think it's that bad, but Mayor Young should know."

"Ronnie Cass was murdered," I said. "And Mayor Young does know. That's why he canceled the performance."

Bobbie released the bear heads. They dropped to the grass and rolled toward my sneakers. I scooped the heads up, sat cross-legged, and rested them and their fur bodies on my thighs.

"When the divas couldn't find her, you went to their trailer," she said.

I nodded. "That's where I found her. I spoke to Detective Nichols about it and then came back here to tell Mayor Young that the show had to be canceled."

Bobbie sat back against the bookcase. I shifted my weight and sat next to her with my bare legs straight out in front of me. We were roughly the same height, and our feet—hers shod in her signature Tretorns, mine in K-Swiss to go with the tennis outfit—lined up next to each other.

"Earlier today I talked to Ronnie at her trailer. She was in a crappy mood, but maybe that's because Jayne

slapped her after their rehearsal. That's the last time anybody saw her alive."

"Ronnie was no princess," Bobbie said. "She's always
making fun of my nonprofit. There have been times I
wanted to slap her myself." She picked up one of the bear
heads off of my knee and stared into his face. "But she
didn't deserve to die."

"She had one of your bears," I said.

"Ronnie never bought a bear from me. She's always
saying they're stupid and that women my age shouldn't
be playing with toys."

I adjusted the teddy bear head that was on my thigh.
"Can you believe Mayor Young isn't going to cancel the
festival? He said there's been too much invested into promoting it and since the murder happened in the trailer, which
was parked across the street, it won't affect the proceedings.
Except for the fact that now there's no headlining act."

"He's going to ignore Ronnie's murder?"

"That's the impression I got," I said. I forgot for a
moment that I was resting against a canvas wall and
leaned back. My weight threw the whole tent off-center.
I leaned forward, eyes wide, arms out, hoping none of
the bear-laden bookcases would tip. A few swayed, but
none fell to the ground. I relaxed my arms and slumped
forward. "He's a typical politician. He should have made
a public statement and canceled this whole thing."

"A lot of businesses would be out a lot of money if he
did. Think about what it takes for them to make the arrangements to run their businesses and also staff booths
here while the festival runs. Just yesterday I saw Catch-22
moving in equipment. This year they're serving scallops."

"I know. I sampled some earlier today."

"They're serving them on checkerboards. Imagine the investment in their setup and food prep, and then add in custom checkerboards in bulk so they could fit the festival theme. The exposure to somebody like them is huge. The mayor promised every business a crowd like they've never seen, and he got the highest participation rate ever."

"His publicist offered the audience a twenty-five-dollar festival food credit. Will that help offset any loss of income for the vendors?"

"Probably not. I bet he'll tell the vendors they have to comp it."

"How do you know so much about the vendor agreements?'

Bobbie pulled her knees up to her chest and rested her head against them. "Because I had to deal with the mayor myself. The only way I could be a part of the festival was if I donated teddy bears as giveaways. Publicity for me, added value, and something to add to his press release."

I shook my head. "I wish Mayor Young would get over his obsession with giving Proper City national exposure. After what happened at Halloween, he should have accepted that we weren't destined for rapid growth and big-city problems. Why'd he want to be our mayor anyway? We're a small town of people who like to throw costume parties. We're not exactly a metropolis."

Several months ago, a developer had worked behind the scenes to change the zoning of Proper City so he could turn it into the next hipster vacation spot. The mayor's office had green-lighted his plans—overlooking important issues that put the town in danger—all in the name of growth of the taxpayer base.

It was an ongoing issue with the Proper City town leaders. Our residents were made up of two disparate segments that could be boiled down to the haves and the have-nots. Wealthy residents had moved to Proper City to avoid the expensive state taxes of living in California. Many of them established their wealth through the lucrative casinos in nearby Las Vegas. The city planners responded to the needs of this growing wealthy community by wooing upscale restaurants to open within the boundaries of our tax base. Occasionally talk of a light rail resurfaced, but nobody believed Proper City would warrant a stop on a futuristic transportation system designed to shuttle people between nearby cosmopolitan cities.

"I think Mayor Young's plan is to build his platform with us and then move on up the political ladder. First stop: Proper. Final destination: the White House. Make him an Abe Lincoln costume and call it a day," said Bobbie.

The thought of Mayor Young in an Abe Lincoln costume caught me off guard and I laughed. But then, the idea of someone from Proper as the president was funny too, for more reasons than one.

Proper City had been founded in the late 1800s by a prospector named Pete Proper. In his zeal to strike gold before the rest of the miners who were looking for it too, he struck a deal with the big man upstairs: if he found it first, he'd give up all of his vices. He did, and he did. Pete left the ladies, the gambling, and the moonshine behind and established a town for other like-minded individuals.

Proper City quickly became known for clean, family living until Pete died in 1930. Word spread quickly, and the people who'd gotten rich off the vices that Pete renounced came back and brought their scofflaw friends with them. We were close enough to the California/Nevada state border to attract criminals who wanted an easy way to escape California jurisdiction. Families who'd hoped to put down roots packed up and left. Proper City started a slow decline for the next twenty years.

But tides turn, and during the boon of the fifties, the Clark County city council announced plans to breathe new life into what was left of Proper. Small, single-family houses popped up like dandelions along streets that were named after storybook characters. Tax incentives were offered to families eager to find affordable housing. Development included the bare necessities of a town looking to grow: a library, a post office, and a grocery store. Soon, a string of mom-and-pop stores opened along the main road. Some made it work, others folded quickly, turning their property over to the next tenant with a product and a dream.

The thing about making up a town that looked like something out of *Grimm's Fairy Tales* was that it was never able to shake the element of make-believe. Families started throwing theme parties based on where they lived: Christopher Robin Crossing, Rapunzel Road, and Thumbelina Thircle. That's exactly what it said on the street sign and on official road maps: *Thumbelina Thircle*. It was a pocket of houses built around a circular cul-de-sac. Apparently thumbody in thity planning had a thenth of humor.

Theme parties soon became costume parties, and thus, Disguise DeLimit was born. My dad, who had started working at the store as a stock boy, saved up his earnings and eventually bought the business from the original owners. Soon after, he met my mom and they fell in love. Their own dream of raising a family and running the store was shattered when she died while giving birth to me. I never knew her. After school, I'd moved away to Las Vegas for several years but came back after my dad's heart attack. Now it's just me, my dad, and Soot, my cranky cat, head of the anti-mouse division of the store.

Personally, I loved the town of Proper. I loved working in a store that made costumes that encouraged people to have fun and play dress-up. But as popular as those pictures were on our city's website, I suspected they'd undermine the agenda of a mediocre mayor with political aspirations.

The urgency of getting everything ready for the opening performance had vanished with the reality of Ronnie Cass's murder, and even though the mayor expected us to carry on, I felt as though something was out of order. I sensed that Bobbie felt it too. For the first time in a week, she ignored the tasks that had to be done.

Bobbie took the other bear head from me and collected the bear bodies. "No matter how much time and effort I put in to him, he's never going to be the same as he was. Should I give up and move on?"

I wanted to lie and say that he'd be perfect, but that was the thing about reality. You learned that sometimes there was no light at the end of the tunnel.

Before I could think of something to say to console her, the front flaps to the booth pulled open and a man dressed in powder blue scrubs came inside.

"Bobbie," he said, apparently startled to recognize her in the booth. "I didn't mean to eavesdrop, but I couldn't help overhear your conversation. I don't know who you're talking about, but people are people. They deserve to be treated like humans, not like something you're willing to throw out with the trash."

Bobbie stood up and I followed. "We weren't talking about a person," she said. "We were talking about—" I grabbed her arm and gave it a tug. She looked at me and then her eyes followed mine to the object in the man's hand. It was the teddy bear that had been sitting on the table inside Ronnie's trailer.

Chapter 5

"IT'S OKAY. THAT must have sounded funny." She stood up. "Dr. Lemming, this is Margo Tamblyn."

He looked back and forth between our faces and then held out his hand. "Call me Chet," he said.

I knew from experience that costumes and uniforms could change the first impressions that people formed, and Chet's scrubs had that effect on me. A small plastic ID card was clipped to the bottom of his top. DR. CHET LEMMING, it read. He had short salt-and-pepper hair. It was neatly trimmed into a style that parted on the side and dusted his forehead. Short, one-inch sideburns defined his face further.

He smiled, a grin too broad for a first meeting where he'd kicked things off with a lecture about how to treat people. I felt like he was going for "good-guy doctor," but instead, the vibe I got was "sleazeball."

"Where did you get that?" I asked.

"What, this?" He looked down at the bear in his hand.

"I found him out there on one of the tables. Figured some little kid dropped him. I was on my way to lost and found." He looked up and, for the first time, seemed to take in the bookcases filled with similar bears that lined the walls of the tent. "What is this place? Some kind of stuffed animal factory?"

"These are the bears I sell to raise money for charity," Bobbie said. "Somebody came in here earlier and damaged a couple. They might have taken that one, I don't know. I didn't see it happen."

Chet handed her the bear. "I bet some kid was playing a prank and swiped him when you weren't looking."

Bobbie took the bear and tucked him into a vacant spot on the bookcase. Chet was doing a poor job of hiding the fact that he was staring at my outfit. "You any good?" he asked.

"With what?"

"Tennis. My wife and I used to play doubles but she lost interest. I could use a new partner."

"I don't play tennis," I said. "I just like the outfit."

"Huh." He turned back to Bobbie. "Well, Bobbie, you take care. I'd better go find my wife. She's probably mad that I missed her performance, but nothing I could do about getting stuck at the hospital."

"Your wife is a diva? Wait, are you married to Jayne Lemming?" I asked.

"Last time I checked." He chuckled, as if he'd said something funny. "You know where I can find her?"

"I haven't seen her for a while," I answered honestly. I glanced at Bobbie, who was busy spreading out the remaining undamaged bears on the bookcase. "She probably went home. Did you already check there?"

"No, I came straight here from work, thought maybe I could catch the tail end of their performance. I guess that's life. If you see her, let her know I was here."

"Sure," I said. I put my hand on Bobbie's arm to keep her quiet until I was sure he had left.

"Why didn't you tell him about Ronnie or about why the divas weren't performing?" Bobbie asked. "When she tells him, he's going to wonder why you didn't."

I held up a finger to silence her. "Hand me the bear he was carrying." She picked the bear off the bookcase and held him out. I took him and tipped his head.

"What's wrong? Chet said he found this bear on a table out front. You don't believe him, do you?"

"This is the bear I saw in Ronnie's trailer."

"How can you tell?"

"The red stitching by his neck is loose, see?" I turned the bear and showed her. "The stuffing is coming out."

Bobbie took the bear and thumbed at the torn threads. "How did Chet get it?"

"I don't know, but it sure seems like Jayne's husband was inside Ronnie's trailer after she was murdered."

IT had been a long day. I helped Bobbie secure her booth and we went our separate directions. In place of the patrons who had come to see the opening performance were security personnel, dressed in blue T-shirts, yellow reflective mesh vests, and baggy khaki cargo shorts. A few wore baseball hats with a patch depicting a pair of black-and-white dominos on the front. The security guards milled around, holding flashlights and walkie-talkies newer than the one I'd seen Ebony using earlier that day.

For the next eight hours or so, the park would be in their hands.

I drove my Vespa scooter back to Disguise DeLimit. A small Winnebago was parked out front. I pulled up behind it and knocked on the back door. When there was no answer, I drove around back and parked in the space by the door.

Disguise DeLimit was a two-story building: the first floor being the store and the second being where I lived. The separation between the two often blurred, especially when I forgot to close the door at the top of the stairs, letting my cat, Soot, have the run of the shop. I found him curled up on a black velvet cape that was lined in red satin. Just as well. Nobody rented the Dracula costume in May.

Costumes filled the walls and racks of the store. Accompanying props sat in adjacent bookcases and shelves. Colorful wigs lined an upper shelf next to a whimsical hat assortment. On the left side of the store—the right if you were entering from the customer entrance on the street—was a chrome fixture filled with bright, fluffy ostrich and marabou feather boas like the one I'd seen on the floor in Ronnie's trailer. In addition to the occasional gangster and moll parties that were a favorite any time of the year, the boas sold well during prom season. The rack was picked over, and I suspected that more than one high schooler had helped deplete our stock.

In the year since I'd been in charge of the store, I'd made a few minor adjustments here and there. I'd created a five-dollars-or-less wall for off-season accessories and wired speakers close to the ceiling so I could play music that coordinated with whatever it was I was promoting at the time. I'd painted over the costume ads that had been glued to the walls in the dressing rooms and turned the small spaces into themes: clown dressing room, western dressing room, gangster dressing room, fifties dressing room. I mounted small buckets next to the mirror in each room and filled them with props that were no longer in sellable condition. People could play dress-up behind the velvet curtain, deciding what it was they wanted, and then come find me to locate the very same item in stock so they could buy it.

I found a note from Kirby, my part-time employee, on the counter.

Margo—

It was a good day. We're running low on boas and bow ties, both because of prom. Varla's going to drop off the backdrop for the window tomorrow.

Kirby

PS: Remember I have a swim meet tomorrow.

PPS: I have to talk to you about something.

I left the note next to the register and yelled upstairs. "Dad? I'm home. Are you up there?"

"In the kitchen," he said.

I climbed the stairs. Dad and Don sat at the 1950s Formica-and-chrome kitchen table that Dad had acquired on one of his scouting trips. He was supposed to focus on costumes, but frequently got distracted by anything free.

"We're on a roll," he said. "Do you mind if we keep working here? Or are you expecting company?"

"Stay as long as you want. Your bed has to be more comfortable than the bed in the Winnebago."

My dad stood. "Margo, you and I have an agreement. Now that you're back in Proper City, I don't want you to feel like I'm crimping your style."

"Besides, we're taking the Winnie to Moxie," Don said. Moxie was a town about an hour to the northwest of Proper. "There's a meteor shower expected tonight, and we all know that meteor showers are just a thinly veiled diversion for known alien activity. I even bought an Orion SpaceProbe Equatorial Reflector telescope so we can see the buggers clearly."

"So you expect people to believe you just because you said you saw them?"

"Don't be silly," my dad said. "We've spent the past week rigging a camera to the telescope so we can capture images. With any luck we'll have next month's *Spicy Acorn* cover story before we turn in for the night."

"Carry on," I said, "and tell Mulder I said hi." I helped myself to a handful of sunflower seeds from the bowl on the table in front of them and then took a shower. By the time I was done, the staff of *Spicy Acorn* had left the building.

I headed downstairs and worked on filling our inventory. About twenty minutes into my project, there was a knock on the front door. We were long past regular store hours, but curiosity got the better of me. I pulled the bottom of the retractable shade that covered the front door. A pretty girl with long, straight black hair and a thick sheaf of bangs stood on the other side next to a tall panel of cardboard.

I unlocked the door. "Hi, Varla, come on in."

"I'm sorry it's so late," she said. "Is Kirby here?"

"He left a few hours ago," I said. She seemed relieved, though I didn't know why.

Varla was dressed in her uniform of black. Tonight it was a V-neck T-shirt, skinny jeans, and a thick belt that cinched in her waist. A silver chain with a heart decorated her neck. I studied her face, unsure if she'd been hoping to see him or hoping to avoid him. "Is that the backdrop for the window?"

"Yes, I finished it this afternoon, but it had to dry." She leaned the cardboard against a rack of pinstriped suits and unfolded each side to reveal a giant Sorry! game board. "What do you think?"

"Another masterpiece," I said.

"Great," she said. She looked around the interior again. "I, um, I'm going to need a special dress for, um, a date," she said. "Do you think I can look around while the store is closed?"

"Sure," I said. I was starting to understand why she'd asked about Kirby, why she'd shown up after his shift, and most of all, why Kirby said he had to talk to me about "something."

Varla wandered the store for about ten minutes, pausing by the eighties rack of big-shouldered suits. She looked at two and put them back, and then picked up a vinyl miniskirt with a race car printed on the front.

"Are you shopping for something in particular?" I called out to her.

"I'm not exactly sure what I'm shopping for." She put the skirt back on the rack. "But thanks for letting me look." She tucked her long black hair behind her ears and started out the door. "Um, Margo? Don't tell Kirby that

I was looking at dresses, okay?" she said. After I agreed, she left.

There's only so much distraction you can get from unpacking a box of feather boas. Even Soot, who normally could entertain himself for hours with the colorful items, sat stoically by the end of the rack, staring at me as if waiting for me to talk. I did some of my best talking with Soot. He was a patient, understanding listener and, usually, allowed me to reach my own conclusions in good time.

"How was your day?" I asked. He kept one eye open but didn't answer me. "Mine wasn't good. You know Ronnie Cass? She's one of the Double Ds." I scooped him up and ran my left hand over his gray fur while my right arm cradled him. "She's dead. Somebody broke into her trailer and murdered her."

As if he recognized that I wasn't just talking about the weather, Soot settled into my arm and started to purr. I rubbed between his ears a little more and then ran my hand over his belly fur. He wriggled around, kicking his feet in the air, until he'd turned himself over and draped his arms over my shoulder. He jumped from my arms and swatted at a stray feather. Seconds later, already bored by the toy, he lowered himself to the ground, put his paws out in front of him, and rested his head on them. For a second I thought he was going to close his eyes and go to sleep, but he kept watching me.

"She was at the rehearsal at four—well, she was late, but apparently she's late all the time. But then when she didn't show for the performance at seven, I went looking for her and found her in her trailer across the street from the festival. That means somebody killed her in her trailer in broad daylight. What does that say about Proper City?"

I'd been so caught up telling Soot about Ronnie that I'd lost track of the boa display. When I stopped talking, I saw that I'd overfilled the rack. Instead of colors dangling easily, the feathers were squished together. After a few customers flipped through the rack, the feathers would get twisted together, and then tear out when someone tried to separate them. I couldn't leave it like this.

I went to the stockroom and assembled a second rack out of chrome components. Kirby had mentioned that the boas were selling well because of prom. No reason we couldn't maximize that with a boosted display and a promotional price. I rolled the new rack back to the store, moved the pink, white, and turquoise boas to it, and spread the green, orange, black, and yellow out on the original rack. I'd make a sign in the morning and roll one out front. When I was done, I collected the empty plastic cellophane wrappers that had fallen to the floor and carried them to the trash can. On top of the trash was a copy of my dad and Don's conspiracy newspaper. They'd made notes about the layout and corrections in red marker. After the acorn recipe was an article that suggested the greeting card industry was really a front for the defense department. If this was the kind of hard-hitting news they were planning on reporting, we'd all be safe. I folded the papers together and tossed them back in the trash. That's when I noticed the writing on the backside. *Ronnie C. Saturday*, followed by a telephone number.

The handwriting was Don's.

Chapter 6

THERE VERY WELL may have been another Ronnie C. in Proper City, but the coincidence of this saying *Saturday* and Ronnie being murdered on Saturday was too much. I cringed internally at the thought that Don wanted to turn the murder into an article for their burgeoning paper. He had to have more class than that. Didn't he?

I pulled the pages out of the trash and carried them upstairs. I'd talk to him about this when he got back from Moxie. The last thing I remember thinking was this: *What possible conspiracy could Don think was tied to Ronnie's murder?*

THE next morning, I woke to the sound of Ebony's voice. "Margo! Girl, where are you?"

The sleep fog slid from my brain and I threw back the covers. Sunlight sparkled through the window, landing on a purple velvet pimp suit I'd worn last week and never rehung.

"Up here," I said.

Ebony had seen me in my pajamas before, so I didn't bother trying to change out of them for her sake. By the time she joined me in the kitchen—with her bichon frise, Ivory, tucked under her arm—I'd put a half cup of blueberries, a scoop of vanilla yogurt, and a banana into the blender. I added some almond milk and hit liquefy. Ebony set Ivory on the floor and he immediately chased Soot into the hallway. Ebony's lips moved, but I couldn't hear what she had to say.

"What?" I asked when I turned the blender off. I poured the contents into two tall glasses and handed her one. She pulled a brown bottle out of her pocket, unscrewed the top, and squeezed an eyedropper of something into her smoothie. "B-12. For stress. You want some?"

"No thanks."

Ebony found a spoon in a drawer and swirled the supplement into her smoothie. "What are you doing in your pajamas? It's after nine."

"It won't take me long to get ready. What's up?"

"This festival. The whole thing is spiraling outta control. It's like that publicist unleashed a family of squirrels around a support group for people with attention deficit disorder. Now I'm dealing with live-tweeting and Instagramming and Facebook updates—all in the form of a festival scavenger hunt that doesn't exist. Who said I could implement a scavenger hunt in addition to everything else? And do you know that flowered freak set up a selfie station? Complete with a festival backdrop. With dominos printed all over it. Now I gotta invent half a dozen things to keep people from thinking about the fact that one of those Domino Divas died. What a world we're living in." She reached up and took hold of the gold medallion she wore around her neck. Her thumb ran back and forth over the surface in a spot that was shinier than the rest. Ebony had been rubbing her medallion for luck for as long as I could remember.

"Do you have another act lined up to take over the entertainment?"

"Exactly how many local acts are named after board games? Go on. Take a guess. And if you can come up with more than one, eliminate any that don't include the word 'domino.'"

"So what are you going to do?"

She didn't answer, at least not out loud. She tipped her head and looked down at my hips, and then tipped her head to the other side and pursed her lips. "What are you looking at? Ebony, why are you here?"

"You're about her size," she said.

It took only a moment to realize what she was about to suggest. I set my glass on the counter and crossed my arms over my pajamas. "Oh, no. I'm not taking her place. That's weird. And wrong. And I'm not a sixty-eight-year-old dancer."

"You got to help me out here," she said. "The mayor is breathing down my neck."

"Think about what you're asking me to do.

"I'm asking you to put on a costume. You wear some kind of costume every single day. If you hadn't told me you were still in your pajamas, I might have thought that was what you were planning to wear today."

"I don't wear pajamas in public."

She acted like I hadn't said anything. "True, you'd have to make your costume, since Ronnie, well, took hers to the great dance floor in the sky, but you can do that in no time."

"It's not right on so many levels. It's icky."

Ebony put her hands on her hips. Today she wore a cropped black sleeveless top covered in suede fringes. Soot and Ivory ran out of the bedroom, through the kitchen, and down the stairs. Ebony's stare never left my face. "If you wanted a job as an office assistant and another office assistant died and somebody offered you the job, would you turn it down because it was 'icky'?"

"I'm not an office assistant and it's not the same thing. She was murdered, Ebony. Somebody killed her in her trailer while she was getting ready for her performance. Why?"

"Aha!" Ebony said, pointing her finger at me. "I knew it. You're not going to just walk away from this. You *want* to be involved."

"I *should* walk away from it. Murder is dangerous business. I should not get involved, and I should let the police investigate it and do their jobs." It was like we'd temporarily traded places.

"I agree with everything you just said. Stepping into the routine in Ronnie's place is you helping me out when I really need it. It's not you being involved in her murder investigation. In fact, it's probably safer than you being involved in her investigation because you'll have to practice with the divas, and between working in the store and performing, you won't have any time to get into trouble. So?"

I looked away from her and my eyes landed on the *Spicy Acorn* newspaper I'd found in the trash. If I was involved in the routine, I'd know if Don tried to talk to the rest of the divas and exploit the murder in the name of conspiracy. I'd also be able to keep an eye on Jayne Lemming and, therefore, her husband, Chet, who found the teddy bear from Ronnie's trailer.

"I'll do it," I said. "On one condition."

The initial look of success that had flashed across her face froze and morphed into furrowed brows. "Just 'cause you're gonna be a diva doesn't mean you get to demand a bowl of green M&M's like J.Lo."

"It's nothing like that. It's just—we should retire the blue domino mask and let me pick another color."

"I don't mean to speak ill of the dead, but that Ronnie doesn't deserve to have you fill her domino mask." She opened her arms and squished me into a tight hug. When she let go, she pulled a CD from her back pocket and handed it to me. "Here's the music."

We worked out the details as best as we could. Ebony said she'd handle the mayor for now. Her eyes glowed with an unspoken idea that she could implement on short notice. I was afraid to ask.

She picked up her smoothie from the table and swallowed several gulps. "So, you wanna talk about it?"

"About what?"

"About finding her body."

"How'd you know it was me?"

"Word gets around."

"Does everybody know?"

"If they don't, they will soon. It's not the kind of thing people can keep quiet." She finished her smoothie and set the empty glass in the sink. "I heard it from Joel V. Truth is, that's one of the reasons I came to you. I know you'll respect what happened and you won't turn it into some kind of opportunity. You'll do the thing, and then when it's over, you'll move on."

I glanced at the newspaper on the table. Her words—*"turn it into an opportunity"*—were exactly what I'd thought when I'd discovered Don's notes in the trash.

After Ebony left, I called Don and left a vague message on his voice mail. I dressed in yellow tights and a yellow and black striped bumblebee costume. Instead of stuffing the body with pillows to make it full and round like I suggested to the people who rented it, I cinched it with a wide black belt and slipped on black ballet flats. I poured what was left of my smoothie into a bright yellow plastic tumbler and went downstairs. When I reached the store, I slipped on a yellow plastic hair band that had two antennae attached to the top. The antennae bobbled around over my head while I finished my smoothie.

Almost everything I owned was in some part a costume, thanks to the costume shop. I'd been wearing clothes from our inventory for as long as I could remember, and if high school peer pressure hadn't changed me, then I doubted anything would. You can take the girl out of the costume shop, but you can't take the costumes off the girl. That was my motto.

I unlocked the front door to the store and a hot breeze swept over me, like someone had left a fan inside a preheated oven. I rolled the racks of boas onto the sidewalk. Soot assisted. He wasn't the most active of cats on a regular basis, but this morning the neon feathers were

too great a temptation. I made a sign that read: INDULGE
YOUR INNER DIVA! And then, regretting the choice of
words, threw it out and made up a new one. INDULGE
YOUR INNER GLAMOUR GAL! FEATHER BOAS: $7 FOR ONE,
2 FOR $10. I fed the sign into a magnetic sign holder, stuck
it to the rack, and shooed Soot back inside.

Since I'd be alone in the store today, I found the supplies needed to make up a domino costume and carried
them to a display table out front. After clearing off gold
doubloons, a treasure chest, and a couple of colorful par-
rots that easily attached to the shoulder of the pirate costume, I set to work. First, I traced a series of circles onto
black felt and cut them out, stacking them on the edge of
the table like poker chips. Next, I rolled out the white felt
and, with a tape measure, marked off large rectangular
shapes. I cut four rectangles to piece together for the front
and back of the costume and four more narrow ones for
the sides. The last piece was a white rectangle that I'd
attach to the top of the costume with a slit for my head.
All in all, it was a pretty easy costume to assemble. As
the machine chugged along the fabric, I thought back to
yesterday. I kept wondering what had happened between
the rehearsal and the performance, and then something
hit me like a ton of dominos.

When I'd talked to Ronnie after rehearsal, there'd
been no sign of the slap from Jayne. She hadn't even
mentioned it. I lifted my foot from the pedal and stared
at the fabric in front of me. The diva who'd performed at
the rehearsal had had red threads on the side of her costume, and I knew why. It wasn't the costume that I'd
made. Ronnie had been dressed to perform when I found
her. That meant a non-diva had shown up for rehearsal

in her place. Why? Had the diva impersonator been planted to keep us from looking for Ronnie? If I hadn't gone to her trailer to find her, how long until someone else would have? Or worse: Had the person who had taken her place been the killer, adopting her identity in order to fly under the radar?

As crazy as my thoughts were, I knew I couldn't ignore them.

I called the police station and told the desk sergeant that I had information related to Ronnie's murder. Minutes later, Detective Nichols arrived at Disguise DeLimit.

"Ms. Tamblyn," she said when she entered. She scanned my bumblebee costume but said nothing.

She wore what I'd come to think of as the Detective Nichols costume: white T-shirt under a black jacket and trousers. Silver chain at her neck. Small hoop earrings hugging her lobes. Silver watch strapped onto her left wrist. Low-heeled shoes that appeared to be both comfortable and practical. If we carried the costume in the store, I'd rent it with a badge, a blond wig, and a tube of lip gloss—scowl optional.

"I've heard you have information that you withheld yesterday," she said.

"I didn't withhold anything. It's something I remembered—more like worked out—this morning."

"I'm listening," she said.

"I don't think Ronnie performed at the rehearsal yesterday. I think the person in the blue domino mask was pretending to be her."

"What makes you think that?"

"First of all, she showed up late with her wig and mask in place, so nobody got a good look at her face. She didn't speak to anybody. And she didn't seem to know the routine very well, kept bumping into the others."

She made a note on her tablet. "What else?"

"Jayne slapped Ronnie at rehearsal, but when I talked to Ronnie at her trailer, there was no sign of redness on her cheek."

"Is that all?"

"What else do you need? That's pretty big. The impostor might have been the murderer. Or she was an accomplice, someone who knew what was going to happen. Whoever it was knew what Ronnie would be wearing. Somebody could have killed her, then put on a spare costume and performed as her so nobody knew she was dead. What does the coroner say? Did he come up with a time of death?"

"Ronnie's trailer was parked in the sun and wasn't air-conditioned. Time of death isn't an exact science, especially in this case. Without evidence, we can't assume that it *wasn't* Ronnie at the festival for the rehearsal."

"You can check if the costume she was wearing when she was murdered has red threads on the side. There was a needle with red thread inside the trailer, so probably somebody tore the dress and had to do alterations."

"I'll look into it," she said. Her voice was calm and controlled.

"What about the bear?" I asked.

"What bear?"

"There was a teddy bear inside Ronnie's trailer when I found her. But later that night, Chet Lemming had the bear. He said he found it. You secured the scene, right? How did Chet get the bear if it was secured in her trailer?"

"Chet Lemming?" she repeated. She tapped the end of her stylus and made another note. "He's Jayne's husband, isn't he?"

"Yes. He said he found the bear lying on a table at the festival, but he could have made that up. I don't know why he'd be in Ronnie's trailer, especially after she was murdered and you'd secured the scene, but I can't figure out any other way for him to get that bear."

"How do you know it was the same bear?"

"It had some damage around its neck. Your team took photos inside the trailer, right? Have them check the pictures and see if there was a bear on the table. It was there when I was. If the trailer was secured, they should be able to go in and see if anything else has changed."

"Are you advising me on how to run my investigation?" she asked.

"Detective, I don't have evidence. I only have what I saw and what I think. I know that's not enough. I'm trying to help you here."

She tucked her hands in the pockets of her trousers and leaned back against a pair of giant foam dice. They toppled over and she stumbled. I'd been planning to redo the windows into a Boggle theme, but hadn't had a chance to finish the concept.

"I appreciate you calling me with this information," she said after she regained her balance. "I'll send some officers back to Ronnie's trailer to check things out and compare with the photos."

I held out my hand and she shook it. Detective Nichols and I were probably not destined to become friends in the foreseeable future, but what the heck. I could be civil.

Business was slow. Two ladies came into the store shortly after noon. I helped them choose and reserve ten small princess costumes for their granddaughter's birthday party. A newly engaged couple came in after them and wandered around, getting ideas for their theme wedding. Before they left, they'd reserved the Dread Pirate Roberts and Princess Butterbean. I hinted around about getting an invite until they confessed they were going to elope to a chapel of love in Las Vegas. A private ceremony in costumes that awesome? Inconceivable.

I took advantage of the lack of customers to work on the windows. I'd installed a curtain rod directly inside the street-facing display. This way I could redo the windows in private and unveil them when they were complete. The door to the store was next to the window entrance. If any customers arrived, I'd hear the bell over the door and, most likely, see them too. Today I didn't expect much in the way of foot traffic. Word of Ronnie's murder would have spread around town. Between that and the festival, people wouldn't be thinking much about costumes.

I dressed several mannequins in colorful fishnet tights, white vinyl boots, and sleeveless dresses that curved out from the body and ended above the knee. They were based on the player tokens from the game of Sorry! and would be perfect with Varla's backdrop. I maneuvered the oversized board game into the window and then set each mannequin on a cart, slid a wooden incline into place, and pushed the cart along the ramp until it was inside. I pulled white bobbed wigs onto each mannequin and finished with oversized bubble hats that matched the color of the dresses. It took a few attempts before I worked out their arrangement, but I got things pretty close. I'd have to check the real Sorry! board game to figure out what other props I could put into the window, but I'd need to see it from the street first. Mostly happy with it, I reached up and pushed the velvet curtains to the side. I hadn't expected to see a face pressed up against the glass, and I screamed.

As soon as I recognized Gina Cassavogli, owner of Candy Girls Costume and Party Store, the scream turned into a groan.

When you have a town of people who entertain in costumes, it stands to reason that sooner or later more than one costume shop will open. Disguise DeLimit had had a long solo run under the original owners and then my dad, but a few years ago, the inevitable happened. Candy Girls, a superstore that carried cheap plastic party props and flammable costumes that came prepackaged, had opened on the opposite side of town.

Candy Girls had become the go-to employer for the eighteen- to twenty-eight-year-old female crowd. They probably handed out applications during sorority rush. They kept their prices low thanks to their inventory suppliers in China, and somehow reinvented themselves to suit whatever crisis arose in town. At one point they'd added "condolences" to their flyer after costumes and catering—a marketing move that, fortunately, hadn't gained traction.

Gina Cassavogli was the store manager. Recently divorced and in her late thirties, she was tackiness personified: caked on makeup, neon high heels, short dresses, and cheap plastic jewelry. Today, she was in all turquoise, including her eye shadow. I would have made a comment, except that I was dressed like a bumblebee. It seemed best to let this one fly. I came out of the window and met her on the street.

"Getting ideas for your next display?" I asked.

"Cut the crap, Margo. I know you're the one who found her and I want to know what happened. The police won't tell me anything."

"Found who? Ronnie?" I asked. "Why are you asking the police about her?"

Gina paled. "I—she—" Her eyes filled with tears. She raised her hands to her face and brushed away tears as they appeared. "You need to tell me what you saw in her trailer."

"What makes you think I saw something? And why do you think I'd tell you?"

She dropped her hands to her sides. "Because you know what it's like to lose a parent."

"What are you talking about?"

"Get with the program, Margo. I thought you were good at figuring things out." Her voice started out shaky but gained strength. "I mean that Ronnie Cass was my mother."

Chapter 7

I QUICKLY DID the math in my head—or as best as I could without a calculator. Ronnie was in her sixties. Gina was late thirties. The ages fit. Ronnie could have been Gina's mother. And then I remembered Ronnie's attitude, her demands, and the way she supposedly treated the other divas. Even if the facial resemblance was hidden under a layer of Gina's heavy foundation and liberally applied blush, I couldn't deny that the apple hadn't fallen far from the tree.

"I'm sorry for your loss," I said automatically. It was a phrase I'd heard my whole life when my father told people that my mother was on another plane. I hated to hear it, but I'd come to respect what it stood for. "When did you find out?" I asked.

"The police notified me this morning."

"Detective Nichols?"

"No, two officers. Why would I talk to Detective Nichols? Ronnie and I weren't close. We barely spoke. Why am I telling you this?" She crossed her arms over her turquoise tank top. "I want to know what you were doing in her trailer."

"Let's talk inside the store," I said. I walked in and Gina followed. Soot crouched by the base of the rack with the boas and hissed at her. She jumped. I turned my head and laughed, and then sobered quickly when I realized that, regardless of her normal disposition, today Gina got a pass.

"Can I get you anything? Coffee, soda, water?"

"Stop acting like we're friends. We're not. If you weren't the one to find her, then this conversation would never be happening."

"Gina, I know we're not friends, but you just found out that you lost your mother. It's completely understandable that you're angry."

"I'm angry because not having a mother at all would have been better than having Ronnie for one. She was self-absorbed and greedy and always had to be the center of attention. All the time. Being late for everything she was ever invited to—attention. Resurrecting the divas—attention. Demanding her own trailer—attention. Sleeping with—never mind. This is so like her." She looked at my head and then stepped back and scanned the bumblebee outfit. "You are really weird, Margo. You know that?"

A very small part of me wished I wasn't wearing the antennae headband, but I wasn't going to take it off now. "I think you should talk to Detective Nichols," I said. "She knows everything I know, and I'd rather you heard it from her."

"Heard what?"

"About your mom."

"What's to know? The original act for the festival was supposed to be *Clue: The Musical*. Only Ronnie convinced the mayor to bring the divas out of retirement instead because of the domino connection. Candy Girls did the costumes for *Clue*. We should have had the contract for the festival. Even after she made him change everything, we should have done the domino costumes too. How hard do you think it is to sew a couple of circles onto a couple of rectangles? But no. She couldn't let me share in her limelight."

"If another act had already been chosen, how'd Ronnie convince the mayor to change his mind? Was it because the divas would bring in bigger crowds and be better for Proper City?"

Gina rolled her eyes. "Ronnie doesn't care about Proper City. She didn't even care about the festival until she heard the game theme. Next thing you know, it was a done deal. Part of the agreement was that the mayor removed all evidence that the community theater was ever involved. All publicity went to Ronnie. You know the rest of them didn't even want to do it? I mean, it's been fifty years. And then, she's so selfish, she demanded a trailer for herself and she refused to rehearse. She managed to screw her group, me, and the mayor all at the same time." She swatted at the bright green boa on the end of the rack. "I guess you could say the mayor got screwed twice."

"How's that?"

"How do you think she convinced him to scrap his original plans and hire the divas in the first place?" She opened her mouth and pretended to stick her finger down her throat, letting me know what she thought of anybody having sex with Mayor Young. "We all should have known better than to expect anything from her."

We stood face-to-face for a moment that felt like an hour. "Talk to Detective Nichols," I said a third time.

In a swift motion, she grabbed the antennae off my head, threw it to the ground, and stomped on one of the round bobbly balls. The plastic crushed under her heel. She balled up her fists and then stormed out of the store.

I located a broom and dust bin wedged into the space next to the register and cleaned up the mess. Pictures of car parts had been taped to the inside of the case that held colorful masks and small accessories. Red marker had bled through the back of the page. I flipped it up and saw a phone number below the name Varla. I let the page drop back into place. Kirby's business, not mine.

I tried to find props for the window but was too distracted by Gina's visit. When she first showed up, I'd been blinded by an overwhelming need to give her a break and be nice, but as time went on, I became more and more focused on her anger. One thing was clear: there'd been no love lost between mother and daughter.

THE rest of the day was quiet. I spent the afternoon working on the Sorry!-themed windows and finished with lettering for the window that read: YOU'LL BE SORRY!

After I was done, I pulled every costume that related to board games out of the stockroom. Ebony needed more items for her giant Monopoly—I mean, Properopoly—setting. In a back corner under two boxes of plastic pistols, I dug out a top hat, a small plastic toy car, and an unused trash bin and spray-painted them silver. The upside-down trash bin was the best I could do on short notice for a thimble. I'd ask my dad, who was handier on the sewing machine than I was, to make a dog out of silver fabric. Ebony's Properopoly would come together yet.

A few minutes after seven, I locked up the store and tallied the few receipts from the day. The real money this time of year would come from the festival. My dad had never created costumes for the headlining act of the festival, but now that I was in charge, I'd seen it as a unique opportunity, something a store like Candy Girls would never be able to do. But because of the murder, the domino costumes had a morbid quality. Would people want to dress like the dancers now? When they'd been announced as the headlining act, their image had been linked to the robbery fifty years ago. Was their memory forever tainted by scandal?

The festival would be going strong until ten, so I had plenty of time to grab something to eat there. Considering the number of restaurants with booths at the festival, I might as well kill two birds with one stone.

I left my scooter behind the store and walked to the corner and waited for the Zip-Three. The Zip lines were a series of repurposed yellow school buses that covered the network of streets around Proper. They were driven by retired senior citizens who were looking for something to fill their time. There were four in total, and with the exception of the really out-of-the-way parts of town where hardly anybody wanted to go anyway, one of the four would take you to almost any Proper City destination.

About two minutes after I arrived at the Zip stop, the

sound of a labored engine blocked out everything else around me. I looked up and down the street—the Zip-Three ran the length of the Main Line, the one road that ran from end to end of the city—and saw what was making the horrible sound. A once-yellow school bus, now covered in a rudimentary mural of dice and domino game pieces, approached and then screeched to a stop in front of me. A cloud of blue-black smoke chugged out of the tailpipe as the doors opened.

The driver, a full-figured black woman with an elaborate hairstyle that had been gelled into place around her face, waved me in. "Trust me. It's better in here than it is out there." I climbed on. "I swear Andy Caplan tried to jump this thing over the dip on Thumbelina Thircle and he cracked my oil pan. Been burning oil since I started her up this morning."

She was right, it was better inside the bus, but not by much. She picked up a can of Lysol and sent a stream of it through the air. "I'd sit in one of these front seats if I were you. The back ones are closer to the exhaust."

I sat in the front on the right side of the bus. "I'm no mechanic, but isn't it a bad idea to drive around with a cracked oil pan?"

"You think? Problem is this festival. I can't take the day off because everybody wants to go to the park. And now that that publicist got these buses painted for the festival, he wants us to double up our shifts so people don't have to wait longer than fifteen minutes to catch the next bus. Do you know how long it takes to drive Main Line Road end to end and make stops? Thirty-seven minutes is the best I ever clocked it and that's with me skipping three stops. Darn near impossible, I tell you."

She hit the gas and the bus lurched forward. I fell back against the torn green seat. Despite what the driver had said, she arrived at the park in record time.

"What happens to the Zips at night?" I asked.

"We park them in the lot behind the high school. Second row behind the regular school buses. Why?"

I scanned her dashboard—Big Gulp, bobby pins, value pack of Twix candy bars, and more—until I spotted a pen and a scrap of paper. "Call Dig Allen. He runs a towing company, but he's really good with cars. His shop is just past the high school. He might be able to fix things for you overnight." I scribbled the name of Dig's company on paper and tucked it under the corner of the Twix package so it wouldn't blow away.

"I know Dig. He taught my youngest how to change his spark plugs." She looked up at me. "I'll tell him to bill the festival. That'll show that publicist." She pulled the lever to release the door and I hopped down the stairs and waved good-bye.

The drop-off spot for the Zip-Three was on Main Line Road by Rapunzel. The festival was across the street from me. Ronnie's trailer was still parked alongside of the curb. Yellow crime scene tape had been affixed to the seal around the door, sliced through, and then covered up again. It must have been after I'd asked Detective Nichols to look for the teddy bear. Which meant she knew the answer to my question and I didn't.

I hated when that happened.

Even though I was in the conspicuous black and yellow striped bumblebee costume and yellow tights, I was more covered up than yesterday, so I dropped down on my hands and knees and looked under the trailer for the blue domino mask. There was nothing to the left of me, but to the right was a small grate for water runoff.

It was an inside joke among Proper City residents: if you wanted to hide your valuables, put them in a sewer grate. Our desert town saw about two inches of rainfall a year if we were lucky. The city planners who designed and built our town had come from cities around the country and didn't understand the idiosyncrasies of the desert climate. They would have done better to put up rattlesnake crossings and BEWARE OF TUMBLEWEED signs, but nobody had known to tell them otherwise.

The grate, as I expected, was dry. I scooted to the right, twisted my head, and closed one eye so I could try to peer inside it. If the blue domino mask had blown under the trailer, it might have fallen inside the grate.

I turned on the flashlight app on my phone and tried to use it to get a better view. The phone slipped from my hand and fell into the sewer. And landed not on a blue domino mask, but in the lap of a small brown teddy bear that sat just below the grate.

Now how did he get there?

Chapter 8

WHO WOULD PUT a teddy bear in a sewer grate? And how? It wasn't like it could have fallen in there. I fed my fingers through the slats under the trailer and yanked. The grate rattled but didn't come free. Three of the four corners were secured by screws. I said a quick prayer to St. Jude, the patron saint for hopeless cases, and tried to fit my fingers through the slats. Apparently St. Jude was otherwise occupied because my case remained hopeless.

It was one thing to have dropped my phone down a sewer grate. It was quite another for someone to have unscrewed the grate, put a bear in there, and then screwed the grate back on.

I remembered the scavenger hunt that Mayor Young had asked Ebony to plan on short notice. Had she done this? It was an odd spot to use to hide something considering the location of Ronnie's trailer. There was an easy way to get an answer. I adjusted the hem of my bumblebee outfit and headed back to the festival.

I found Ebony talking to Dig Allen, of the towing company that I'd suggested to the driver of the Zip-Three. Ebony often bragged about how she could still fit in the clothes she wore in high school, and she proved it most days of the week. Today she'd paired hip-huggers with a white T-shirt that had a pair of dice printed on the front. The decal had cracked thanks to too many washings over the years, but Ebony didn't seem to mind. Her trademark gold medallion hung around her neck, matching shiny gold hoop earrings.

Dig held a torch for Ebony even though she was ten years older than he was. Dig's wardrobe consisted of vintage bowling shirts with the sleeves torn off to show his biceps tattoos: an anchor on one side and Tweety Bird on the other. His usual appearance was like Mr. Clean with toffee-colored skin. Today, he wore a black wig that looked suspiciously like the one we rented with Moe from *The Three Stooges*. He was dressed in a baggy peach-colored jumpsuit. A large hole had been cut out of the front exposing a second layer with cartoon drawings of a rib cage and internal organs. Similar holes were on his arms, left thigh and shin, and right knee and ankle. A red clown nose rested on his face. Not a lot of men would seem confident while dressed like the body in Operation, but Dig seemed okay with it.

"What could she possibly have offered you to get you to dress up like that?" I asked.

"Ebony said she needed help with the kids," he said. "I'm good with kids so I figured what the heck."

"Where'd you get the costume?"

"Jerry made it. He dropped it off at the tow yard before he and Don headed out to Moxie."

"You knew they were going to watch the meteor shower?"

"Meteor shower. That's what they told you?"

"Yes. Why?"

"I'm pretty sure your dad was trying to give you some privacy in the event you wanted to have company at the house."

"No, I'm pretty sure he and Don were trying to get photographic evidence of extraterrestrials. Did he say anything about the store? About the way I was running it?"

"No. He did have a hard time finding the clown shoes. Said something about how they were always on the shelf next to the gorilla feet and why would you move them?"

"Because I put all of the feet together," I said. "Sometimes when people don't know what costume they want, they look at the shoes. And when they see the feet, they make a decision. It's good business."

Dig held his hands up and the plastic sleeves of his jumpsuit dropped to his elbows. "Hey, don't put me in the middle of it. Maybe he was put off by the fact that you didn't approve the change first."

Ebony put her hands on her hips. "Listen, yo. This woman here doesn't have to report to anybody. She's a full-grown independent costume shop manager. She holds the keys to the kingdom. Ain't nobody going to tell her how to do her job. Isn't that right, Margo?"

"Darn straight," I said.

Ebony and Dig looked at me as if I'd actually said a curse word. "Come on, you know I've never been able to curse around you," I said to Ebony. "Not since I was seven and asked you about the words somebody spray-painted on the side of the school and you washed my mouth out with soap."

Ebony crossed her arms and tipped her head to the side. The layers of her hair moved ever so slightly, as if she were the star of a shampoo commercial in the seventies. "If I recall, you were so traumatized by the experience that I ended up taking you out for a root beer float a half hour later."

"Something had to get the taste of Ivory soap out of my mouth."

"Girl, you think I use Ivory soap? My skin looks like this because I use one hundred percent pure cocoa butter. Have my whole life."

Dig looked at Ebony's bare arms appreciatively. "That cocoa butter is working for you," he said.

Ebony crossed her arms and lowered her head so she was staring down Dig in his Operation patient costume. "Little man, are you going to make Ebony regret asking you for help?"

"Dig is always available for Ebony." Something inside of his suit made a buzzing noise. He patted his chest and hips, and then reached inside the costume and pulled out a cell phone. "Dig's Towing," he answered. He turned his back to us and stepped a few feet away.

Ebony looked at me and shook her head. "Do you see what I have to put up with around here?"

"You love the attention and you know it." She smiled at me. "Remember that scavenger hunt idea? Did you start working on it yet?"

"Nope. I decided to take a stand. Too many people are trying to take control of this festival." She tapped herself on the chest. "Ebony is in charge. About time all these men around here recognize it."

"Who else is getting in your way besides Joel V. and the mayor?"

She put her hands on her hips. "Tak Hoshiyama, that's who. He zoned out this whole time and then took off for parts unknown and left me handling the complaints. You didn't chase him away, did you?"

"He had interviews," I said.

"He should be looking for work around here," she said. "How are you two supposed to have a relationship if he takes a job in Minnesota?"

"Michigan," I corrected. "That's where his interview is today. And it's not that simple."

"It's not that difficult either." Ebony's cell phone rang and she took the call. She held up a finger and turned around. "You tell those rich kids to stay off that playground." She hung up and turned back. "I gotta go. Kids think they can get away with more at the end of the day. Those slides weren't built to accommodate high school boys."

I scanned the grounds. Parents and children strolled around, but not as many as I'd seen in previous years. "Attendance is a little light this year, isn't it?"

"Hard to get into the spirit of the thing when all anybody can talk about is the murder. If I wasn't under contract, I'd cut my losses and let this thing go down in flames."

"Were the Domino Divas that big of a deal that people really were going to come here from all over to see them reunite?"

"You're too young to know what they meant to Proper City, but yes, they were a big deal. They gained national attention with their routines. Better than any sports team we had. You know who could tell you about them?"

"Who?"

"Your dad's friend, Don."

I felt a chill shudder through me as I remembered Don's handwriting on the back of the discarded issue of *Spicy Acorn*. "What does Don have to do with Ronnie?"

"They were pretty hot and heavy before she left town."

"Don Digby? The same guy who thinks Elvis is alive and well and running a secret branch of the DEA?"

"One and the same."

"So what happened?"

"Girl, you know Ebony doesn't go in much for town gossip," she said. "You'd better ask him if you want to know the skinny."

Dig rejoined Ebony and me. He pulled the black Moe wig from his bald head and spun it on his index finger like a Harlem Globetrotter spinning a basketball. "I gotta split. Tow job just came in and it's going to be a late night."

"That reminds me. The mayor doubled up the Zips and the Three is in bad shape. I told the driver to come see you."

He pointed to his phone. "That might be the job. Somebody from the mayor's office said there was a broken down vehicle on the Main Line. I gotta get my truck and take care of it. See ya, ladies." Dig reattached the red ball to the end of his nose. It lit up like Rudolph's. Ebony shooed him away. He smiled, touched his forehead and held his hand out in a tip-of-the-invisible-hat gesture, and left.

"So," I said to Ebony, "you needed help and you called Dig? He's going to get a hero complex."

"I needed a clown."

"He's not a clown. He's the patient from Operation. Why'd you need a clown? I don't know any clown-themed board games."

"It's a festival. I don't care what the mayor says, every festival needs a clown. And Dig is five foot ten and bald. He was the right man for the job."

"Dig is bald by choice, not by genetics."

Ebony pointed her finger at me. "You might be a full-blown woman in charge of that costume shop, but you're always going to be a baby girl to me. Don't you forget it."

"Okay, fine. Now, you were about to tell me about Don and Ronnie."

"No, I wasn't. Don't try to trick me, it won't work. If you want to know about Don and Ronnie, you have to ask him." She pointed to a small red and white striped tent on the edge of the festival grounds. "They got back this morning and asked for a better location. Don't tell Tak. That's their tent. Go crazy, but remember. There's a reason you haven't heard about this. It was a long time ago, and when two people break up, one of them usually holds a grudge."

I turned away and headed toward the *Spicy Acorn* tent. Even though the festival attendance was light, a crowd of people milled about outside the striped tent. As I grew closer, I realized that people were waiting to get inside. One man stood out, and not only because of his bright, copper-colored hair. Grady O'Toole would have stood out any-where at the festival, dressed as he was in a suit and tie.

Grady was the single most charming guy I'd ever met even if he was six years younger than me. His father owned a couple of casinos in Las Vegas, which put his

family securely on top of the Proper City food chain. He
lived in Christopher Robin Crossing, a development of
mansions designed for the wealthy contingency of Proper
City. A. A. Milne would have rolled over in his grave if
he knew.

Grady hadn't seen me, so I approached quietly and
tapped him on his left shoulder and then ducked over to
his right side. He turned to look one way, and then the
other. I laughed, having pulled off one of the more popular gags I remembered from the sixth grade.

"Margo! I thought I might run into you today."

"Is this your first visit to the festival?"

He nodded. "Yes. I came to talk to your dad."

"Why?" I asked. Grady had been known to throw
around his considerable wealth to host costume parties
for his crowd, but if that's what he wanted, he needed to
talk to me. "I'm in charge of Disguise DeLimit now," I
added.

"I heard. I almost came to you first, but this is really
more about Jerry."

"What are you talking about?"

Grady pushed his blazer open and tucked his hands
into the pockets of his trousers. He stood straight and
puffed up his chest a bit, projecting an air of self-
importance. "My dad said it's time I did something with
my life. He gave me two months to find a business opportunity to fund. Philanthropy, he called it. I think he
expected me to write somebody a check, get listed on
their board of directors in a non-voting role, and get on
with my life."

"Sounds like you," I said, only half joking.

"Hey, I resent that! Besides, Dad might have something. People don't think too much of me except for my bank account. But look at the kind of the guys you date. They're not rich, but people respect them because of their jobs. People think they're making a difference."

I knew there was more than one reason that Grady had avoided mention of Tak's name. Ever since I'd met Grady, there'd been an undercurrent of flirtation between us. On more than one occasion, he'd asked if I'd gotten tired of Tak's attention. I'd always laughed it off, but couldn't deny that secretly I found Grady's persistence flattering.

Grady's thoughts about philanthropy sounded honorable enough, but I didn't like the way he eyed my dad's booth while he said them. Before I could cut to the chase, a man in a Grateful Dead T-shirt, dirty Birkenstocks, and a full mousy-brown beard approached us. He held out a closed fist. Grady balled up his own fist and brought it down on top of the Dead Head's, who then repeated the action.

They turned to me. "I'm Finn," the Dead Head said. "Are you one of them?"

"Depends which 'them' you mean. I'm Margo. I'm with the nuts." I pointed toward the *Spicy Acorn* booth with my thumb stuck out like a hitchhiker.

"These guys are right on," he said. "They've been talking about how the government's been spying on us." He held up a copy of *Spicy Acorn*. "Their newspaper opened my eyes to things I never even thought about. Best booth at the festival. You think they're hiring?"

"I'm pretty sure they're keeping it a small staff." I looked at Grady. He shrugged and smiled, and then stepped away from us and toward another cluster of people. I turned back to Finn. "If their message is so popular, why is everybody outside and not in there listening to them?"

"It's exactly what they've been telling us. Once the man found out what they were saying, he'd come after them. It just lends credence to their message, you know? Speak the truth and watch out for authority."

I looked around. "What man?"

"The G-man. Except in this case, he sent a woman to do a man's job." He smiled and made a fist and held it out. "Equal rights, man. Power to the people."

I was getting nowhere. "Excuse me," I said. I moved past the crowd and went into the tent. Amid cries of protest, I turned around. "My dad's booth," I said. "Family emergency."

When I went inside, I realized that I'd been more correct than I thought. Detective Nancy Nichols stood in front of Don Digby, and she was in the middle of reading him his rights.

Chapter 9

DON, DETECTIVE NICHOLS, and my dad all turned to face me. Their expressions covered a range from outrage, annoyance, and concern. The concern was in my dad's face. I could tell he wanted me to turn around and leave. I took a breath to speak, but my dad moved his head very slightly from side to side. Detective Nichols appeared to give me a moment to react.

"I need to talk to my dad," I said.

The detective put her hand on Don's arm and guided him toward the exit. Once they left, a few cheers went up from outside. I recognized Finn's voice out front: "You can't shut down the truth!"

My dad rushed past me and pulled the zipper on the tent flaps down to indicate that the booth was closed. "Do me a favor, Margo. Behind the table is a sketchpad. Make a sign that says we'll return tomorrow. I need to do damage control." He rushed around the booth, packing up copies of *Spicy Acorn* and stuffing them into boxes.

I put my hand on his arm. "Dad, stop. I don't think the detective wants to talk to Don about conspiracy theories," I said gently. "I think this has to do with Ronnie Cass's murder."

"What could Don possibly know about the murder? He and Ronnie were a lifetime ago." He buzzed around the tent stashing supplies. I wrote out his sign and he reached under the tent and propped up the sign out front.

I settled into a chair. "So there *was* a Don and Ronnie? They actually were a couple?"

My dad stopped what he was doing and sat down too. "Yes, there was a Don and Ronnie. He loved her. He even bought her a ring. But Ronnie had an agenda that didn't include marriage to a poker-playing male nurse who likes the blues. She wanted to be rich and she wanted to be famous. Don wasn't going to give her either one of those things."

As I listened, I noticed a figure hovering outside the tent, close enough to hear us. I held my finger up to my lips, and then pointed toward the wall. Though distorted, it appeared to be a misshapen man in a top hat. Whoever he was, he was dressed in costume.

"It's getting late and the festival is about to close for the night. Let's secure the booth and head home," I said in a loud voice. I pointed to the shadow again. In a lower voice, I added, "We can talk about this later."

I could tell that my dad wanted to argue with me, but the shadow hadn't moved. "I'll finish up here," he said equally loudly. "Why don't you go check in with Bobbie?"

"Good idea."

I left the booth quickly, looking at the spot where the eavesdropper had been. And there he was, dressed in a black tux and red bow tie, thick white mustache, and a cane. Our eavesdropper was a cardboard cutout of Rich Uncle Pennybags, the millionaire character from Monopoly, propped up on a dirt patch outside of the conspiracy theory booth.

I felt silly for imagining that someone had been listening to us, but instead of admitting my error, I headed to Bobbie's spot at the festival. She was talking to Joel V.

Today he was dressed in a pink and white striped shirt, a pink and orange floral necktie, and orange pants. The man did not shy away from color. Bobbie pointed to me. "Here she is now," she said.

Joel turned to me. "Bobbie says you made domino costumes for the bears."

"That's right. It was a last-minute idea. Bobbie and I were unpacking the bears, and the two thoughts just merged. You know how ideas do that sometimes."

"Yes, but now if we expect any kind of profit, we have to scrub any mention of the dominos from the festival."

"Wait a minute," Bobbie interjected. "The festival is a Proper City tradition. It's not a moneymaker. I've approached the mayor's office about fund-raising for the past five years and for five years I've been shut down. And I'm a nonprofit. The message has always been, this is for the residents of the city. Everybody who participates is responsible for funding their own booth, donating their materials and time. There are no financial winners here." She picked up one of the small bears. "That's why I'm giving these away."

"Maybe that was the case in the past, but not this year," Joel said. "I saw the agreement myself. Ronnie had Mayor Young sign a contract that paid the Domino Divas fifty percent of festival income in exchange for the use of their name and logo."

"Is that public knowledge?" I asked.

Joel straightened up and adjusted his floral tie. Guilt slid across his face, like a kid who'd just tattled on his brother for swiping a cookie before dinner. He raised his hand and held two fingers up in a Scout's honor gesture, then pointed them at Bobbie and me. "Let's not turn this into a thing. The mayor is counting on me to fix this so people aren't distracted by the tragedy."

"That's pretty callous," I said. "The mayor should be worried about what it says about him that he's willing to gloss over the fact that a woman was murdered at the festival."

"She wasn't murdered at the festival. She was murdered in her trailer that was parked on an adjacent street. There is a difference." Joel picked up one of the bears. His hand gripped the back of its head, causing the bear's face to scrunch up. "I have a proposition for you. Because of the original agreement with the Domino Divas, everything from this festival has their logo on it."

"Ebony already asked me to take Ronnie's place so the divas could perform and I said yes, so if that's what you were going to ask, don't bother."

"You're going to be a Double D?" Bobbie asked.

I glanced down at my chest. "This might be the closest I get."

"Not necessary," Joel said. "I found another act. This time tomorrow, *Clue: The Musical* takes the stage." He stared into the face of the little bear and then back at me. "So I'm going to need Clue costumes for the bears. Professor Plum, Colonel Mustard, Mrs. White, Miss Scarlet. Can you do that?"

As much as I didn't like the idea of adding to my work-load, I knew his idea was genius. Tiny bears dressed to match the costumes of the characters from Clue would make everybody forget about the Domino Divas and the murder. Photos of the Clue bears would pop up on social media and within twenty-four hours, people would forget about the Double Ds. Considering it was almost nine p.m., the only problem was when I would find the time to make them.

"If you think you can't do it, I can go to that other costume shop. Truth is, that might be easier since they're making the costumes for the stage show. I need an answer right now. Yes or no?"

"It's going to require an all-nighter," I said.

"A hundred bears in Clue costumes by tomorrow. Yes or no?"

"A hundred!" I exclaimed. "I can't make a hundred by tomorrow." He pulled his phone out and scrolled through his contacts. "Who are you calling?"

"Candy Girls."

"I'll do it!" I said. Joel V. wasn't giving this business to Gina Cassavogli. "I'll do my best. But I need some-thing from you." The idea came to me in an instant. "You must have video or pictures of the divas performing. Can you send them to me?"

"Why do you need that?"

"Posterity." He looked at the rack of costumes hanging next to me. "I made their costumes. I'd like something to show for it."

He didn't look happy. "I don't want word to get out that I did this." He swiped the phone screen a few times. "What's your number?"

Between Detective Nichols taking Don out of my dad's booth and now Joel V. requesting a hundred bear costumes overnight, I'd completely forgotten about my phone falling into the grate under Ronnie's trailer. "Can you e-mail it instead?" I asked.

"E-mail, sure. What's your addy?"

I gave him the e-mail address for Disguise DeLimit. He repeated it into the voice recorder of his phone. "Thanks, ladies. I'll be in touch." He pushed his phone into the back pocket of his striped pants and left.

"What was that all about?" Bobbie asked. "You don't need to see that video. Why the story?"

I held my hand horizontal and slowly lowered it in the universal pantomime for "keep it down." I held my finger to my lips, just in case she wasn't fluent in universal pantomime, and pulled her deeper into the booth. "I don't think Ronnie performed yesterday," I said. "Which means somebody else stood in for her. If we can see that video, really analyze it, we might be able to figure out—"

Bobbie pushed me away. "No, we won't. *We*," she said pointing at me, "need to get to work on a hundred bears in Clue costumes for tomorrow. Leave this alone, Mitty. It's not your problem."

Deep down, I knew she was right. Just because I'd had a little success in the past when crime had come to Proper, threatening Ebony and then my family's store, didn't mean that I knew what I was doing. The same experiences had threatened my life and put a strain on my relationship with Tak. The smart thing to do would be to let it go. Except that somehow my dad's best friend was connected to whatever had happened to Ronnie and

I'd learned a long time ago that friends were as important as family.

"The police need to know what Joel just told us. They need to see that video and check the diva contract."

"So call Detective Nichols and tell her about it," she said.

"I can't. I dropped my phone down the sewer grate underneath Ronnie's trailer."

"I'm afraid to ask this next question. What were you doing under Ronnie's trailer?"

"I was looking for evidence, okay? When I found her body, I saw a blue domino mask on the sidewalk. Ronnie was the blue domino. Detective Nichols says I imagined it because her team didn't find it."

"It's been over twenty-four hours," she said. "Even if you did claim to find it now, don't you think she'd dismiss it? You could very easily take a blue mask from the store and say it was in the grate. Mits, I know you feel like you're in some kind of competition with Nancy Nichols, but she's doing her job and you're kinda getting in her way."

"So you're saying if I found something suspicious in that grate today, nobody would believe me?"

"Did you? Did you find the blue mask in the sewer grate?"

"No, I didn't find a blue mask in the grate," I said. I leaned back and put my hands on my hips. "I found a teddy bear."

Bobbie's face went pale. "In the sewer? Under the trailer?" I nodded. She grabbed my wrist. "Let's go."

Bobbie closed the flaps to her booth. She found one

of the security guards standing by a nearby trash can. "Keep an eye on my booth, please? I'll be right back. Ten minutes," she said, holding up all of her fingers. He nodded.

Proper City had grown dark. We hurried through the patches of dead yellow grass, crossed the street, and came to a halt as we rounded the corner. Ronnie's trailer, which earlier had been parked along the curb of Rapunzel Road, was gone.

Chapter 10

"**WHERE DID THE** trailer go?" I asked. "It was right here."

"Do you have the right road?" Bobbie asked.

"Of course I have the right road." I took a few steps forward and stepped down off of the curb by the sewer grate. It was too dark to see inside it. "Do you have a flashlight?" I asked.

"Hold on." She fiddled with her phone until a beam of light shined out from it, just like I'd done with mine. The fact that the sewer was dark told me my battery had died.

I squatted by the grate and squinted. Two hours earlier, I'd seen my phone drop onto the lap of a teddy bear. Now, I wasn't sure that other critters weren't occupying the same close quarters. I looked up at Bobbie. She bent down, soiling the knees of her khaki pants on the sidewalk, and pointed the light to the grate. Even with only the slim beam from her phone's light, I could make out the shape of my phone resting on top of the bear.

"What does it mean?" Bobbie asked.

"It means that somebody put a teddy bear in a sewer grate. I don't know how or when, or who or why, but I dropped my phone earlier today, so it happened before that," I said. "I thought Ebony put it there for the scavenger hunt the mayor asked her to arrange, but she said she's taking a stand and ignoring his request."

"How long was the trailer parked here?"

"I don't know. A week?"

"You said yourself that there wasn't a lot of room under the trailer. So somebody must have put him in there before the trailer was parked."

"There's another possibility," I said. My knees were sore from squatting so I shifted myself onto the curb and rested my feet next to the grate. My yellow tights snagged on the concrete and a run climbed up my leg. "Somebody put the bear in the grate because they knew the trailer would be parked there. They knew as long as the grate was covered, nobody would look inside it." I looked away from the grate and at Bobbie. "But then Ronnie was murdered. It's too much of a coincidence. That bear has something to do with what happened."

Bobbie turned the flashlight off on her phone and held it out to me. Without words, I took it and made the call I knew I had to make.

TWENTY minutes later, we were joined by Detective Nichols. "Margo, Bobbie," she said. She did not seem surprised by the lack of trailer on the street. I knew as long as she was calling us by our first names, we fell into the category of concerned citizens and not nuisances or suspects. Once she went all "Ms. Tamblyn" on me, I had cause for alarm. "What's this about more evidence?"

I'd made the decision to remain vague on the phone call in order to get her to the scene. Something about evidence hidden in a teddy bear in the same grate I claimed held a phantom blue domino mask sounded a bit fantastic, like the fairy tales the local roads had been named after. When I'd mentioned evidence, she agreed to join us without further questions.

Bobbie and I both stood. When Nancy—as long as we were on first name basis, I figured why not think of her that way?—held out her hand, I shook it. She looked at Bobbie, who looked at me, who took a deep breath and prepared to watch the polite respect we'd been getting from the detective evaporate.

"Earlier today, I came out here to look for the blue mask that I told you about," I said. "The one that I think came from Ronnie's domino costume."

She held her hand up to stop me. "Ms. Tamblyn, you've already told us about the mask. My team checked inside the trailer. We found her blue mask wedged between the bed and the wall."

"You did? But that means the one I saw out here must have been a duplicate. Which supports my theory that it wasn't Ronnie at rehearsal, it was somebody dressed up as her."

I waited for a reaction from Nancy. Her expression remained unreadable. If she ever decided to get into the local poker game, she'd be a worthy contender.

"Margo, I know you like to think that I am a bumbling

small-town cop who can't do her job. I wake up every morning with that in my head. But here's the thing: I'm here because I chose to be here, not because I was shuffled to your district by some vindictive boss. Crime in Proper City has been on the rise for the past decade. I saw it long before you moved back. I became a cop because my dad was a cop. I respect the job and I want to make a difference. I became a detective because I want to investigate. So while I appreciate the fact that you've been forthcoming with the evidence that you've found, I don't want you to get the feeling that I rely solely on you for clues. Do you understand?"

I bristled at her words and heat rushed to my face. "Let me finish. I thought maybe the mask had rolled under the trailer. There's this sewer grate, see? And I thought—"

"That the mask had dropped into the sewer grate. This is all very convenient. I suppose when I look in the grate I'll see a blue mask that will incriminate someone other our current person of interest. Am I right?"

"That's what I thought too, but you're wrong," Bobbie said.

I didn't want to gloat, but I was really happy that she'd asked that question. "When you look in that grate you'll see my cell phone."

"And a teddy bear," Bobbie added.

Nancy looked back and forth between Bobbie's and my faces. "A teddy bear? How'd that get in there?"

"We don't know, but it seems that if a bear was inside of a grate that was under where Ronnie's trailer had been parked, maybe it was evidence in your investigation and we should tell you," I said. While technically it had been Bobbie's idea, I felt I'd earned the right to point it out.

Nancy unclipped a flashlight from her belt and clicked it on. She stooped down above the grate and aimed the beam into the hole. She moved the beam slightly, an inch here, an inch there, and then she straightened up quickly, her eyes wide.

"What?" I asked. "Did you see the bear?"

"No. I saw a snake."

Both Nancy and Bobbie turned to look at me. I held up my hands in surrender. "Don't look at me. I didn't put it there."

Nancy stood up and called somebody. She gave the address and instructed them to bring tools and a net. When she hung up, she turned to us. "I'm delegating," she said. It wasn't like we were judging her.

Bobbie and I moved from our position near the grate to the wall of the building. A police car arrived quickly, and two uniformed male officers got out. Nancy pointed to the grate, pointed to me, and then held her hands in approximately the size of the bear. One officer inserted a bit into a cordless power drill and then unscrewed the corner screws one by one. When he finished, the other officer lifted the grate and set it on the sidewalk. The first officer looked at Nancy. She held out a plastic bag. "Put the bear and the phone in here," she said.

"That's my phone!" I said.

"Like you said, it's evidence. I should be able to have it back to you tomorrow," she said.

The officer reached down and pulled out my phone first, and then the small bear. He was smudged with a dusting of dry dirt, as if he'd been dredged through chocolate powdered milk. The officer put both items into the bag and sealed it. He set it on the sidewalk next to the drill and reached back into the sewer. Bobbie, Nancy, and I all took a step backward, predicting what he'd pull out next.

We were wrong. The snake may not have been hiding under the bear, but a round piece of felt was. It was one of the circles I'd glued onto the Domino Diva costumes.

It appeared as though one of Ronnie's fellow dancers had visited her the day she'd died.

Chapter 11

IF THE DETECTIVE recognized the felt circle, she didn't say. This time, I was keeping my mouth shut and my theories to myself. After all that nonsense about not counting on me for clues, Detective Nichols was going to have to do her own detecting to figure out what I already knew.

After the officers and the detective left, Bobbie and I returned to the festival until closing time. She reminded me that I was expected to make a hundred bear costumes by festival opening tomorrow. I waited at the Zip-Three stop for a few minutes until a yellow school bus rumbled toward me. The doors opened, and the driver, a crotchety-looking old man covered with wrinkles and thin gray hair, looked at me. "If you want a ride, you'd better get on now. I'm the last run of the night."

I climbed on and took a seat halfway back. The bus was already mostly full. The woman next to me wore a tight red satin dress, red fishnets, and red platform shoes.

Her hair was jet-black and parted on the side. It was curled under and the back was held into place with a soft net.

"Nice costume," she said to me. "What are you performing in?"

I glanced down at my black and yellow striped bumblebee romper. "This? I work in a costume shop, so I wear a lot of costumes because it's free publicity."

"Candy Girls?" she asked. "I haven't seen you there."

"No. Disguise DeLimit. Candy Girls is more of a party store, but Disguise DeLimit specializes in costumes only. We've been around a lot longer than they have."

"'We'?" She laughed. "The owners must love you. You sound like you own the place."

"It's a family-run shop. My dad and me. He ran it for most of my life, but I'm back in Proper City now, so I run the shop and he scouts costumes around the country."

The man in the seat in front of us turned around. His face looked far younger than I'd originally placed him thanks to the gray hair that hung down from under a pith helmet. He wore a safari-style jacket over a white shirt and a yellow ascot. Several medals were pinned above his left pocket. "You don't just order your costumes from a catalog?"

"No, we're not that kind of costume shop."

The woman tapped the shoulder of the man across the aisle. He wore a purple tweed blazer with elbow patches over a purple argyle sweater. "Did you hear about her store?" she asked.

"Yeah," he answered. He leaned forward and looked at me. "You ever take custom jobs?"

"All the time. That's one of our specialties." As I talked, I noticed that more and more of the people on the bus were tuning in to our conversation. Not only that, I noticed that their outfits were not everyday outfits, and the direction of the conversation started to make sense. "Are you all actors?"

"We're the Traveling Thespians," the woman in the red satin dress said.

"Not anymore," the man in tweed interjected. "Now we're the Proper City Players."

"I live in Proper City and I don't know you."

"We used to travel up and down Route 15 looking for places to perform. Somebody from the Sagebrush Festival approached us with the opportunity to be the replacement act if we were willing to change our name."

I studied their outfits. "You're performing *Clue: The Musical*," I correctly deduced. The mayor's office hadn't missed a beat. "Professor Plum, Colonel Mustard, and Miss Scarlet," I said, pointing one at a time to the three who had engaged me in conversation.

"Yes!" Miss Scarlet smoothed a few wrinkles out of her red satin dress. "I guess the costumes aren't too bad if you could recognize what they were from."

"Actually, I'm sort of going to be working on costumes based on yours." I explained how I was about to head back to the shop to start working on costumes for teddy bears that were based on their production.

"Clue bears? How charming," said Colonel Mustard.

Miss Scarlet smiled. "How are you supposed to make costumes based on ours when you never saw them?"

"To be honest, I was going to make them up based on the original board game. But why are you in costume now? I heard that you were taking the place of the last act, but when do you start?

"It's not that far from what you're doing. We need all the publicity that we can get, so we agreed to wear our costumes until the festival is over. People see us dressed like this and they ask questions."

"Here's a question: Will you follow me to the store so I can take pictures myself?"

IT was after eleven when the cast of *Clue: The Musical* left Disguise DeLimit. When I couldn't find the battery to the digital camera, I asked them to use their cell phones to take pictures of each other and then I let them browse the store while I downloaded everything onto the store's computer. There was much excitement over our rack of gangster suits and flapper dresses, more understandable when they told me their next production was going to be *Guys and Dolls*.

After they left, I went upstairs to the kitchen. I brewed a pot of coffee and ate a bowl of Fruity Pebbles. Soot sat on the windowsill staring at the glass as if it was sweeps week and he was watching his favorite program. "I don't suppose tonight's the night you want to start helping me make costumes," I said.

"You need help with costumes?" he answered. I jumped, and the cereal bowl, mostly empty except for a little blue milk that I had yet to finish, tipped over and fell on the floor. Soot jumped down from the sill, sniffed the spill, and immediately lapped it up. My dad stood up from outside the window. "Hold on, I'll be right inside."

I put my hand on my chest to calm my racing heart.

His footsteps descended down the rungs of a ladder, and then seconds later, the back door opened and shut downstairs. He made his way up the stairs and joined me in the kitchen.

"What were you doing outside on the ladder?" I asked.

"Trying to get an establishing shot."

"Of what? The festival? Does this have to do with your newspaper? You're not— Don's not planning on doing a conspiracy story on Ronnie's murder, is he?

He gave me a funny look. "No. The footage from Moxie didn't turn out as well as we expected. If I can get the telescope set up on the roof, I might be able to set a timer and capture part of the meteor shower."

Mention of the trip to Moxie set my suspicion meter on alert, but I refrained from calling my dad's bluff. If Dig was right and the reason my dad and Don had vacated the premises was so I could entertain gentlemen callers, I'd rather avoid the ensuing conversation.

My dad rubbed at his eyes. "What time is it?"

"It's after eleven." I poured a cup of coffee. "Stay as long as you want. I'm going downstairs to work." I purposely remained vague. What would he say when he heard I was making costumes for bears—costumes that we not only wouldn't get paid for, but that were based on ones made by Candy Girls? The realization hit me. We'd be getting nothing from me doing this extra work. No word of mouth. No potential business. No income.

"I'm awake now. What are you working on? I can help."

I shook my head. "I don't think it's worth your time. Go to bed. I'll try to be quiet."

I carried my coffee downstairs and reviewed the photos on the computer. The last time I'd made a series of costumes for bears—when you run a costume shop, you don't get picky about clients—I'd learned that it was easiest to simplify and then mass produce. But costumes based on the characters in Clue? I didn't see a way to simplify. Footsteps sounded on the stairs and my dad joined me in the sewing room. He surveyed the photos scattered across the workstation and then picked up a small teddy bear.

"This has to do with the festival?"

"Sort of," I said. "You know that the Domino Divas were supposed to headline the festival, right?" He nodded. "After what happened, Mayor Young won't call off the festival. I ran into this group of actors on the Zip line tonight. They call themselves the Traveling Thespians—or at least they used to. They said they've been performing across Nevada, but somebody from the festival got in touch with them with the opportunity to become the replacement act for the divas."

My dad shook his head. "You have to give Mayor Young credit," he said. "What he lacks in community-building vision, he makes up for with opportunistic thinking."

"I figured it was either him or his publicist."

"Joel V. You're right, this does have publicity stunt written all over it. What does it have to do with costumes?"

"Joel wants to scrub the festival of the divas' presence, so that means no more dominos. Apparently Mayor Young hired these guys to perform *Clue: The Musical.*"

"And now you're making costumes." He spread out the pictures that I'd printed out. "Why didn't you just rent them costumes from our inventory? We have a full set of Clue costumes. I think they've been in storage since Edith and Eddie Green renewed their vows last year."

"I didn't make these costumes," I said. "They came from Candy Girls."

He sat back and studied me. "You're collaborating with Candy Girls?"

"Of course not!" I said. "Candy Girls already had the account. What's weird is that the cast acted like they'd never heard of us. I thought we had strong ties to the local community theater groups."

"We rent to the community players all the time. This must be something new. What did you say they were called?"

"The Proper City Players," I said. I toggled from the screen showing the pictures of the costumes to a new Internet window and typed *Proper City Players* into the search bar. I was redirected to a slick site that announced the upcoming performance of *Clue* as the headliner of the Sagebrush Festival. I was less surprised by the costumes in the photos than the identity of Mrs. Peacock, the newly appointed star of the show.

It was Jayne Lemming.

Chapter 12

"JAYNE LEMMING IS the star of *Clue*? She's one of the divas," I said. "I didn't know she was in the Proper City Players too."

"You know how acting types are. They don't like to turn down roles," my dad said.

"Yes, but Jayne was the choreographer for the divas. Now that Ronnie is dead, the divas can't perform and Jayne is going to be the new star of the show. *New* star. It says so right on their website. Doesn't that seem suspicious?"

"Margo, don't jump to conclusions. You're talking community theater here. *Waiting for Guffman*, not *Black Swan*. Jayne probably knew the festival needed a new leading act. She may have been the one to approach the Proper City Players."

"But don't you see?" I said. "Ronnie's murder should have shaken everybody up. It should have been cause to cancel the festival, or postpone it, or something. But it didn't. The mayor is obsessed with the festival being a success despite the murder. He demanded that the festival continue. He has a publicist spinning it so people forget about the tragedy and still come out and spend their money. And then there's Jayne. Her friend—even if they fought, you'd think they were friends—was murdered. She could be involved. I found a felt circle by Ronnie's trailer. It could have come from her costume. I wish there was a way for me to check."

"Margo, let the police do their job."

"Come on, Dad, you're a reporter now. You want to uncover the truth, right? Jayne should be in mourning and instead, she's in the spotlight. Ronnie is dead and the divas are going to fade into oblivion after this, but Jayne is still going to get her fifteen minutes of fame."

"Some people are like that," he said. "You can ask all the questions you want, but you're never going to change human nature." My dad toggled back to the photos of the *Clue* costumes. "I still don't understand why Candy Girls is making the costumes. Why wouldn't Jayne have them work with us? Her husband was very happy with the Mardi Gras costumes we've done for him for the past five years."

It was unclear to me whether he was truly concerned by the costume situation or if he was trying to distract me. "I think Jayne is hiding something. I don't know what or why, but something about the way she barely even acknowledges Ronnie's death is suspicious. Her lack of sadness is like a big red flag waving in front of my face."

I thought back over my conversation with Gina Cassavogli. Unlike Jayne, she'd seemed upset about what had happened, but not for the reasons I would have expected. She'd asked me to look into the death of her mother, but not because she felt any kind of bond with her. Why had Gina come to me at all? Considering both she and Jayne had said the same thing about Ronnie being out for herself, what kind of relationship did the mother and daughter have? And here they were, two people who should have been close to Ronnie but had moved on awfully quickly.

I yawned. My dad picked up the coffee mug and moved it away from me. "You don't need caffeine. You need power foods. Go upstairs and eat a handful of almonds and a cup of Greek yogurt, and then come back down here. If we're going to produce a hundred costumes by tomorrow morning, it's going to be a long night."

"You're still going to help me? Even if Candy Girls is going to get the publicity for the costumes?"

He put his hand on my shoulder. "Candy Girls is going to get the credit for those crappy costumes, yes. But Disguise DeLimit is going to get the credit for the teddy bears. I'll see to that. Now, go eat some real food and then let's get started."

BEFORE moving back to Proper City, I'd lived in Las Vegas and worked as a magician's assistant. Not one of the good magicians either. Think rickety wooden stage, threadbare velvet curtains, and lots of sequins. The bar had a two-drink minimum, and the doves often tried to escape during the act. I'd learned a few things during those years: among the more important ones, the facts that misdirection is a handy skill and good Chinese food comes cheap at four o'clock in the morning. But the number one lesson I'd learned was that if you don't look at the clock, your body doesn't know it's time to sleep.

Since I'd been back in Proper and in charge of running Disguise DeLimit, there had been more than one time when I'd done things my way instead of my dad's. But tonight, as I watched him work, I was inspired by what he was able to accomplish.

First, he'd located a stack of T-shirt iron-on transfer paper. He measured the small teddy bear and then mocked up a two-dimensional cartoon safari costume on the computer screen. "Go to the stockroom and find the boxes labeled PREEMIE. Bring them out here."

It took me about ten minutes to find the boxes he wanted and another five to dig them out from where I'd stacked the fog machines after Halloween. By the time I returned to the workroom, he'd set up the iron next to our workstation. He opened the box of preemie garments and took one out. He lined up one of the images on the front and ironed it on. The printer chugged out more sheets while he handed the first T-shirt to me and moved on to the next. I pulled one of the small shirts over the head of one of the teddy bear models and turned him to face my dad. "Colonel Mustard is complete."

"Almost complete. He needs his ascot," he said. He picked up a small cutting of yellow fabric, knotted it around the neck of the teddy bear, and tucked the ends in. "*Now* he's complete. Here, you take over the ironing. I'll make aprons for Mrs. White."

We continued that way—with the clocks draped with fabric so we didn't know what time it was—until we were done. I added an accessory to each one: a script for Miss Scarlet, elbow patches for Professor Plum. I was stumped when it came to Mrs. Peacock until I looked up images online and got the idea to cut small cat-eye glasses out of sheets of blue tinted plastic. We took a little creative license, printing out a peacock-feather pattern to iron onto the small white cotton garment. After attaching the cat-eye glasses with glue dots to the corners of their eyes, the Mrs. Peacock bears would be complete.

By the time we pulled the fabric from the clocks, it was after four in the morning. I climbed upstairs, curled up next to Soot on my bed, and fell asleep in the bumble-bee romper.

WHEN I woke later that morning, I wanted nothing more than to go back to sleep. So I did—or tried, at least. I rolled over and found a bear dressed like Professor Plum on the nightstand next to me. He held a sign that read: WAKE UP, MARGO.

I picked the bear up and looked at the clock. It was after ten and the shop would have to be open by eleven. There wasn't enough time to drop off the costumes, come back, and take care of business, let alone take a shower. I stood up and caught my reflection.

Change in plans. I had to make time for a shower.

After the shower, I dressed in a pair of green harem pants, a matching tank top, and a vest trimmed with gold braid. I pulled my wet hair into a high ponytail and wrapped the base of it with gold cord like on *I Dream of Jeannie*. If only I could grant wishes too.

I slipped on a pair of gold Turkish slippers and made a kale and yogurt smoothie. I drank half and poured the rest into a gold genie bottle that I attached to a loop on

the hip of my costume. I went downstairs to pack up the
bear costumes. There were more boxes than I expected
and there was no way I could strap them to my Vespa. I
went behind the counter to the phone on the wall and
called Kirby.

"Hey, Margo," he answered. His voice sounded flat,
dejected.

"Hey, Kirby." I paused. "Are you okay?"

"Yeah. No. Yeah. Whatever."

That was clear. "You want to talk about something?"

"Not now. Maybe later. Do you need me to come to
the store?"

"If you can. When does school get out?"

"I can leave after Spanish class, so in, like, forty-five
minutes. I padded my schedule so I have study hall all
afternoon."

"Perfect."

"Are you going to be around? I want to talk to you,"
he said.

"Sure. See you soon."

There was barely time to get the register open by
eleven. I unlocked the front door and filled a rack with
assorted tie-dyed shirts from the '60s section of the store,
and then made a sign: TIE-DYED SHIRTS: $10, OR MAKE
YOUR OWN FOR $15. I lined up four buckets of water and
added red, blue, and yellow dye to the first three, and a
gallon of half vinegar, half water to the fourth one. I set
a shoebox filled with various sized rubber bands on the
sidewalk and filled the rest of the rack with an assortment
of plain white T-shirts from the stockroom. Two girls I
guessed to be about Kirby's age walked up and stopped
when they read the sign.

"OMG, you can make tie-dye?"

"Like, seriously?" said the other.

"Sure," I answered. "You put rubber bands around the T-shirt and then dunk the T-shirt into the dye. The dye bleeds together into abstract patterns, and the rubber bands make interesting negative space—you know, where the dye doesn't absorb."

They looked at each other. "This is totally epic. Wanna do it?"

"Abso. It's like art class with clothes."

They each selected tees from the rack—I didn't comment on the fact that both went straight for kids' sizes instead of ones that were made for adults—and then I instructed them on how to knot the shirt with the rubber bands and then dunk them. Blue water splashed out of the first bucket and I jumped back so as not to stain my Turkish slippers. The first girl went with a dip into all three buckets, but the second stuck with the red.

After they were finished dunking in the colored water, they submerged their shirts into the last bucket. The vinegar/water mixture would help set the color and keep the dye from crocking—the term for when color transfers onto other garments.

"What's next?" asked the first girl.

"That's pretty much it," I said.

"But they're all wet," she said.

"And they smell like vinegar," said the other.

The one thing I hadn't thought of was the drying process. "The first time you wash it, the vinegar scent will go away completely. But you're right, they do need to dry."

Fortunately, the desert air of Proper would suck the

moisture into the atmosphere in no time. "Wait here," I said. I grabbed an empty rack and a handful of hangers from inside. Out front, I had them remove the rubber bands and hang the shirts on the rack. "They'll be ready in fifteen minutes," I predicted. "In the meantime, come on inside and browse."

Hanging the drying shirts out front served the secondary purpose of luring in customers. By the time Kirby arrived, I'd sold fourteen T-shirts and had had to refill the blue dye bucket twice—although the second time was because a child had tipped it over. Blue water flowed across the sidewalk, leaving a trail to the sewer grate. As atrocious as it was, I was thankful he hadn't tipped over the more ominous, blood-like red.

After tending to the buckets, I went inside and found Kirby behind the counter, a dirty rag and an assortment of car parts scattered in front of him.

Kirby Grizwitz was a tall, lanky high school senior. He had wild curly hair and a swimmer's body, broad shoulders, narrow hips, low body fat. He'd found his way to a job in the store under my dad's management. As I'd gotten to know him, I'd learned of his crush on Varla, the head of the high school drama club. We'd worked out a deal where the drama club would provide us with the occasional backdrop for our widow displays in exchange for a 20 percent discount on costumes for their annual performances. This meant Varla had become something of a regular, a fact that left Kirby in a constant state of embarrassment when she was around, even though he'd proven his creativity in the form of costumes over Halloween when he'd convinced the swim team to help with the unexpected crowds.

"Hey, Margo," he said in the same voice he'd used on the phone earlier.

"Hi, Kirby. What's this?" I asked.

He sighed. "My parents said I can't get a dune buggy until my sophomore year of college. So I have two choices: drive my mom's minivan or my dad's minivan."

"Or assemble your own car from the ground up?" I asked, indicating the parts on the towel in front of him.

"I've been spending a lot of time at the dealerships out at the end of Main Line Road. Red Harkonnen has a dune buggy on his lot that I can almost afford, but it needs a lot of work. He said I could work on the carburetor in my spare time since it's just sitting there not going anywhere."

I was impressed. "I didn't know you knew how to rebuild a carburetor."

"I don't." He picked up the book in front of him, displaying the title *Auto Repair for Dummies*. He set the book back down. "Auto Shop's been no help. I missed the last couple of classes because of swim meets and now my grades are slipping. If my grades drop any lower, I'll lose my scholarship to college in the fall. None of this is going as planned." He tossed the metal piece that he'd been holding onto the counter and it bounced off of another piece, and then knocked into a smaller bolt. The bolt rolled to the end of the counter and fell. Soot, appearing from under the rack of fringed flapper dresses, ran forward and tapped it a couple of times, and then swatted it across the highly polished concrete floor. It skidded against the surface and disappeared under a bookcase filled with slippers shaped like Godzilla feet.

"Great," Kirby said. He tossed the rag onto the counter next to the other car parts, but didn't make a move to retrieve the bolt.

"Come on. The two of us can move that bookcase without unloading it. I've been meaning to rearrange that wall anyway."

He followed me to the bookcase and we each took a side. Slowly, we shifted it away from the wall. "Bring your end toward me," I said. Kirby scooted his side in a semicircle. As he looked down at the floor to make sure nothing was in his way, the bookcase tipped. Furry Godzilla feet showered the floor. Soot, who had caused the impromptu floor move with his game of hide-the-bolt and now oversaw the move of the bookcase like a curious onlooker, jumped out of the way and scurried up the stairs.

Kirby righted the now-empty bookcase and dropped onto a lime green beanbag chair that sat close by. "I'm sorry. I can't do anything right these days."

I scooped up several Godzilla feet and set them on the empty shelf. "You seem distracted. What's up? This all can't be about a car."

"Angus O'Toole," he said. "Captain of the football team."

"What does this Angus O'Toole have to do with anything?"

"He likes Varla."

The picture came into focus. "Does Varla like him?"

He looked at me like I'd missed a vital part of the conversation. "Did you not hear me say he's the captain of the football team?"

"So what? You're the captain of the swim team."

"It's not the same."

"I don't see why not. Swimming is as cool as football."

"You can't compare the two. He's out there on the field padded up to look like a warrior. I'm on the side of a pool stripped down to a Speedo."

Kirby had never before indicated that there was a class distinction to the jocks at his school. Last I'd heard, the swim team was undefeated, something that couldn't be said for any of the other sports teams. There was a reason the Proper City High School mascot was the prawn.

"Do you really think Varla cares about football players? She's the president of the drama club. I didn't think drama people mixed with the regular jocks."

He shrugged. "They don't, usually, except that Varla's different. She acts like she doesn't need anybody."

"The old hard-to-get routine."

"She's not a game player. She's independent and she does her own thing. But it's hard to compete with the homecoming king."

"I thought you said he was the captain of the football team?"

"He's both. You know how high school works." He looked down at the toe of his Converse sneakers and bounced his feet against each other. "Her birthday is next week too, and he's taking her out this weekend. I wanted to do something special for her, but what's the point? No way can I compete with him."

"I think you're projecting a lot onto this Angus guy. What makes you think he can impress her more than you can? Maybe he'll buy her a cake and think that's good enough."

"Angus *O'Toole*. Grady's little brother. Remember Grady? Their family is rolling in money. Angus is like a pit bull with red hair. He's capable of buying her more than a cake."

I was beginning to see why Kirby was depressed about his chances. "I don't care how much money his family has, you have the entire creative staff of Disguise DeLimit at your disposal," I said. "We can talk more about this later. Right now I have to go see Dig about a car."

"Sure."

I left Kirby with instructions on the tie-dye process and then caught the Zip-Two. Minutes later, I got off and walked half a block to Dig's Towing.

Dig's business was a small property set a few blocks away from the Main Line. Though his primary income came from roadside assistance, he always had a few cars scattered around the lot that he tinkered on throughout the day. Today, the lot was empty except for a long, yellow Zip bus in front. I recognized the graffitied images of dice and game pieces that I'd first noticed last night.

"Dig?" I called out.

"Under here," he said. A few seconds later, he wriggled out from under the bus and stood up. "Whoever's idea it was to go with repurposed school buses for the Zip line was a genius. School buses are easy to work on. But this thing"—he waved a wrench at the bus—"is a nightmare. The wiring is held together with electrical tape and bubblegum."

I laughed. "Come on, it can't be that bad. Besides, you're Dig. You can do anything."

He bent his arm in front of him and flexed his bicep, making Tweety Bird jump twice. "Make sure you tell

Ebony that," he said. "What are you doing here in the middle of the day? Shouldn't you be at the store?"

"Kirby's minding the store," I said. "I'm here because I need some transportation."

He glanced at my outfit. "I'm all out of magic carpets."

"I'll take whatever you have. I have to take a couple boxes of costumes to the festival."

"How big are these boxes? I don't have any trucks. Except mine, and you're not driving my tow truck."

"I don't need a truck. The boxes are about the size of shoe boxes. Six of them."

"What kind of costumes fit in boxes like that?"

"Teddy bear costumes."

"'Teddy bear costumes,'" he repeated, with a look that suggested he didn't believe me. "You finally run out of human customers?"

"Hey, at least the teddy bears stand still for their fittings," I said.

I followed Dig inside his office and waited while he sorted through a bowl of keys. He pulled out a set with BUICK written on the tag and handed them to me. "It's a Le Sabre. Around back. Not the best-looking car in the world, but I just gassed her up so you'll be in good shape."

"Thanks." I took the keys and tucked them into a hidden pocket on my harem pants.

Dig tipped his head to the side. "I haven't seen Tak Hoshiyama around much lately. You didn't scare him off with the way you dress, did you?"

"I dress like a person who runs a costume shop. Why should that scare him? He dresses like a city planner and that doesn't scare me."

"He have any luck finding a job?"

"I don't know. I mean, nobody around here is hiring. The mayor kept him pretty busy zoning out the park for the festival, but that's done now. He's been on interviews for the past two weeks. Other than that, it's freelance work."

"He's been doing a lot of freelance work," Dig said. "One of these days a company is going to offer him a steady paycheck. What's going to happen then?"

"If it's a job he wants, he'll probably take it."

"What happens to you?"

"What do you mean?"

"I mean, long distance doesn't work. You're here. If he doesn't want to be here, then maybe that's a sign."

"Sign, schmine. You've been spending too much time talking to Ebony."

"See, that's the difference. Ebony wants to be in Proper City. I want to be in Proper City. All I have to do is convince Ebony that she wants to be with me."

"How's that working out for you?"

"She'll come around."

We walked around the back to the Le Sabre. "Thanks for the loaner," I said to Dig. "I'll bring it back as soon as I drop off the costumes."

"No rush. I'll be working on that yellow beast out front for the rest of the day."

"You can't work under the bus after the sun goes down," I said. "How will you see anything?"

He tipped his head to the side. "Easier to work on it from the inside than underneath, anyway. I was only down there to grease the hinges on the trapdoor."

"What trapdoor?"

"On the bus. All buses and trailers have them. You

never noticed that? Must be one of the people who likes to sit in the front."

"I like to keep the driver company."

"Sure, sure." He wiped the back of his hands across his dirty jeans. "In the back of the bus, there's an access panel. Twelve inches by twenty-four, usually. Big enough for me to open up, light the bus from underneath, and work on it from inside. Gives me a rush with my head hanging upside down like that, but it's good for the circulation. Not as good as a headstand, but better than nothing. Why are you looking at me like that?"

I turned off the engine to the Le Sabre and got out. "You're saying trailers all have trapdoors that can be accessed from the inside?" He nodded. "All of them?" He nodded again. "Show me."

He led me into the bus and about three-quarters of the way to the back. He'd unbolted one of the seats, leaving a one-foot-by-two-foot opening exposed in the floor. Through the opening, I could see the gravel of his parking lot.

"Did you have to take the seat out to get to the panel?"

"Nope. I did that so I'd have room to keep my tools close." His brow furrowed, and he jutted his chin out at me. "I never knew you to be interested in auto mechanics before. What's this all about? You're acting like it means something."

I stared through the access panel at the ground. "It does. It means Ronnie Cass left somebody a message before she was killed."

Chapter 13

I PROMISED DIG that I'd explain everything when I returned the car, and then I left. I'd spent too much time with him to begin with, but I'd learned something valuable. A trapdoor meant Ronnie could have been the one to put the teddy bear in the grate under the bus. But why? What message could she possibly have hidden in a small, plush animal?

I'd barely ever heard of Ronnie before the festival. But she'd brought the divas back together and out of retirement, negotiated an unprecedented festival contract, and then someone had killed her. It couldn't have to do with their performance. There had to be more at the heart of it. I was going to have to find out more about Ronnie Cassavogli. But first, I had work to do.

I drove Dig's loaner car back to Disguise DeLimit and found Kirby refilling the bucket of blue water. His hands and forearms were stained, making him look like he was part Smurf. I added a capful of dye to the bucket while he held it, and then waited inside while he carried it back out front. His mood had improved, though not considerably.

I'd learned firsthand that when money was no object, fun for rich kids was to try to outdo each other. I wondered if Grady's brother, Angus, had inherited the same sense of competition and if he saw Kirby as his worthy opponent.

"Did you mean what you said about helping me with Varla's birthday?" he asked.

"Of course I did! And Varla is a creative, so I bet she'd be more impressed with what we can all pull together than with Angus's money. Ebony will probably help too, if you don't mind me talking to her about this."

"Really?"

"I don't see why not. You're practically part of the family. Do you have any ideas?"

"I'd like to throw her a party."

"How many people? Do you have a guest list?"

For the first time since I'd returned to the shop, Kirby showed a spark of interest in what might happen. He was a competitor and had led the Proper City Prawns to many a championship while he'd been captain. My pep talk seemed to have worked enough to put him into the same competitive spirit.

"No, but I can make one. It could be a big party, like the whole school could come. Hey, maybe coach can get permission from the principal to let me use the gymnasium?"

"Find out as soon as you can. If he says yes, call me and I'll check it out when I return the loaner car to Dig."

"Angus would never think of something like this. He only hangs with the jocks and the cheerleaders. Varla's friends with everybody. She's like the only person I know who gets along with all of the cliques: the band kids and the debate club and the jocks." Kirby jumped up in a swift motion. "This is great, Margo. I wasn't even going to ask for your help because of the festival and the stuff going on with Don. You're awesome."

My stomach turned slightly at the mention of how many other things were going on in my life, and Kirby's mention of Don let me know that gossip had spread beyond the border of the festival and the conspiracy crowd. Kirby held out a fist, I made my own, and we knocked knuckles, the eighteen-year-old's version of a handshake.

I packed the small Clue bear costumes into shoe boxes, carried them to the Le Sabre, and drove to the festival. When I arrived, I stacked the boxes on a handcart and pulled them to Bobbie's booth. Joel V. and the mayor stood with her. The mayor had his arms crossed over his chest.

"Margo!" Bobbie called out when she saw me.

"Sorry it took so long," I said. I lined the boxes on the table, opened the flaps, and exposed the costumes. Bobbie grabbed a teddy bear, put a Colonel Mustard costume on it, and then knotted a small yellow ascot around its neck and repeated the process. I grabbed a bear and pulled a tiny Miss Scarlet dress onto its body and then draped a small black lace mantilla over its head.

"This would go faster if you helped," Bobbie said to the two men.

Joel's face lit up as the photographic possibilities occurred to him. "She's right. The mayor dressing the bears in costumes? That's perfect for social media. I'll get pictures."

No sooner did Joel speak the magic words than the mayor grabbed a Mrs. White bear. He set a small white bonnet on top and held the bear next to his face.

Joel snapped pictures. "Keep working," he said. "I'll get some spontaneous shots. Keep it natural." He moved about us and tapped the screen of his phone. At one point he cleared his throat. When Mayor Young looked at him, Joel patted the tummy of his orange and white striped shirt. The mayor sucked in his gut and resumed dressing the bears.

"Wait a minute!" Joel said suddenly. "I have an idea." He turned around and left.

Without a camera pointed at him, Mayor Young lost the motivation to help. Bobbie and I continued dressing bears since they showed no signs of dressing themselves.

"How'd you meet up with Joel?" I asked Mayor Young. "He's not local, right?"

"He comes highly recommended from some celebrity friends," he said. He placed a special emphasis on the word "celebrity," as if running in high-profile circles made him more important. "I've been pleased with the job he's done so far."

"What exactly is his job? It can't be all Instagram and Facebook posts, right?"

"Oh, no. Joel's been working with my office to raise the profile of Proper for months now. He came on board long before the festival actually started. Actually, he was the one who had the idea to pull the Domino Divas out of retirement for the festival. Once they signed, he put out stories to the media, teasers about their identity, who they were, what they'd won, all the kind of stuff the press loves. He even leaked a few nuggets about their past to spice things up. They picked up on it right away too. I wasn't sure, you know, that going with them was the right idea, but Joel convinced me that we were sitting on a gold mine. No pun intended." He laughed, apparently having made a joke that neither Bobbie nor I got.

Joel returned with two of the actors from *Clue*. They oohed and aahed over the bears, and then posed with the mayor while holding their plush mini-me versions. Joel tapped away at his screen, pausing every now and then to wave Bobbie and me out from the background. "This is it," he said. "Exactly what we need to shift gears and blow this thing up." He turned around and walked away, head down and thumbs tapping the screen at a rapid rate. I was surprised that he didn't walk into anybody.

As soon as the publicity shoot was done, the mayor was too. He tossed a half-dressed bear onto the table and nodded at us. "Get these things set up for sale immediately. What's your cost?"

"Five dollars each," Bobbie said.

"Charge fifteen and we'll split the profits," he said. He thanked the actors each and extended his hand for a shake. Colonel Mustard saluted and Miss Scarlet blew him a kiss. The mayor looked confused for a moment, and then he smiled, nodded, and left. The actors headed back toward the stage, leaving Bobbie and me with the balance of the work.

"Nice math," Bobbie said. "I pay for supplies and we split the profits. Two fifty profit for me, seven fifty profit for Proper." She picked up an armful of bears and moved them to an empty shelf on the bookcase. "If he doesn't use some of this money to fix the pothole on Main Line Road when this is done, I'm going to put polyester fiber-fill in his gas tank."

"Bobbie!"

Once the bears were dressed, I left Bobbie to her

booth and went to see if there was an update on Don's situation.

The red and white striped tent had twice as many people out front today as it had yesterday. Most of them were reading *Spicy Acorn* newspapers. I read the headline over the shoulder of a woman in a Proper City sweatshirt. "Truth Teller Detained: Who's Keeping Secrets Now?" I bypassed the crowd and went into the booth. My dad stood next to a table of newspapers, handing them out to everybody who came in.

"I thought *Spicy Acorn* was going to be a monthly thing?" I asked.

"Special edition," he said. "Don called me last night. He's being held because of this thing with Ronnie."

"They can't think he had anything to do with her murder."

"They know there's a connection between them and he doesn't want to talk about it."

"But that was a long time ago, right? That's what Ebony said." My dad nodded. "I still don't get it. So they dated when they were teenagers. I bet a lot of people around here dated way back. Why's it so important now? And why does anybody care that the divas reunited? They were a big deal in the late '60s. I see how that would make them a local novelty act, but why would that sell tickets?"

He sat down on the brown metal folding chair behind the table and gestured for me to sit on the one in front. "Sit down. This could take a while." He handed Grady a stack of newspapers. "Take over for a few minutes."

Grady pushed the stack back toward my dad. "I'm your financial backer, not your staff."

My dad pushed the newspapers back at Grady. "You

want to be a newspaperman? You need to learn from the ground up. Handle the crowd out front. I need some privacy." Grady glanced at me, and then shifted the stack of newspapers from in front of him to his side. He nodded, as if my dad had said something profound, and went to work.

I rested on the chair inside the booth. My dad sat across from me. He wore a white shirt and black tie under a black suit. A small ID card was clipped to the lapel. The word PRESS was in all caps next to his picture and name. On the bottom, it read: SPICY ACORN: CHEW ON THIS.

"This is a case of something that happened a long time ago. Most people don't talk about it around Don, so you wouldn't have heard it."

"Is this about the gold robbery?"

He nodded. "The story has gotten watered down over the years, but to fully understand what's happening, you should hear the facts." He cleared his throat and drank some water from a paper cup. "The last time the divas performed, there was a robbery at the Proper City Savings and Loan. Right across the street from their stage. Rumor had it that the robbers knew about the performance and took advantage of the act—used it as a distraction, so to speak, although some people think the divas might have been in on the whole thing."

"I heard the only thing stolen was some gold."

"That's right. It was the first gold that Pete Proper struck when mining."

"Where was it kept?"

"In the lobby of the savings and loan, locked under a case. It was on display for the residents to see when they came in. People used to say that Pete wanted people to feel like their money was safe there, so he put his on display for everybody to see."

"How much gold are we talking about?"

"About the size of a brick."

"I don't know anything about the value of gold," I said. "Is that a lot?"

"Back in Pete Proper's day, that much gold was worth about nineteen dollars."

"What would it be worth today?"

"Close to two million dollars."

Chapter 14

I WHISTLED. TWO million dollars was a lot of money. "Was there any evidence?"

"There was too much evidence. The interior of the bank looked like someone had dumped the contents of a trash truck on collection day. It took the police weeks to sort through what they found inside the lobby. A surprisingly large amount of it was traced back to residents of Proper—envelopes, receipts, the kinds of things that people throw out without thinking too much about it. Remember, this was 1968. Forensic science wasn't what you hear about today."

"The robbers buried the scene in evidence to hide their own tracks," I said, understanding the genius behind such a plan. An investigator would be required to bag and tag whatever was found at the scene, just like Detective Nichols had bagged and tagged my phone, the felt circle, and the teddy bear from the sewer grate. The team would waste precious hours sorting through what was found and cataloging everything. If anything could be traced back to someone's trash, that person would have to answer questions.

"Did they ever link anybody to the crime?"

"They found a domino mask among the trash and concluded that one of the divas had been in on the robbery. Their performance was supposed to start at five, and because one of them was late, they didn't go on until 5:42. The robbery took place at 5:23."

"How do you know the exact time?"

"The clock was unplugged. The cord was torn off and used to tie the doors open. It was one of the only solid pieces of evidence that they had."

I crossed my legs and brushed some dirt off of my gold shoe. "Let me guess. The mask they found was blue and the diva who was late was Ronnie."

My dad nodded and the two of us grew silent. I didn't know what he was thinking, but I suspected it was something close to what I was thinking. That it was hard to ignore the fact that Ronnie was murdered before the first performance of the divas since their implication in a bank robbery when they were teenagers.

"So people think the divas had something to do with the robbery. What does that have to do with Don?" I asked.

"The day of the robbery was the same day Don proposed. He had the ring in a safe-deposit box at the savings and loan and he took it out that morning. The bank manager confirmed it. That was a sticking point in the investigation: Why did he take it out that day? Did he know something about the robbery? It was suspicious timing."

"Don's a smart guy. If he was going to rob a bank, he wouldn't make a mistake like that. Besides, if he was going to rob the bank, he'd get his stuff back anyway, right? So why take it out first?"

"That's the argument he used, but it didn't exactly paint him in the most innocent light."

"What happened with him and Ronnie?"

"Speculation about their involvement put a lot of pressure on the relationship. Don wanted to elope, but Ronnie seemed to like the attention. Instead of getting engaged, they broke up. Ronnie left the divas and moved to Las Vegas in search of fame."

"As what? A performer?"

"A personality. She wanted to be a star. It started on the small stage, her telling her story, and then slowly, her audience grew. She used what happened in Proper, turned Don into fodder for her act. She used to sell T-shirts that said 'My Boyfriend Robbed the Savings and Loan and All I Got Was This Lousy Shirt.' It practically destroyed his reputation."

"What did he do?"

"Don enlisted in the army and tried to put it behind him. Eventually the story died down. People lost interest in Ronnie when they saw that there wasn't much more to her act than exaggeration. She moved away for a while. When she moved back, the gossip surrounding her started up again for a whole other reason."

"Why, because she'd done something scandalous when she was in Vegas?"

"Depends on your definition of scandalous. When she moved back to Proper City, she was Mrs. Wharton Young."

Chapter 15

"RONNIE WAS MARRIED to the mayor?" I asked.

He nodded. "It was a short-lived marriage. I don't know the details. Back then, there were lots of rumors around town, but Don distanced himself from it all. And as his friend, I thought it was better to ignore the gossip instead of participating in it."

"But you must know something," I said.

My dad was quiet for a few seconds. He picked up a stack of newspapers, flipped the top one around so it was facing the same direction as the others, and then lined up the edges. When the stack was neat, he set it back down on the table in front of him. He'd never been overly concerned with neatness, so I knew it wasn't a compulsion toward right angles that made him straighten the pile, but he was conflicted. His loyalties were toward Don, but whatever had happened all those years ago might be threatening Don's freedom today.

After close to a full minute of silence, he spoke. "They

split up. Ronnie did her thing in Vegas, and Don enlisted in the army. It got to the point where it seemed as though she and Don had wanted different things all along. She was driven toward a level of notoriety and fame that he didn't understand, and he pulled away from everybody except for his closest friends. He grew suspicious about a lot of what was happening around him."

"Don was always suspicious though, right? I mean, he's a conspiracy theorist. That's his nature. He didn't just wake up one day and say, 'Hey, maybe the world really is flat and the government's been lying to us all along.'"

"He always had a curious side. That's why we got along so well. We liked to question what we were told. But that was the defining year for him. Maybe, in a way, it's easier to believe in a vast conspiracy against the public than to believe that some people are inherently evil. Before the robbery, Ronnie was a good foil for Don. She laughed off his theories but accepted that he questioned everything. They complemented each other. I think a part of him believed that if someone like her could see him as he was and still love him, maybe he needed to let go of some of his suspicions and start trusting the world."

"You mean there was a time when he was willing to give up what he believed because of her?"

"It was more like he was willing to back-burner things. But so much happened in 1968. The world changed. On a big scale, there were political assassinations. On a local scale, the hippie movement was gaining momentum. The separation between the teenagers and adults was a gap almost too broad to span. The bucolic town that you grew up in was different then. Kids were experimenting with drugs and challenging authority. They were exerting their voices in ways that the previous generation never thought possible. That's one reason why Don was under suspicion of the bank robbery. A lot of people wanted a kid to be guilty so they could lock him up and send a message to the rest of the generation."

"So Don and Ronnie were suspected of being involved. Don stayed here and Ronnie went to Vegas. When did she meet Mayor Young?"

"It was a couple of years later. She never quite made it the way everybody thought she would, but when she came back to Proper, it was on the arm of Wharton. He was an up-and-comer in local politics, and she was the pretty young thing from the city of sin. They gave each other what they both wanted: her, respectability, and him, sex appeal."

I pictured the mayor, skinny limbs and rotund belly, dressed in his thin dress shirts, seersucker pants, and goofy round rocker-bottom sneakers. Ronnie herself had aged from too much sun and booze. But back then, who knows? It was hard to think that any woman would go for him unless there was something else to be gained in the union.

My dad interrupted my thoughts. "When Ronnie came back to Proper, Don tried to pretend that he was over her, but it all came back. At first, he defended her leaving town and making a name for herself. But the more famous she got, the less she wanted to talk to him. One day we overheard a reporter asking her about her past, and she glossed right over him, said there hadn't been anybody worth mentioning until Wharton."

It sounded to me as if Ronnie Cass had an iron in

every fire. In the six degrees of separation game, she was
Kevin Bacon, connected to the mayor, Don Digby, Gina
Cassavogli, Chet and Jayne Lemming, and probably half
of the town. It stood to reason that she'd made an enemy
somewhere along the way, someone who had murdered
her. But had it been a recent action that triggered the
violent act? Or something she'd done almost fifty
years ago?

I took a copy of *Spicy Acorn* and left my dad to his
audience of fellow theorists. Don would have loved the
scene, a group of like-minded individuals who believed
he was being detained because of his desire to expose
"the truth." But there had been more than the whim of
part-time conspiracy theorists behind my dad's de-
meanor. He was worried about Don. The crowd out front
could spin the situation however they wanted, but my dad
knew there was something more than the desire to in-
convenience Don at the root of the detective taking him
away from the festival.

I found an empty table at the back of the park and
borrowed a pen from the snow cone cart next to me. On
the back of the newspaper, in the space left blank for a
mailing address, I made some notes.

Ronnie Cass

Engaged to Don Digby
Short marriage to Wharton Young
Child: Gina Cassavogli (Who is father?)
Rift with divas
Murdered
Possibly involved with bank robbery 50 years ago

Came out of retirement for this year's festival. Why
    now? Why did other divas agree?

I was so involved in my note-taking that I didn't notice
that I was no longer alone. A shadow fell across the page
and I looked up.

"Mind if I join you?" asked Tak Hoshiyama.

"You're back!" I said, a little too eagerly. "I mean, hey,
nice to see you again."

He picked up the genie bottle that I'd set on the table,
closed his eyes, and rubbed it. "I wish I could find a
woman willing to speak her mind." He opened his eyes
and set the bottle down.

"Hey," I said, trying to act cool.

"Hey."

Tak was the son of a Japanese father and a Hawaiian-
born mother, resulting in Asian features, black hair, and
naturally red lips. His strong brow made him appear as
though he were deep in thought most of the time. I'd
teased him that he spent too much time calculating the
interior dimensions of wherever we were, but I guess
that's the side effect of being good with numbers.

Tak and I had dated occasionally since we first met
about a year ago. It was after a client of the costume shop
had been murdered at his birthday party—the client's,
not Tak's, although Tak had been a guest. Tak had an
uncomfortable knack for guessing what I was thinking
before I said it. His dad, a proud Japanese man, hadn't
liked the fact that Tak, a Princeton graduate and former
city planner for the Clark County District Attorney's office, had prioritized spending time with me, a costume
shop owner, over finding another prestigious job.

Despite a comfortable connection, I couldn't shake the fear of the inevitable: that he'd get a job somewhere else and leave me behind in Proper. Whether or not he sensed those thoughts, like he read the rest of my mind, was unspoken. I thought I'd done a good job of hiding my own insecurities, though Soot and I had had a couple of heart-to-hearts about the subject.

Tak himself had realized that working in his parents' restaurant and helping me reorganize the stockroom of Disguise DeLimit wasn't what he wanted out of life. Jobs for analytical city planners with Ivy League degrees weren't plentiful in Proper City, which meant the jobs Tak interviewed for weren't local. A month ago, it was Pennsylvania. Last week, it was Texas. This week, it was Michigan. All of which might have been the moon in terms of starting a relationship, which explained the "occasional" in our dating status.

It had been my own decision to move back to Proper City and take over the costume shop. I knew this was where I wanted to be, but I couldn't say the same for him. We'd agreed to keep things laid-back between us so as not to complicate anything.

Sometimes I hated being a grown-up.

I didn't know how long Tak had been back in town. He wore a gray T-shirt over black jeans, and red Converse sneakers. His black hair was cut into a more businesslike style than when I'd met him, neatly trimmed and held into place with a product that left it looking shiny and wet. It was parted on the side and dusted his forehead. He pushed his hand into it, moving it away from his face, but when he let go, it fell back into the same spot.

"Sit. Talk. Tell me. How were your interviews?" I asked.

"Okay."

"Just okay? What'd you do, spill coffee on the head of human resources?"

"Nothing quite that bad. How are things around here?"

I looked to my left and to my right to see if anybody was within earshot. "You really haven't heard anything?"

"My plane got in about an hour ago and I have an appointment at"—he looked at his watch—"four thirty. I haven't even been home."

"You came straight here? Why?"

"Why do you think?" He lowered himself onto the bench next to me. Under his direct stare, I felt my cheeks grow warm. I tried, unsuccessfully, to hide my smile.

"I think you wanted to get some of your parents' fried rice before your next appointment."

"You forget I can make my own fried rice whenever I want. Want to guess again?"

"You got tired of only seeing people dressed up in businessman costumes and needed some variety."

"That's a little closer to the truth." He grinned.

The easy familiarity that Tak and I maintained when we were together was not something I was used to. Sometimes I felt like I'd known him my whole life. But times like now—him being playful and me being distracted by Ronnie Cass's murder—I felt like we were worlds apart. I looked down at the newspaper in front of me and shifted my arms to hide the notes I'd been taking.

"What's going on?" Tak asked. He glanced at the paper in front of me. My handwriting was mostly covered by my forearms, but the words "bank robbery" and "murdered" were visible. He put his hand on the corner of the paper and tried to tug it out from under me. I pressed down harder to keep it where it was.

"There was a murder two days ago. One of the Domino Divas, the headlining act."

"It happened at the festival?"

"Close. In their trailer. It was parked on Rapunzel Road." I smoothed my hand over my hair and twirled my ponytail around my finger. "I found her body. And when I was in her trailer, I got stabbed—not by a person, but by a needle—and it turned red—not the needle, but my hand—and now Detective Nichols is holding Don Digby because of something that happened almost half a century ago."

I had a tendency to get things mixed up and turned around, especially when things were already as jumbled up as they were right now. Tak had demonstrated an ability to untangle my thoughts, but this time even he seemed confused.

He reached his hand out and put it on the side of my face, and then brushed his thumb across my lips, which temporarily made me forget the murder, the bank robbery, and the six degrees of separation between Ronnie Cass and everybody else.

"There's someplace I have to be, but I want to keep talking to you about this. So, dinner? Tonight?"

"Sure," I said. "Your parents' restaurant?"

He nodded. "I'll stake a claim on one of the private rooms." He dropped his hand from my face but his dark brown eyes held mine. "I missed you." He kissed my forehead, then stood up and left.

I watched him make his way out of the park to his gray RAV4. I'd missed him too, but I couldn't let myself think too much about that. It was inevitable that he'd get a job offer somewhere else and that would be it. It would be easier for me if I never let myself get attached. Still, I should enjoy it while it lasted. Right?

I looked down at the notes I'd scribbled on the back of the newspaper. I was almost out of room and I'd hardly scratched the surface of what I knew. Or what I thought I knew.

Did I really know anything?

I sat back and tapped the pen against my front tooth. In the distance, Ebony stood with her hands on her hips giving Mayor Young an earful. I waved my hands to get her attention. She said one last thing to him and then came my way.

"That mayor wouldn't know his head from a hole in the ground."

"What's he done now?"

"He's all hopped up about this Clue thing. I told him maybe we should just move on, focus on the rest of the festival and not the headlining act. But he's all Clue this, Clue that. He wants to know how to run a festival, he should *get* a clue."

"But I'm completely off the hook, right? You're not lobbying to resurrect the Double Ds with me as a stand-in, are you?"

"You're officially in the clear. Don't get me started on the divas. Do you know what I found out today? We have to pay them every time we use their name. I don't mean on merchandise sold either. If that publicist gets up in front of an audience and mentions "Dominos" or "Divas" or "Domino Divas"—per their contract—it's a hundred dollars. Flat fee." She looked over both shoulders to make sure nobody was within earshot. "That's four hundred dollars right there if anybody heard me."

"What happens now?"

"Don't know, don't care. I'm not saying I'm happy about what happened, but at least the festival gets to keep the proceeds from the merchandising instead of being a fund-raiser for a bunch of high-kickin' baby boomers."

I could have pointed out that Ebony herself was a baby boomer, but it seemed this wasn't the appropriate time. "Whose idea was it to get the Double Ds out of retirement?" I asked.

Ebony looked at me as if I were a child asking questions about why the sky was blue. "What difference does it make now?"

I shrugged. "It seems to me that if they'd performed, they'd be cleaning up in terms of merchandising. So even though there was bad blood between them, financially it made sense for them to get over their differences."

Ebony's expression changed. "Not necessarily. I saw the contract. Ronnie incorporated the act six months prior to the festival. She was the sole proprietor. All of the money they made from coming out of retirement went to one pocket: hers."

Chapter 16

"BUT CONSIDERING NONE of the other divas seemed to like her, why would the rest of them agree to something like that?" I asked.

Ebony shrugged. "You'd have to ask them. Hard to say what motivates people to do anything. Maybe they got tired of being treated like little old ladies. Sixty-eight isn't old. If you got it, you got it."

"Do you 'got it'?"

"You know I got it."

"Did they have it?"

She considered the question. "They were passable."

"It doesn't make sense," I said. In my mind, new questions surfaced. Had the remaining five members of the group known that Ronnie incorporated them as a single entity or had she kept that detail to herself? What had she offered them to get them to agree? Did someone say yes to Ronnie's proposal because they'd been holding on to a grudge and knew they'd have the opportunity to kill her?

Ebony shrugged. "Don't underestimate the power of ego and fame," she said. "Ronnie may have benefited financially, but maybe the rest of them wanted to come back so they could be in the spotlight again." She tipped her head to the side and smoothed out a couple of flyaway strands of hair that weren't cooperating with her *Charlie's Angels* blowout.

"If that was the case, you'd think they'd be more excited about it. From what I saw, there wasn't a lot of love lost between them. Especially Jayne and Ronnie. Maybe— What?"

"No." Ebony leaned in and pointed a shiny blue fingernail close to my face. "I don't want to find out that you're poking your nose into this murder. I know you're worried about Don. We all are. But that fancy-pants detective can't hold him for no reason. Don wouldn't harm a fly even if he suspected it was carrying a mutated form of Agent Orange."

As much as I agreed with Ebony in theory, I couldn't pretend that all would be fine if we just waited out Detective Nichols's investigation. There had to be something stronger than the fact that Don and Ronnie went to the prom together fifty years ago. Innuendo that led the investigation to Don's door. Detective Nichols would have to either turn up hard evidence to hold him or let him go.

The items in the grate were suspicious too. After seeing the trapdoor in the trailer at Dig's tow yard, I felt certain that Ronnie could have put the teddy bear there. But why? The process of unscrewing the grate and hiding the bear was laborious. If someone was in front of her, threatening her life, she wouldn't have had the time or the privacy to complete that task.

But the killer could have too. Whoever had hit Ronnie in the head and ended her life would have had all the time in the world. No spectators. No questions. He or she could have committed the murder and then gotten into the sewer grate through the trapdoor inside the trailer. Why? Was there something hidden in that bear that they'd been planning to retrieve?

There was a good chance that Don's history with Ronnie would quickly become the talk of the town if it wasn't already. That meant whoever killed her now had a scapegoat. An unwanted thought of lone gunmen theories and patsies popped into my head.

There are two sides to every relationship, but in this case, only one could talk. One person who could tell me about what had really happened when Don and Ronnie broke up. One person who could shed light on things.

I had to find a way to talk to Don.

I left the festival while it was in full swing. Families were milling about, patronizing the various booths. Even though the mayor had arranged for there to be state-of-the-art video-game consoles with the intent of attracting the high school crowd, a surprising number had congregated around arcade games that played digital versions of dominos. Ebony's talent with a theme was making it hard to escape the tragedy that had occurred.

It was five thirty. I went back to Disguise DeLimit. The phone was ringing.

"Disguise DeLimit," I answered.

"Hi, who is this?"

"Margo Tamblyn. Are you in the market for a costume?"

"You're Jerry's daughter, right?"

"Yes."

"Can you tell me anything about Don Digby's relationship to Ronnie Cass?"

My stomach twisted. "Who am I talking to?"

"Or the gold. Can you tell me about the gold? One quote, that's all I need."

"Have a nice day," I said, and hung up the phone. It started to ring almost immediately. My business sense overrode my paranoia and I answered, experiencing almost a replica of the first conversation, this time with a woman. By the third time the phone rang, I let the answering service pick it up.

I went upstairs to get ready to meet Tak. Even though it was May, the dry desert air would turn chilly when the sun went down, so I changed out of the genie costume and into a uniform from an out-of-business ice cream shop over leggings, and then slipped on ballerina flats. Not much could be done about hair that had been in a ponytail all day, so I tied a scarf around the base of it. Soot, who had been watching me patiently, let out a howl that could probably be heard at the Sagebrush Festival.

"What?" I asked. He gave me the stink eye. I sat down on the bed next to him, took a deep breath, and let it out. "Okay, I know. It doesn't make a lot of sense to keep seeing Tak when it can't go anywhere. But I'm a big girl. I won't get hurt if I already know that."

This time his meow was less audible but more judgmental—at least it seemed that way to me. I ran my hand over the dark gray fur on his head, and then scratched the patch between his ears with my index finger. "It's not like I met a lot of smart, attractive men when I lived in Vegas. You know that. You were there too."

Shortly after I'd moved to Las Vegas, I answered an ad for a roommate and ended up living above a Chinese food restaurant. It wasn't on the main strip—or even the strip next to the main strip—but it was affordable, and Crystal—the resident advertising for a roommate—was nice. We were both struggling to make ends meet, and oftentimes dinner consisted of egg rolls from the restaurant below us.

One particular day while recovering from a cold, I'd gone downstairs for a bowl of egg drop soup. The candy store next door to us had put a sign in the window: FREE KITTENS. A family of four walked out with a tawny kitten nestled against the chest of the boy. Whether under the influence of extreme cuteness or Benadryl, I'd never know, but instead of getting the egg drop soup, I went into the candy store and inquired about the cats. Ten minutes later, I walked out with a dark gray bundle of fur and an industrial-sized bag of cat food. Soot and I had been together ever since.

My time in Las Vegas had started out rocky. I'd taken whatever jobs I could: receptionist for a real estate agent, vintage clothing store sales associate, and concession stand clerk for a theater. Eventually, I answered an ad for a magician's assistant. Magic Maynard wasn't the best magician, which was why his show was at a dive bar on a side street away from the main strip, but he paid me every week and let me design my own costumes. I spent the better part of those years in sequined bodysuits and fishnets under cutaway tuxedo jackets that I got when one of the chapels of love cleaned out their inventory.

Crystal spent her days auditioning at the main casinos. She stood in for me when I first came back to Proper, but she never got the hang of the doves, so Maynard replaced her with someone else. Last time we talked, she'd been working on an act as a Taylor Swift impersonator. I guess when you're determined to make it, you learn to create your own opportunities.

My hand had gone slack. Soot bent his head into it and pressed slightly, and then swatted at it with his paw a few times to make sure I got the message to keep petting him. I caught his paw between my thumb and forefinger and rubbed it a few times until he pulled away, meowed again, and jumped off the bed. He skulked to the kitchen and sat below the window, staring up. The wall phone rang again as I was filling Soot's bowl. I ignored it and refilled Soot's water too. I checked the litter box, scooped out two suspicious clumps, washed my hands, and left.

HOSHIYAMA Kobe Steak House sat a couple of miles east of Disguise DeLimit on the left-hand side of Main Line Road. Unencumbered with boxes of bear costumes and the like, I was able to take my scooter. The helmet sat awkwardly on the top of my head, squishing my ponytail down. It was a short ride, and a few minutes later, I was parked in a space close to the front of the restaurant.

I'd fallen in love with teppanyaki-style cooking long before I'd met Tak. Ebony and my dad had taken me to Vegas for my sixth-grade graduation and told me I got to choose the restaurant. Considering I was twelve, they'd probably expected to get off with a Happy Meal and a supersized order of fries, but once I'd spotted Mori's Steakhouse, I'd been smitten. Add in the fried rice, onion volcano, and green tea ice cream, and I'd never been the same.

Hoshiyama Kobe Steak House had moved into Proper City while I lived in Vegas, so I hadn't experienced their menu until my recent return. Tak's parents had been running the restaurant for several years, slowly converting the interior to a more authentic Japanese style. The exterior was a dark brown wooden building with a small plaque and menu posted, but inside, the hostesses wore kimonos and the chefs wore white mandarin-style cooking shirts and chef's hats. Paper lanterns hung at varying levels from the ceiling, glowing with soft battery-operated tea-light candles, and displays of swords, knives, paintings, and objets d'art were placed in the front lobby, giving visitors something unique to see while waiting for their table.

Tonight, the restaurant was mostly empty. Teppanyaki restaurants, most famously Benihana, were popular destinations for special occasions, but aside from celebrations, most people didn't think of them when considering takeout or a typical Tuesday night meal. The festival would pull people away from the existing restaurants too, which was why so many of them chose to participate. Tak had promised to get us a private room, but it appeared as though that would be unnecessary. We could have our pick of the tables and still enjoy our privacy.

I scanned the interior, looking for him. A pretty brunette woman in a pink and orange floral kimono approached me. "Good evening," she said with a slight bow. "Are you waiting for the rest of your party?"

"Tak Hoshiyama. I'm meeting him. Is he here yet?"

She looked confused. "Tak isn't coming here tonight,"

she said. Something about her expression had changed, but I couldn't read the emotion that had replaced her initial politeness.

"Are you sure? He said he was going to meet me in one of the private rooms. Maybe he's there now?"

"I think there's been some kind of mix-up. Maybe you should call him?" Her eyes cut to the phone that sat on the hostess station, and then she looked down toward the carpet.

"You're not telling me something," I said. "I don't know who you think I am, but I'm—I'm Tak's girlfriend." It was the first time I'd spoken those words, and guilt shuddered through me. "I mean, we're not—you know—but we do go out together, and I don't know if he's seeing anybody else, but I'm not, so—"

The light behind the rice paper screens that separated the private room from the main dining room went on, casting a muted orange-pink glow onto that corner of the restaurant. The doors slid open, slowly.

"He is here. I'll just go surprise him," I said.

"No, you can't—" she said. She put her hand on my arm and held me back. Startled, I looked at her, and then back at the open doors to the private room. Standing in the orange-pink glow next to Tak was Detective Nancy Nichols.

Chapter 17

OF ALL THE people I could have imagined being with Tak behind closed doors, this one was my least favorite. Not because she was conducting an investigation against my dad's best friend. Not because she and I had been at odds twice before over crimes in Proper. But because she actually *had* been Tak's girlfriend, for real, for a while, before he'd moved to Proper City himself.

He'd never told me about their breakup, their relationship, or the terms of their coexisting in Proper City now. I liked to think that the fact that he spent time with me meant something, but seeing them together, across the restaurant, coming out of a room that I knew to be both private and intimate in setting, scrambled everything I'd been comfortable thinking and left me feeling poached.

While I hadn't spent much time listening to the not-so-subtle hints of the hostess, it seemed like there was no time like the present to change that. "Oh," I said. "I'll just be leaving." I looked at the hostess stand. "Is this the takeout menu? Great, thank you. That's just what I need." I left the restaurant as quickly as I could, sure that they'd recognized me, feeling ridiculous. I had my helmet buckled on and the scooter engine started by the time Tak caught up with me. I probably could have gotten out of there too, if he hadn't stood directly in my path.

His mouth moved but with the helmet on, I couldn't hear what he said over the engine. I pointed to my ears and shook my head. He came closer and cupped his hands around his mouth.

"What are you doing here?" he asked.

"You invited me."

"Didn't you get my message?"

"What message?" I asked, which seemed to work as well as "No, I didn't," in terms of answering his question.

"I called you and asked if we could reschedule."

"My cell phone is still with the police and the store phone's going crazy with reporters. I stopped answering after the first two and let the service pick it up."

"Turn off the scooter and take off the helmet. We need to talk."

I thought back to my conversation with Soot about being a mature adult who could handle the situation with Tak. I owed it to Soot to act like that mature adult. Cats like him preferred to know that their owners were emotionally stable. I turned off the engine and unbuckled my helmet. The scarf that I'd tied around my ponytail stuck to the inside of the helmet, which made it difficult to extricate my head from the plastic casing.

"Did you or did you not tell me to meet you here for a da—for dinner?"

"I did."

"So I did not get that wrong? Because the hostess acted like maybe I'd gotten that wrong. And when I saw you and Detective Nichols coming out of the private room, it sure felt like the hostess was right, which meant I wasn't, which meant that you hadn't asked me here, which you say you did, so I'm confused."

"After that, I'm confused too." He held out his hand. "Come back into the restaurant and I'll explain."

"Is there a back door? I'd rather not walk past the hostess again."

"I just saw a party of seven go inside. There's light staffing tonight because it's been so slow lately, so she'll be busy serving the miso and the salads. Come on. You have a limited window to maintain obscurity." He grinned.

I took his hand and swung my leg over the scooter, hopped a couple of times until I had my balance, and locked the helmet to the seat. He kept holding my hand even though I was off the scooter. I didn't mind.

I half expected to find Detective Nichols waiting for us in the private room. When Tak slid the doors open and led me inside, I felt an unexpected release of tension, as if weights had been tied to my hands and feet and were suddenly removed. But then I realized I hadn't seen her leave, which meant she knew of a back passageway, or she could be hiding behind the other set of rice paper walls or under the table—

"Nancy left out the back when I came after you."

"So there *is* a back door."

Tak dropped my hand. "Margo, sit down. We need to talk."

"I don't want to," I said. Soot, I felt, would have been embarrassed by how quickly I abandoned my mature adult act.

"Why not?"

"Because if I sit down, you're going to tell me how you and the detective are getting back together, and how you don't want to see me anymore, and I can't move away because I just moved back a year ago to take over the store, so we'll see each other all the time, and I won't be able to get fried rice anymore because it'll remind me of you." I remembered the takeout menu in my pocket, but bit my tongue. Not the time to mention that my subconscious had seen this coming.

"I used to think I could read you pretty well," Tak said. "It wasn't just a body language or facial expression thing either. The first time I met you I felt like I'd met you before. But you're so off base right now, I don't even know what to say. Why do you think Nancy and I are getting back together? Why do you think I don't want to see you anymore? Where did that come from?"

I chewed the inside of my mouth and stared at the table. I knew where it had come from. A big fat overwhelming ingrained-in-my-DNA fear of abandonment that I'd been carrying with me since the day I was born. The day my mom had died.

I knew the story of my mom and dad. Jerry and Celeste had met shortly after he'd bought Disguise DeLimit from the original owners. Together they'd taken over the daily running of the costume shop. They were the picture of newly married bliss, and then my mom had gotten pregnant. Nine months later, I arrived, but complications during her pregnancy had created a situation where only one of us would survive.

That day, she passed the torch to me. For the past thirty-three years, it had been me and my dad. He managed Disguise DeLimit while raising me by himself—at least until Ebony happened into the shop, saw a five-year-old girl dressed like a fireman, and figured I could use a female influence in my life. The two of them did the best they could to make me turn out normal, but considering my school clothes came from the costume store and my surrogate mom sometimes kept a plastic pistol in her Afro, normal was a stretch.

I'd spent time with more than one therapist trying to get over what they all termed "survivor guilt," or the residual feelings that maybe I should have died so my biological mother could live. A few specialists added in the extra prediction that I'd have trouble connecting with people in my adult life, a side effect of the irrational sense of abandonment I'd developed. I almost wished I'd never heard the theory because it had turned out to be freakishly accurate, leaving me wondering if the suggestion had never been planted, would I be more suited to handling the ebbs and flows of adult relationships?

This was the type of conversation I usually had with Soot, who had taken the place of a rotating cast of therapists when I moved back to Proper City. One woman, an unlicensed counselor named Willow, pinch-hit when Soot was busy chasing mice in the stockroom. But otherwise, I was on my own to sort this kind of stuff out. See how well that has worked out for me?

"Okay, you don't have to tell me what you're thinking, but I do have to tell you something. You know I've been looking for a job. It's rough out there. Maybe if I was fresh out of college, I could find something, but I'm not. I'm competing with people who are ten years younger than I am."

"But you're smart and you have experience."

"That's all true, but there's an explanation for why I haven't been excited about any of the jobs that I've interviewed for. There's a reason why I want to stick around Proper City even though my employment options are limited."

He was quiet for a moment. I didn't say anything.

"I got a job offer today. It's not exactly what I was looking for, but it's a lot closer to what I do than helping around the restaurant."

"Congratulations," I said. My words felt empty of emotion and I hoped Tak didn't notice. "When will you be moving?"

"I won't be." I looked up at his face. I'd expected to see a smile, but I didn't. He was serious, the kind of serious that said that what sounded like good news was possibly bad news parading around in a sheep's costume.

"The Clark County District Attorney called. With the incorporation of Proper City looking more and more like a reality, the mayor's office has approved a bill to fund city expansion at the district level. A portion of the money is being used to create a position that works closely with the police department to advise on the expansion. That's what I worked on before I left my job. Turns out they're willing to set me up in a satellite office to focus on future growth in Proper."

"So you're going to stay here? In Proper?"

"Yes."

"That's good news, right? All you have to do is set up a temp office and you're good to go."

"I have a temp office." He paused. "At the police station."

Neither one of us said the obvious second half of the sentence. That he'd be staying in Proper City, working alongside Detective Nancy Nichols, every day of the week.

Chapter 18

AFTER THE BOMBSHELL, I wasn't sure how I felt. It seemed inappropriate to suggest that I had to leave the restaurant so I could go home and talk things over with my cat, so I stayed. I even managed to ask a few questions about how this all had come about. It quickly became obvious that he'd been nervous about telling me, and that somehow allayed my fears. Not to mention the fact that when somebody who's been looking for a job for months finally gets one, you're a pretty crappy person if you make it all about you.

Eventually, conversation turned from Tak's new employment opportunity to what had been going on around Proper. Sometime between him coming to see me at the festival earlier today and now, he'd been briefed on the details of the murder of Ronnie Cass.

"Who told you?" I asked. "Earlier today, you didn't seem to know any of this."

"Nancy told me. I don't think she would have normally talked to me about it, but Don kept interrupting her. He's not doing himself any favors."

"Maybe he was interrupting her because she arrested the wrong person. Did she ever think of that?"

"Don was let go earlier today. She didn't have enough to hold him."

"They why did you say he kept interrupting her? What did he do?"

"He keeps calling the police station, asking to speak to her. Demanding is more like it. He said he had information that could help lead to the capture of Ronnie's murderer."

"He's cooperating. He's trying to help."

"He's borderline making sure the case is thrown for good. Every time he makes the claim that he has information that could help in the investigation, the police have to take him seriously."

"I should hope so," I said.

"The law is like that for a reason, but Don's information *isn't* helping, it's diverting attention from the real investigation. He keeps talking about bank robberies from fifty years ago and illegitimate children and pointing the finger at Chet and Jayne Lemming. His behavior isn't entirely unexpected considering his love of conspiracies, but it's not a good strategy if he wants to cooperate."

I sat up straighter. "Maybe he *does* know something. Don's very in tune with what's going on around him. That's the benefit of being a bit on the paranoid side. He might have seen or overheard something. He might really *know* what happened."

"Or he might be throwing a bunch of red herrings at the police so they get lost in a blizzard of dead ends."

Like the evidence found at the bank robbery fifty years ago, I thought.

By the time our food arrived—prepared on one of the cooking surfaces out front and delivered to our room so as to maintain the "private" part—I'd lost my appetite. Tak hadn't been gung ho on how I'd gotten involved in recent crimes in Proper, but he'd understood why I had. First, Ebony's freedom had been at risk. Then, I'd almost lost the store. He hadn't judged me during either of those times. He hadn't tried to talk me out of being involved either.

But tonight, we were on opposite sides. His new job was funded by Mayor Young and was a by-product of the desired city incorporation. His base of operations would be inside the police department working alongside the town detective every single day. His background and grasp of mathematics and calculations led him to being an analytical person, systematic in his approach to everything. He was on the side of rules, regulations, and leaving things to the police.

I already knew that sometimes life wasn't like math. You could add two and two, but if there was an unknown variable at play, you wouldn't get four. Was this what things were going to be like after Tak took this job? Spending time alongside his ex-girlfriend, would he become *her* confidant, someone to bounce theories off of?

"You said Don was released? How come?"

"Nancy brought him in for questioning, but she didn't have enough for a warrant. He was there for twenty-four hours, which is the maximum she can detain him."

"She took him in yesterday."

"That's right. She let him go this afternoon right about

when I got there. We were twenty minutes into our interview and he started calling."

I looked at the time on the clock on the wall. Yesterday, Don had been taken away from the festival around four o'clock. It was closing in on eight now. If Don had made enough of a nuisance of himself in the four hours after he'd been let go, then Don had something worth talking about. And even if Nancy didn't want to listen to him, I did.

I balled up the napkin that sat in my lap and set it on the table next to my barely touched plate of food. "Will you judge me too harshly if I back out of tonight? I've had almost no sleep over the past two days, and the carbs in the fried rice just hit me. I think I need a very long nap."

Tak studied me for a few moments without saying anything. His deep brown eyes bounced back and forth over my own, and I knew there was a chance that he knew exactly what I was thinking. There was also a chance that, after he'd made all of these arrangements for us, he'd be insulted.

I put my hand on his arm. "I really am tired," I said. "I was up most of last night making costumes for teddy bears for the festival. I know it's barely eight, and I'd really like to spend time with you, but I think I'm going downhill."

"Truth is, I'm a little jet-lagged myself. I think I synced with Michigan time right before I flew out today."

"So how about tomorrow night? We'll have a proper celebration for your new job."

"Isn't any celebration in Proper a proper celebration?"

"I guess you'll have to wait and see."

Tak found a couple of takeout containers and helped me pack up half of the food for later. He knew about my penchant for Fruity Pebbles and wanted to make sure if I did get hungry later, I'd have a more acceptable meal available. I think he considered the bowl-of-cereal-for-dinner thing an insult to restaurateurs everywhere.

If he doubted my sincerity earlier, he had proof while he walked me to my scooter. I stifled two yawns and gave up the third time, turning my head the opposite direction and gulping down air. He stood patiently while I unlocked the seat to the Vespa, pulled my helmet out, and tucked the takeout containers inside.

"Are you okay to drive?" he asked.

"Sure. It's two miles."

"I think we should put the scooter in the back of my truck and let me drive you."

"Not necessary."

"Then I'll follow you."

"Tak, I'm not going anywhere but home. You can trust me."

"Who said anything about not trusting you? You're stumbling around like you polished off a bottle of wine."

"Maybe you slipped something into my fried rice."

"Margo, come on, this is serious."

"I'll be fine," I said. I remembered a time, not too long ago, when I'd been in a dangerous situation and had wanted nothing more than for Tak to check on me. "You know what? You should follow me and make sure I get home safely."

He smiled. "You got it."

And that's exactly what happened: I drove home on

my scooter with Tak not far behind me. And after I parked out back and waved good-bye, I went upstairs, turned on the light to my bedroom, and changed into black sweats and a baseball hat. I turned the light off, made sure Tak's SUV was nowhere in sight, grabbed the keys to Dig's Le Sabre, and drove to Don's house.

DON Digby lived in arguably the smallest house in Proper. About five hundred square feet in total, it was a small brick box that sat between the Department of Water and Power and the abandoned schoolhouse where a portion of Proper City's residents had been educated. After he'd retired from being a nurse, he'd made it his mission to live small and reduce his carbon footprint.

I parked the Le Sabre out front and approached the door. Before knocking, I slipped a piece of paper underneath. *Frohike's here. Open up.* I tapped lightly on the door and it opened almost instantly.

"Hurry up," he said. "You don't know who's watching."

For the briefest of moments I worried that Don had lost it. I stepped inside and he closed and locked the door behind me. "The news has created a feeding frenzy. People keep driving past, shouting my name and asking where I hid the gold. I can't turn on my TV or radio because all I see are reports that aren't even true. It's like the mayor sicced his PR person on me and I'm the flavor of the month."

"People are stalking you?"

"When I got home today, there were holes in my yard. Actual holes. People were digging."

"Digging for what?"

"For the gold that Ronnie took from the bank fifty years ago."

"But that's just a story, right? Wrong place, wrong time. You and Ronnie didn't rob the bank."

"I didn't, but Ronnie did. That's the reason we broke up."

Chapter 19

"RONNIE ROBBED THE bank?" I asked, shocked at the news.

"Sit down, Margo. I'll get some tea. It's a long story, and you might as well hear it."

I lowered myself onto a brown tweed chair but then stood up almost immediately. The room was a study in brown, sort of "eccentric professor," the type of setting that called for a costume with elbow patches and argyle. A map of the world that was marked with locations of UFO sightings hung from the ceiling, separating the living room from the corner with Don's bed. The walls were lined with floor-to-ceiling bookcases filled with bound reports and record albums. His love of blues and soul music was as great as his suspicion of the government. I ran my hand over the spines of a row of old cordovan leather books with faded gold letters, and then lifted the lid on the record player to see what was on the turntable. Sonny Boy Williamson.

As I wandered around the tiny room, I couldn't help but think about how different Don must be now from the eighteen-year-old who had been in a relationship with Ronnie. In 1968, Don had been Kirby's age. The memory of Kirby's angst over Varla was still fresh in my mind. Was that how Don had felt about Ronnie?

He returned with two steaming mugs, one in each hand, and a folding aluminum TV tray tucked under his arm. He twisted at the waist and I took the TV stand and set it up. He set one mug down and then sat on a small footstool and drank from the other—the mug, not the footstool. I sat back in the tweed chair and cupped my mug, waiting for him to talk.

"Your dad and I weren't sure whether we should tell you any of this or not," he said. "It's water under the bridge. Ancient history." He took another pull on his mug and then set it on the floor. "How did she look?" he asked quietly.

My heart went out to him. For as long as I'd known Don, he'd been happy to be on his own. I'd never asked why he didn't date, because that was too close to asking why my own father didn't date. Both men could be filed in the category of eligible bachelor: single, financially solvent, unencumbered by ex-wives. I knew a lot of the women in Proper viewed my dad as a catch, but I'd never really thought much about Don.

I'd spent the past few days trying to block the image of Ronnie's body from my mind, but for Don I conjured the image back up. "She was in her costume," I said. "Ready to perform."

He smiled and nodded. "Ronnie loved performing. She was like an athlete suiting up for a big game. She put on that wig and that mask and could do anything. And she did."

"You said she robbed the bank. How do you know for sure?"

"Because I helped her." At my startled expression, he laughed. "Not like you think. I didn't know I was helping her at the time."

He grew quiet. I wanted him to tell me the story, but I knew it was something he'd kept to himself for a long time. The clock on the wall ticked like a metronome, counting out beats of silence. An occasional drip from the faucet behind him provided a counter rhythm. It struck me as funny that the house next to the DWP had a leaky faucet.

"She knew I liked puzzles, so she'd try to come up with things to stump me. Sometimes riddles, sometimes impossible situations. Every once in a while she told me a story that she pulled from those two-minute mystery books, ones where she knew the answer because she flipped to the back page to read the solution. She used to ask me about conspiracies too. She said that's why I liked them, because it was as if there was a big secret out there and I was constantly trying to figure it out. She said one day I'd figure her out too. I told her as long as I lived, she'd always be a mystery to me. My enigma," he added, almost as if he was talking to himself.

I was having a hard time justifying the snappy, arrogant, self-centered Ronnie with the woman Don described. Every person who'd talked about her had shared the opinion that she only looked out for herself, except for him. Something big had happened to her after she left Proper. Something that had forever changed the person she once was into the woman I'd found dead in a trailer.

"How serious was your relationship?" I asked.

"Ronnie and I had talked about marriage. I even bought a ring and had it inscribed. I kept waiting for the right time, but I was scared. We were just kids, but we didn't feel like it. We thought if we didn't capture what we felt it would vanish. Ronnie used to talk about us making a name for ourselves. She said Proper City was too small for us, and I said that no matter where we went, Proper would always be a part of us. I think that's how she got the idea, because she started to say that Pete Proper was our guardian angel. Pete Proper would always look out for us."

"But, Don, it's one thing to say the founder of the town is going to look out for you and another to rob a bank and get away with a brick of his gold."

"She had this game she'd play. It started out being 'How much would we need to disappear?' and then it turned into 'How could we get it?' and from there it became 'There's gold sitting right there in that bank. Let's figure out how to steal it.' It seemed innocent at the time, but it was also a way to rebel against authority. *Bonnie and Clyde* came out in 1967, and she wanted us to be like them. Talking about robbing banks and disappearing. And it was somehow okay because we never talked about robbing the citizens of Proper who kept their money there. It was always about Pete Proper's gold. And like she said, he stole it in the first place."

"So you two came up with a plan?"

He shook his head. "It was just talk. She never wrote any of it down, and eventually we moved on to something else. Then the Domino Divas were booked to dance at a concert that would take place right out front and all of her free time went into that. Practicing around the clock, designing costumes, promoting the show. She contacted agents and scouts from Las Vegas and California. It was supposed to be her break and she wanted every single person to be there to see it."

I was starting to get an idea of why. "That was the day of the robbery, wasn't it?" I asked. "She had a plan. She got everybody to show up at the dance concert so nobody was around to catch her."

"The news broke later that day. The alarm had been cut. The display case had been drilled and the gold was gone. The interior of the whole savings and loan was a mess. Trash everywhere. And it was wet. Like the roof leaked after a bad rainstorm."

"But it doesn't rain in Proper."

"No, it sure doesn't. That was just part of the enigma." He grew silent again.

"That's the second time you mentioned an enigma." Curiosity had taken over for me, a desire to know everything that had happened, the inside scoop, and why Don was so sure Ronnie was behind it.

"Have you ever heard me or your dad talk about the '23 enigma'?"

I shook my head.

"It's the belief that most incidents and events are connected back to the number twenty-three. William S. Burroughs wrote about it. Smart man."

"Don?" I prompted, unsure how we'd segued to a novelist from the Beat generation.

"The bank was robbed on February third at 5:23. Two

three. Two plus three is five. Twenty-three. And twenty-three dollars was left behind on the bank counter under the velvet box that held Ronnie's engagement ring."

"That doesn't sound much like coincidence anymore."

"No, it doesn't."

"I know it's no consolation, but at least she didn't take the ring."

He looked up at me, his eyes filled with a sadness that spoke fathoms about the pain he still felt. "But she did. The ring box was empty."

Chapter 20

THE WAS NO easy way to ask the next question. "Don, I heard somebody say that you had a safe-deposit box at the bank and that you emptied it the day of the robbery. Is that true?"

He leaned back and stared up at the ceiling. "There are no records that show that I emptied my box that day. Besides, there was only one thing in my safe-deposit box—the engagement ring. I kept the key on my key fob and Ronnie knew it. She could have made a copy at any time and replaced it without me even knowing. The story has gotten a little twisted over the years. Thing is, my box was the only one that was empty after the robbery."

"So people assumed you were involved because in addition to everything else, your box was singled out."

"Yep. Talk about a conspiracy to implicate me." He laughed, but it was hollow. I could see why Don believed that what people saw wasn't always the truth. He'd lived it himself. And like any good conspiracy, it was back in the media gaining steam, making him the center of attention over something that had happened too long ago to be news.

"What happened after the robbery?"

"There was an investigation, but it led nowhere. Too much evidence. As soon as I was cleared, I enlisted in the army. I couldn't stay here. Life was different then and I needed a chance to make my own fresh start."

"But you came back."

"I served my time, but I'm not an army guy. Too many things I didn't trust. Too many people who had secondary agendas. Proper City is home, so I came home."

"Detective Nichols thinks you're doing the same thing again. Calling her with tips to investigate Ronnie's murder to distract her from what happened. She thinks you're more involved than you admit. She doesn't have enough for a conviction yet, but you need to tread carefully."

"Ronnie was supposed to be my future. Apparently I was a poor judge of character back then. But this isn't a game now. This is my life. For fifty years I've accepted that a lot of people think I was part of that robbery. I had patients who demanded a different nurse because their life savings was in that bank. I still get e-mails from people who ask me where the gold is. Once a month I have to edit the Wikipedia page about that robbery to keep my name out of it. Now somebody killed Ronnie and it's all coming back. I had to unplug my phone because the reporters won't leave me alone. Strangers are digging in my yard. I don't know what she got into in the past fifty years, but it didn't have anything to do with me. She made it clear that I wasn't a part of her life when she came back, so I moved on." He stood up. "I'm not going to let them vilify me again. This is as much my town as anybody else's."

I stood up too. "Thank you for telling me the truth," I said.

He smiled. "I told you my version of what happened. The truth is still out there."

THE next morning, I rose bright and early. I'd fallen asleep while trying to sort out everything Don had told me. There were details in his story that I hadn't heard before, but there was still a lot of information for me to discover. What I knew was that Don hadn't held back. He hadn't been evasive. If he was involved—in either the bank robbery or the murder—he wouldn't have opened up like he had. He reminded me of a pressure cooker, with everything building up on the inside, needing a release from the history that haunted him. Me showing up on his doorstep gave him that release, except it didn't change anything. If Detective Nichols suspected that he did it, then no amount of pressure release would make a difference.

There was one detail that nagged at me from Don's story, though. The reason Ronnie had been suspected of the robbery in the first place: the blue domino mask that had been found at the scene of the crime. The Domino Divas had been at the top of their game when the robbery took place, and they'd been scheduled to perform that very day. It was almost too obvious . . . unless another diva was involved. And the one who appeared to have a grudge against Ronnie was Jayne.

The sun was just starting to break over the horizon,

which told me one thing: if I hurried, I could make it to Jayne's morning class of yoga in the park. I texted Bobbie and told her to join me, and then dressed in tights, a leotard, and an oversized sweatshirt à la Olivia Newton-John, the "Physical" era. A few minutes later, I joined Bobbie at the PCP.

Bobbie had taken up yoga after her stint with rehab. She'd needed an outlet for stress and, apparently, spending her days surrounded by teddy bears hadn't been sufficient. She'd tried to convince me to join her, and I had on more than one occasion.

Today she sat on a pink rubber mat with one leg in front of her and the other leg pointing straight up toward the sky. She tipped her head toward the vacant blue mat next to her. I dumped my bag and assumed the same position (or tried).

Because the festival was taking place on public property, the planners couldn't tell the yoga class to find another place to meet. But still, only a handful of women were scattered about on colorful neoprene mats, twisting into pretzel-like shapes while calming melodies trickled from a boom box. Jayne, dressed in an outfit remarkably similar to mine but lacking the irony, faced the group. She sat in what I thought was the lotus position: cross-legged with her feet resting on top of her knees. When she spotted me, her face colored to a flush. She looked away and called out another pose that allowed her to turn around and hide.

I spent much of the next forty-five minutes contorting into unfamiliar poses, hoping for a good time to ask some questions. I almost missed my window when Jayne called out the final position—instructing us to close our eyes and lay flat on our backs with arms overhead and feet pointed to the sky—and counted us down from twenty to one. It wasn't until somewhere between seven and four that I opened my eyes and realized she'd been packing up her own belongings, probably so she could make a quick getaway. I jumped up and approached her.

"Do you have a minute?" I asked.

"Not really," she snapped, exhibiting none of the Zen calm that one should find after forty-five minutes of yoga in the park.

"This won't take long."

"I'm late," she said. She pushed the last of her belongings into a denim duffel bag and walked toward the parking lot. I jogged a few steps to catch up to her and then fell into step.

"I was wondering if you were planning on doing anything for Ronnie? A memorial or a tribute or something to commemorate her contribution to the Domino Divas?"

"Let's see. She patented our name and made herself the sole proprietor of the operation, which basically told the world that the rest of us didn't matter. The contract she signed gives us nothing. I'd say Ronnie established that when she died, the Domino Divas were done. So no, I'm not really feeling like spearheading a memorial, if you know what I mean."

"Why did you all agree to get back together? If it wasn't for the money, then what did she say to convince you?"

Jayne ignored my question. We had reached the parking lot. She reached into her bag and pulled out a full set of keys. She clicked the black plastic fob and a dirty gold sedan beeped. With longer strides, I made it to the car first and blocked her ability to open the door.

"I already know you and Ronnie were friends once."

"Those days are long gone."

"Doesn't it bother you that somebody killed her?"

"Not really. Ronnie put herself at the front of the line. We're all going to die someday. Her day came first."

A few other yoga class attendees caught up with us. Jayne smiled at them and wished them a good day. When they were finished, she reached out to me and tried to push me out of the way. I stood my ground.

"What happened between you two?"

"Nothing 'happened.' We just grew apart." She pushed me again and this time I shifted out of the way. She threw her yoga gear in the backseat, climbed into the car, and started the engine. She put the car into reverse and backed up slowly even though I still held the door open.

I kept my hand on the door and walked with the car. "If nothing happened, then why did you slap her after rehearsal?" I asked.

She glared at me for several seconds. "Because a long time ago Ronnie took something that belonged to me. The only reason I agreed to this farce was so I could get it back." She grabbed the inside door handle and yanked it shut. The power locks clamped into place and she swung wide and then peeled out of the lot.

Chapter 21

THE STATEMENT CAME out of left field. I watched the sedan pull onto the Main Line Road and speed through a yellow light. At the rate she was driving, she'd get a ticket for a traffic violation before she got home.

Bobbie had stayed behind, packing up first her own belongings and then the ones she'd packed for me. By the time she joined me in the parking lot, Jayne's car blocks away.

"I know you don't do this every day, but yoga is supposed to make people calm down and help you deal with your stress, not the other way around," she said.

"Try telling that to your instructor." I pointed down the street. The only evidence of Jayne's car were the fading taillights that grew ever smaller as she increased the distance between us.

"What did you say to her?" Bobbie asked.

"I asked her why she slapped Ronnie at the rehearsal."

"And?"

"She said Ronnie took something that belonged to her."

Bobbie didn't seem surprised. "She was probably talking about her husband. There've been rumors about Chet Lemming since I first started volunteering at Landis House."

"Isn't that where you did your first teddy bear fundraiser?"

Landis House was a women's shelter on the north side of Proper. Originally an apartment building, it had changed hands several times before becoming a temporary residence for women in need. The mortgage had long since been paid off, and the owners willed the deed from generation to generation to keep it privately owned. Outsiders might not even notice the structure, a nondescript building of craftsman design that was maintained by the women who lived there and a small team of volunteers.

To anybody who didn't know Bobbie's history, they might have wondered what it was that drew her to help them, but I knew.

Bobbie had first learned about them in rehab. A few of the women at the clinic said they'd gone there when they'd needed a safe place to stay while getting on their feet. Bobbie listened to their stories, about leaving abusive relationships, getting over addictions, taking control over gambling problems. Some of the women had young children who'd only known a life of instability. It was after hearing these stories that Bobbie got the idea to start a nonprofit that made and sold teddy bears to raise money. Landis House had become the first beneficiary of her now-famous teddy bear fund-raisers.

"I've been volunteering at Landis House since getting

out of rehab. One day a month Chet comes out to Landis House to give general checkups after his shift at the hospital. The women who live there aren't exactly looking for a new relationship, but that doesn't stop him from crossing the line of appropriate bedside behavior. It's not that hard to imagine that he cheated on Jayne at some point."

"I get the idea that Chet is a ladies' man, but seriously? He'd cheat on his wife with her friend? That's the stuff of slimeballs."

"It takes two to tango," she said.

I turned away from Bobbie and stared at the street in the direction Jayne's car had driven. "True. I wonder if it's easier for Jayne to hold Ronnie accountable. I'd think after a while, a wife would get tired of being married to a man like that."

"What makes you think she's not?"

"She's still married to him, isn't she?"

"Yes, but nobody said they have a healthy relationship." Bobbie bent down and retied the open laces on her left sneaker. When she stood back up, she said, "You could always get his side of things."

"I bet that would go over well. Knock on his front door and ask how long he'd been having an affair with his wife's best friend." I rolled my eyes. "With my luck she'd be in the kitchen making macaroni."

"I was thinking more along the lines of something less obvious."

"Like what?"

"If you can come to Landis House this afternoon, I can try to get you alone with him."

"I can't. There's nobody else to run the store." I chewed my lower lip and thought for a couple of seconds. "You said he works at the hospital before coming to Landis House. Do you know when he starts?"

"The free clinics open up around eight. Why?"

I grabbed Bobbie's forearm and twisted it so I could check her watch. "It's seven thirty now." I looked back up at her. "No time to spare." I hugged her and said good-bye.

THERE was a short list of things I wanted to accomplish before opening the store and a narrow window of time in which to accomplish them. I made a banana and peanut butter smoothie, fed Soot a can of tuna-flavored cat food, and dressed in generic blue scrubs that we'd ordered from a uniform company. On any other day I would have draped a stethoscope around my neck and a surgical mask over my mouth, but today's outfit wasn't about accessorizing, it was about blending in.

I drove the Le Sabre to the hospital. If time permitted, I could swing by the high school and then return the loaner car to Dig when I was done. I parked in Lot D, which was designated for visitors. I had a vague memory of how the hospital was laid out thanks to my dad's first heart attack. Memories of that day flooded back as I walked across the street and stood in line to pass through the metal detector. Tears welled up in my eyes and I blinked rapidly to hold them in. When the blinking proved ineffective, I tipped my head backward, succeeding only in running into the person in front of me.

"Sorry," I mumbled. I swiped my hands across my cheeks to brush away the tears that had spilled. "The hospital brings back bad memories," I said.

The woman glanced at my scrubs. "Don't you work here?" she asked.

The problem with being so comfortable dressing in costume was that sometimes I didn't remember I was wearing a costume. It was one thing to dress like I fit in so as not to be noticed. It was an entirely other thing to lie about it.

"No, I don't. I'm here to see one of the doctors."

Her expression changed. "Oh, honey, I'm so sorry. You go on in front of me."

For a small town, we had a decent hospital, thanks mostly to the wealthy residents who knew even money couldn't stave off potential health issues or accidents. I walked through the emergency waiting room, around the corner, and up the stairs to the area designated for weekly clinics. It was the one concession to the lower-income families in town. Different days of the week were designated for broad health concerns: vaccinations and flu shots, blood pressure tests, weight-loss consultations, and the like. Doctors rotated through on a somewhat regular schedule. Today's board featured general physicals conducted by Dr. Chet Lemming.

I approached the window. "Hi, I'm Margo Tamblyn," I said. "I'm here to see Dr. Lemming."

"Sign in," she said.

"Do you know how long the wait is? I have to be somewhere in a couple of hours."

"Sign in," she said again. She glanced up and tapped the clipboard with the back of her pen. "Dr. Lemming sees patients in order of arrival."

I took a seat on the end of a row with a pretty woman with long, straight blond hair. Three girls matching her coloring giggled and squealed as they ran around the reception room. A fourth girl, smaller than the others, sat in the chair next to the woman, hugging a threadbare blanket to her chest. The mother caught me looking at them and smiled. I smiled back.

"Sorry about my girls," she said. "They don't realize this is a hospital."

"I think that's a good thing."

"The staff doesn't like it," she said in a whisper. "If I could afford a sitter, I wouldn't be at the free clinic. But Dr. Lemming, he's good with the kids, and he renews our prescriptions whenever we need them." She rolled her eyes. "Even if he is a little overzealous with his stethoscope."

It was starting to seem as though my initial impression of Dr. Chet Lemming was spot-on.

"Has he ever—you know—been inappropriate?"

She laughed. "He's a big flirt, that's all. You get a physical, they're going to weigh you, take your temperature, check your blood pressure, and listen to your heartbeat. All part of the routine."

The door next to the reception desk opened and a woman in scrubs printed with cats stepped out. "Margo Tamblyn?" she said.

I gathered my things and glanced sheepishly at the woman and her girls. Embarrassed that I'd been called before her when she clearly had been there longer than I had, I held a closed fist up to my mouth and faked a cough. She put her arm around the girl next to her and pulled her closer, as if shielding her from my imaginary germs. I followed the cat woman through the hallway and into exam room number four.

"Wait here. The doctor will be with you shortly," she said.

"Aren't you going to weigh me or take my blood pressure or temperature?" I asked.

"Not necessary. The doctor will be with you shortly," she said again.

There were no clocks in the exam room, and I still didn't have my cell phone back. I wished I'd brought a magazine from the lobby with me. I quickly bored of the poster on the wall, an artist's rendition of the pulmonary cavity illustrated in bold shades of red and blue. I hopped down and wandered around the small space. A series of framed posters that illustrated various internal organs in colorful graphics hung on the wall.

The door to the exam room opened just as I was pulling a pair of blue rubber gloves from a box next to the sink. I shoved the gloves into the back pocket of my scrubs and sat back on the exam table. Chet entered. He stared at the contents of a light blue file folder, flipping through pages. I recognized my handwriting on the top one.

"Open your mouth," he said. He held a large wooden tongue depressor in my mouth. "Say ah."

"Ah," I said. He shined a light into my mouth, and then threw the tongue depressor away and moved the light to my ears.

"You're here for a physical?" he asked.

"Actually, I wanted to talk to you."

He clicked the end of his pen and wrote something in my file. He placed the flat end of his stethoscope on the outside of my scrubs and put the earpieces into his ears.

"Breathe in through your nose, out through your mouth," he said.

I took a few breaths until he appeared to be finished, and added, "About Ronnie Cass."

He stopped writing mid-word. He glanced up at me and then back at the paper, but his writing didn't resume. "What about Ronnie?" he asked.

"She was murdered a couple of days ago, and I heard"—I took a deep breath—"I heard that you had a relationship with her."

"Oh yeah? Where'd you hear that?"

"Your wife."

He pulled the pen out of my file. "My wife is a disturbed woman," he said. "I thought it would be good for her to get back involved with the Domino gals, give her a chance to recapture her youth, but gossip has a way of coming back to life. Maybe it wasn't such a good idea to stir up old wounds."

"Gossip about your affair or gossip about the bank robbery?"

He held my stare for a few uncomfortable moments and then clicked the pen off. He reopened my file and flipped back to the top page. "Margo Tamblyn," he read aloud. "You're Jerry's daughter, aren't you?"

It was one of the more familiar questions I'd gotten since moving back to Proper. My dad was popular around town, not just because of running the costume shop, but also because he'd lived there his whole life. In a small town, people got to know each other, either through school board meetings or poker games or other social activities.

"Yes," I said. "I moved back to Proper last year and took over the costume shop. My dad says he's done the

costumes for your Mardi Gras parties for the past few
years."

"He and Don Digby just started up some kind of publication, didn't they?"

"Yes, a conspiracy newspaper. It's nothing."

He flipped the file shut. "Doesn't sound like nothing.
Is this some kind of undercover exposé?" he demanded.
"Forget anything I said here. And you tell Jerry he'd
better watch what he prints. One word about me or my
wife and I'll slap him with a lawsuit for defamation of
character."

Chapter 22

CHET DIDN'T GIVE me a chance to respond. He stormed out of the exam room with my folder and left me alone with little more than a pocket full of blue rubber gloves. I counted to sixty to see if he'd come back. He didn't.

I left the exam room and stopped at the reception desk. "I don't know if I'm supposed to wait or not," I said. "Dr. Lemming left in the middle of my exam."

"Dr. Lemming got paged for an emergency," she said. "We're trying to get another doctor to come in to take over for him, but it's going to be a couple of hours. You can wait if you like."

"No thanks," I said. I left the clinic.

The blond mother of four from the waiting room caught up to me in the parking lot. "Excuse me," she called out.

"Did I drop something?" I asked.

"No, but that receptionist lied to you. I don't know what happened in that exam room, but Dr. Lemming didn't get paged for an emergency. He came out front and told the women behind the glass to 'get that woman out of this clinic.' What happened back there?"

"Nothing. Well, something. I accused him of cheating on his wife."

"Everybody knows Dr. Lemming cheats on his wife. There's a line of women just waiting for her to ask for a divorce so he's available. I don't think that would have upset him like this."

"But that's all I said."

"Did he deny it?"

"Not exactly," I said. I thought about what he had said. *My wife is a disturbed woman.* He'd all but fingered Jayne as Ronnie Cass's murderer, and then threatened my dad with a lawsuit if he printed anything that could potentially harm him. It could mean nothing.

I didn't think it meant nothing.

I drove to the high school. I'd been living and breathing the Sagebrush Festival for weeks, and shifting focus to Kirby's dilemma was a welcome respite. I parked next to the tennis courts in a space marked VISITOR and entered the building the same way I had back when I was a student.

A long hallway framed out with blue-gray metal lockers stretched in front of me. To my left was a trophy case that housed various plaques, awards, and ribbons, and photos that documented the achievements of students who had come and gone. A couple of old yearbooks were displayed in the background, navy blue covers with gold writing embossed on the front. I had one like it, as did my dad and Ebony. I used to love flipping through the pages, looking at photos of the people I'd only ever known as adults.

Across the hall from the trophy case was the principal's office. I entered. A younger version of Grady O'Toole was waiting in one of the otherwise vacant chairs. He wore a blue letter jacket with yellow sleeves. The name ANGUS was embroidered above a patch that featured a shrimp in a football helmet.

"Hi," I said to him.

"'Sup."

"Do you know if the principal is here?"

"If he is, he's keeping me waiting out here for nothing." He scowled. A young blonde entered the office and let herself behind the counter. Angus's attitude changed dramatically. He sat up and dusted off the sleeves to his letter jacket. Considering how hot it had been lately, I got the feeling he wore the jacket out of vanity, not necessity. I guess we all wear costumes.

I approached the blonde. "I'm here to see the principal. Margo Tamblyn."

"You're the one who made that great lab rat costume for the chemistry teacher for Halloween," she said. "That was the best costume *ever.*"

"Thank you."

She reached down behind the counter. "Principal Stanley was expecting you. He said the gymnasium is a go as long as you can hold off on setup until Saturday morning."

I felt my neck prickle with the knowledge that whatever we said could be overheard by Angus. I tucked my chin and pretended to rub my cheek against my shoulder, giving him a sly over-the-shoulder look. He was busy texting and probably hadn't heard a word.

"Sure, that works for me. Can you tell him I said thanks? And please, it's a surprise. Not a word to anybody."

She glanced at Angus and smiled. "You got it."

I left the office. The task had taken less time than I anticipated, so I paused by the trophy case and looked at the photos until I spotted the swim team. Kirby stood proudly in the middle of the rest of the men, hands behind his hips, feet shoulder-width apart. They were suited up in the navy and yellow tracksuits they'd raised money for by working for us last Halloween.

My eyes traveled over additional awards in the case. Of a series of black-and-whites, one caught my eye. It was a candid shot that had been taken on the football field. While a few people stood in the background, the subject was a pretty brunette in a majorette costume. There was something familiar about her face, though I had to look at the caption to confirm what I thought. "Young and Ready to Take on the World," it read. In parentheses after, someone had written *Ronnie Cass*.

WHEN I returned to Disguise DeLimit, the door to the stockroom was open and Soot was standing guard by the entrance. Booker T and the MGs played over the speaker system. I put my hands on the doorframe and leaned in.

"Dad?" I called.

The response was muffled. A few seconds later, Richard Nixon stood up from behind a stack of boxes. He held his arms out on either side and made peace signs with his fingers. I crossed my arms over my chest and shook my head at him.

"Let me guess. You are not a crook."

"The man was president for seven years. He helped desegregate schools, put women in his cabinet, and created the Environmental Protection Agency, and his most quoted line is denial. Poor guy. Makes a good costume, though. Everybody recognizes Nixon." He pulled the mask up and rested it on top of his head. "I'm in the lead on an eBay auction of president masks. I'm thinking we can do a whole political corner. Campaign buttons; red, white, and blue ties; and the masks. What do you think?"

"Can you build a fake voting booth? People could rent it with the costumes."

"Sure. See if Varla can paint a backdrop. I'll bring out the Fourth of July stuff: flags, streamers, balloons."

"And don't forget the donkey and elephant costumes. No reason they can't be repurposed."

"Don'll have a fit. He still thinks Nixon had something to do with the Kennedy assassination. Payback for beating him in the 1960 election." He pulled the Nixon mask back onto his face, gave me the peace sign fingers again, and continued digging through the boxes.

Riffing about costumes and party themes had been one of my favorite activities to do with my dad. Growing up, I'd watched him get an idea and implement it. Once I'd gotten old enough, he'd ask for my ideas. My goal had always been to impress him, to think of something he hadn't. I'd forgotten how good it felt to be part of the brainstorming.

FOR the next several hours, I'd have to concentrate on business, but that didn't mean I couldn't try to make sense of what I'd discovered. I pushed all thoughts of Ronnie and the bank robbery temporarily out of my mind and got the store ready to open. Expecting another quiet day, I grabbed squares of white, yellow, blue, green, red, and orange felt and carried them out front to the temporary sewing station. Since the festival was clinging to the game theme, I was branching out into Rubik's Cubes.

I laid the felt rectangles over each other in perpendicular patterns and trimmed off the excess so I was left with a pile of squares. One by one I pinned them along a straight edge and then sewed them together in three-by-three panels of mixed colors. In total, I made five panels, and then attached four of them along one edge so they created a square. I pinned the final panel to the four edges on the top and cut out a small *X* for my head to fit through. I was in front of the mirror checking the look when my dad—still in the Nixon mask—emerged from the stockroom.

"Turn it inside out," he said. His voice was muffled by the plastic.

"Why?"

"The seams are on the inside right now, so you don't get the sharpness of each square. Turn the whole thing inside out, and the raw edges will create more of the grid that you want."

I shrugged out of the square and gently turned the inside to the out, and then set it on top of my head again. He was right. With the raw edges of the felt squares pointing out, the felt looked more like a Rubik's Cube.

"If you reinforce the seams a second time with heavy-duty thread, the whole thing will be even more rigid," he suggested.

"If I run the sewing machine needle through the felt again, it'll weaken it and increase the chances of it falling apart while being worn. I'll use fabric glue on all of the seams. That should seal the needle holes."

"That's my girl. Always thinking. I'll get the glue." He went into the sewing station and returned with a clear plastic bottle of fabric glue. One end had a long aqua nozzle, like the kind a baker uses when decorating a cake with icing. I took the glue, but before I got to work reinforcing the seams, I set it down and looked up at him.

"Dad, are you worried about Don?"

"He needs to lay low for a bit, but this is all going to blow over."

I thought back to last night. "People are stalking his house and digging up his yard. Even if he never leaves, I don't think he has much of a chance to lay low."

"Don can take care of himself. This situation will work itself out."

"But what if it doesn't? You told me how he changed when Ronnie left. Now all of these stories are resurfacing and they're putting Don in the middle of something he's not a part of. He's like an uncle to me. I want to help him."

"Margo, I don't know that there's much you can do."

"If you really believed that, you wouldn't have started *Spicy Acorn*. You wouldn't have thought it was important for people to know the truth."

Slowly, he pulled the Nixon mask off and set it on the corner of the table that held the sewing machine. He leaned against the table and nodded. "I can't argue with that, now can I?"

Everybody I'd tried to talk to about Ronnie's murder had told me to leave it alone, but I had to talk to someone. I had to talk about what I'd found out so far.

"Dad, I found something out this morning, and I think

I know what it means, but I need to talk it out. Can you pretend for the next hour or so that I'm not your daughter?"

"No."

I braced myself for another lecture, another *Stay out of it, Margo.*

"You're my daughter, and asking me to pretend you're not is asking me to give up my one link to your mother," he said. I looked away. He reached his hand out and rested it on top of mine. "But Don's my best friend," he continued. "If it hadn't been for him, I don't know how I would have gotten through Celeste's death. If you know something that might help him, tell me and we'll see what we can do with the information." He lowered himself onto a small ottoman and waited.

I started talking before I could lose my nerve. "I went to see Chet Lemming this morning. At the West Proper Hospital. I pretended to be a patient in need of a physical to get in to see him, and then I asked him about his relationship with Ronnie Cass."

"Did he deny it?"

"No. He implicated Jayne. And then it was like a light-bulb went off over his head and he asked if I was your daughter."

"Then what?"

"When I said I was, he said you'd better watch what you print in your newspaper, otherwise you'll be looking at a lawsuit."

He sat back in his chair. "Interesting."

"Which part?"

"We started *Spicy Acorn* a few days ago. No advertising, just word of mouth. If Chet knows about us, we must be doing something right." His eyes got the familiar gleam that usually meant trouble.

"Dad, I don't think his reaction was a rousing endorsement of your agenda. He threatened to shut you down."

"Chet's not a dumb guy. He knows that we have the First Amendment on our side and can say whatever we want in *Spicy Acorn*. You say he implicated his wife in Ronnie's murder?"

"He said she was 'disturbed.' That's the word he used. And then he said something about how he encouraged her to get back involved with the Domino Divas. I got the feeling he wanted me to think she was guilty. And then all of a sudden, he made that threat and stormed out."

"He left the exam room? Were you done with your physical?"

"No. I waited about a minute and he didn't come back. The receptionist said he got called on an emergency, but a woman from the waiting room said it was a lie, that Chet told the receptionist to get rid of me."

"What took you to the clinic in the first place? Are you feeling okay?" He leaned forward and put the back of his hand across my forehead.

I leaned back. "I'm fine, Dad. I was following up on a rumor I heard this morning. Jayne Lemming—his wife—said Ronnie took something from her, and Bobbie told me Chet and Ronnie had had an affair. I thought that gave Jayne a pretty big motive for killing Ronnie. *That's* the reason I went to the clinic."

"And he handed you that motive on a silver platter." My dad tapped his index fingers on the tabletop and stared up into the shelf with the mannequin heads and the colorful wigs. I knew he wasn't seeing the costumes; he was searching for answers.

"Dad, when I was in Ronnie's trailer, I saw a lot of pill bottles. And the woman in the reception area said one of the reasons she liked Chet was because he refilled her prescriptions without question. What if Chet's doing something illegal, like writing out prescriptions that people don't need? Can't he lose his medical license over that?"

"I don't know. Maybe *Spicy Acorn* should investigate it."

I didn't know either. But if Chet's livelihood—the very thing that afforded him the luxury car and the mansion in Christopher Robin Crossing—was at risk, what would he do to protect them? Had Ronnie benefited from his underhanded dealings? Had she gotten greedy, demanding more and threatening to talk if he didn't comply? And if so, did the resulting confrontation end in him bashing her head inside of her trailer, minutes before she was scheduled to perform?

Chapter 23

MY DAD LEFT the stockroom and made a phone call. A few minutes later he returned. "I made arrangements to scope out some golf uniforms in Utah. It's a two-person job. Don and I will take the Winnie. I'm going to go upstairs and pack, and then we'll probably spend the night there and head home tomorrow. Call me if you need me."

I nodded. We both knew what he was doing. Golf uniforms weren't in particularly hot demand, and we already had a vast collection from shopping the thrift stores over the years. Dad was making sure Don stayed out of trouble by getting him out of town.

FOR the next few hours, I felt like there was a toxic cloud over my head, interfering with my ability to function normally. Of the few customers who came in, two fell in love with the Sorry! game piece costumes in the windows. I promised to have the costumes removed and ready for pickup the next day. A couple came in looking for something special to wear to the prom. They walked out with our rentals of Queen Amidala and Darth Vader. The prom sure wasn't what it was when I'd gone to high school.

At four thirty, the chimes over the door sounded and Bull Smith, the neighborhood mailman, entered. He was dressed in his usual uniform: light blue shirt, navy blue shorts, navy blue socks, black sneakers. A dusty brown messenger bag was slung across his narrow chest. Bull had been our mailman my entire life except for the two weeks each year that he went on vacation. Over the years his hair had turned white and his skin had tanned. He reminded me a bit of Boris Karloff, except without the lisp and the creepy monster gait.

"Hi, Margo," he said. "Is Jerry around?"

"He's well on his way to Utah by now."

"Figures. You never know what's in those boxes he ships to himself. Every time one shows up at the post office, we take bets. I won fifty dollars the day he got the UPS deliveryman costumes."

"How did you know what was in the box?"

"Same supplier that we use for the postal service, and the word 'brown' was stamped on the outside of the box. Ours say 'blue.' I took a shot and I was right."

I laughed. "Good deduction."

"When you spend your days delivering packages, you start to notice things like that." He reached into the messenger bag and pulled out a slew of bills and preapproved credit card applications. "You tell Jerry I said he's losing his touch. It's time for him to send us something interesting."

I took the mail and thanked him. "I'll give him the message. Thanks, Bull."

"Hold on there, I got one more thing for you." He pulled a thick padded mailer out of his messenger bag. "Official business from the mayor's office," he joked. "Maybe they want some horses' patootie costumes. You know, dress like themselves instead of parading around like you and me." He scanned my scrubs. "Okay, maybe not you."

"The mayor's office?" I said. I looked at the return address. The seal of the mayor's office stared back at me, alongside the address for city hall. I flipped the package over and pulled the tab on the side. Inside was another bundle, this one wrapped in brown paper and tied with a piece of twine. A piece of paper was tucked under the twine. *This should help you find answers. For your eyes only*, it read.

It had to be from Tak, who, because of his new job, had access to files in the mayor's office. I pushed the bundle back into the original packaging before Bull had a chance to see the note. "Nothing important," I said.

"Seems important enough to wrap up twice," Bull observed.

I smiled. "It's from a friend. I think he wrapped it up twice so nobody would see that he was letting them pay for his postage." I held my finger up to my mouth. "We'll keep his secret, won't we?"

"As long as people keep sending things, I've got a job. You tell your friend his secret is safe with me."

I didn't point out that such an acknowledgment would expose the secret. I set the package on the table, pulled a couple of squares of felt over it, and walked Bull back to the door. As soon as his little white mail truck was down the street, I locked the door and flipped the Open sign to Closed.

SOOT sat on the kitchen table sniffing the empty packaging while I read an important-looking document on official Proper City stationary. The date on the paperwork was 1952. The letter detailed the findings of the most recent census that had been conducted, and then outlined the proposed template for what was to become Proper City as I knew it.

All my life I'd known that Proper City had been a census-designed town. As it had been explained to me, after the city had been overrun with criminals, scofflaws, and a corrupt mayor, a new team had been elected on the platform that it was time for a new type of community. Stricter laws cleaned the streets of crime. The recession drove out bootleggers, who sought potentially bigger opportunities in Las Vegas. Once the criminal element had been contained, a task force of city planners had been put into place to pretend they were building a city from the ground up. From that point on, it really was like a version of Monopoly.

The planners had been smart. They proposed everything that a small town would need to encourage community: a library, a post office, a town hall, a police station, a public park, and a savings and loan. Percentages of businesses to residents were established, and zoning proposals indicated how many of each business could move into town. There'd been no zoning restrictions on costume shops, but if there had been, we could have claimed that we were here first. I suspected it was why Candy Girls defined themselves as a party store and not a costume store. Whenever someone planned an event—birthday party, funeral, high school dance, or bake-off, they claimed that was their specialty. "Costumes" had only been added when they saw a way to compete with us.

I flipped past the first page of the file. Why had Tak sent me this? I didn't think it was because of my interest in Proper City. So far, everything I read could be found in the one public library that had had been awarded to our town. One by one I flipped through reports that listed target demographics and how they would be served by everything that was being suggested.

Three-quarters of the way through the file I came to a piece of paper marked "Proper City Savings and Loan." A red star had been drawn on the page next to the subject. A phone number had been written in the margin alongside of the paper.

I reached for the store's phone before reading the document, but the words "Pete Proper's gold" caught my eye. I set the receiver down and read.

In order to build on the city's past and create a sense of community and loyalty, the proposed Proper City Savings and Loan will house a display of gold attributed to Pete Proper's mining efforts. As no gold from Pete Proper's mining efforts has ever been found, it is assumed that he spent, traded, or gave away whatever he had. Source the gold for the S&L from a Hollywood prop company (suggested confidentiality agreement attached).

I sat up and stared at Soot. "Well, how do you like that? If there was no gold in the savings and loan, then what could Ronnie have possibly stolen?"

Chapter 24

THE FIRST PHONE call I made was not to the number in the file. It was to Don. His phone rang three and a half rings before he answered with a tentative and muffled, "Hello?"

Don didn't program phone numbers into his phone, and he wiped his call history every night. It was his way of ensuring he never gave away another person's information. He usually screened his calls and only returned the ones that left messages.

"Don, it's Margo. Can you talk?"

"Margo—hi—what?" He sounded confused, as if I'd possibly awoken him.

"I found something out about the bank robbery, but first I want to make sure you can talk freely."

"Sure," he said. "I'm with your dad and we just crossed the state line. You think Proper City is full of desert? You should get a load of Utah."

"What about Arizona?"

"What does Arizona have to do with anything?"

"Are you on Route 15? You have to drive through the corner of Arizona to get to Utah."

"You sure?"

"That's not why I called. You know how you told me about the robbery at the savings and loan?"

"Sure. Why?"

"I just found out there was no gold."

"That's because Ronnie stole it."

"No, before that. The gold that everybody thought Pete Proper mined, that sat on display in the lobby of the Proper City Savings and Loan. It wasn't gold."

"Then what was it?" He sounded more alert now.

"It was a prop from a special effects company in Hollywood. The early city planners came up with the idea to make people feel connected to the community."

"How do you know this?"

I looked at the papers in front of me. The only reason I knew any of this was because Tak had used his position to get the info to me. It wasn't common knowledge, and there was a very good chance that if it got out, someone would be able to trace it back to him. "I can't tell you how I know it. I just do."

"You have a source," he said, excitement evident in his voice.

"No, I don't," I said too quickly.

"Jerry, did you know Margo has a source? Are they willing to meet?"

We were getting off topic.

"Your dad doesn't know anything about your source either. I want to see your notes, do a write-up. Did you give this information to Detective Nichols? We have to do that. She needs to know this new development. Have you called her? I can call her. Right now."

Panic spread through me. Tak worked with Detective Nichols. He would lose his job if she found out he'd pulled this info and gotten it to me. Not only that, Don's abuse of the tip line had made him appear less than innocent, and adding this info to the rest of the evidence he'd already called in would surely paint him in a negative light. "Don, let me talk to my dad."

A few seconds later, my dad's voice came onto the line. "Are you seriously hurt?" he asked.

My dad had always had a problem with the question, "Are you okay?" He figured that, in most cases, that very question followed up an action or a reaction that indicated that the speakee—the person being spoken to—was definitely *not* okay, and the use of those three generic words undermined the situation. Two minutes after he'd first explained it all to me, he'd slipped on the freshly mopped floor of Disguise DeLimit. His feet had shot out from under him, and he'd landed on his butt. I'd walked over with the mop in hand and, looking down at him, asked, "Are you seriously hurt?"

A Tamblyn tradition had been born.

"I'm okay," I answered. I gave him the highlights about what I'd learned. "Don can't tell anybody about this, not until I find out more." I paused, and then added, "Dad, would Ronnie have known that the gold wasn't real?

"I don't know," he said.

"Think about it, okay? Because it's looking more and more like whatever happened during that robbery has something to do with the reason she was killed."

I hung up the phone and read over the information again. Soot jumped on the table and walked to the stack of papers. As I flipped through, I set each page upside down in a new pile above the ones I was reading. Soot flopped down on top of the pile. I turned a page and he stuck out a dark gray paw and swatted at the paper until I set it down.

"Let's assume the facts as we know them," I said to him. "Number one: the Domino Divas—mainly Ronnie Cass—are suspected of involvement in a bank robbery in 1968. Number two: nothing of value was stolen. Number three: people think she stole today's equivalent of close to two million dollars in gold. Number four: the so-called gold wasn't real. Number five: after the robbery, she left town, thus breaking her engagement with Don. Number five point five: when she returned, she and Mayor Young were a couple."

Soot seemed unimpressed with my recap.

"Fast-forward. Now Ronnie is dead and everybody thinks Don is guilty. What's his motive? It can't be the gold because there was no gold. Is it supposed to be unrequited love? I could find a dozen people willing to testify that Don isn't walking around carrying a torch for Ronnie. I never even knew they were a couple and I've known him my whole life."

Soot shifted his weight onto his back and stretched all four of his paws out, the front two in front of him, the hind two straight behind him. He added a yawn, just in case I didn't realize he was disinterested.

"Am I boring you? Okay, how about this. Two cats make off with a giant ball of string. Then a bunch of years later, one loses his ninth life and the other is held accountable. But the giant ball of string never existed in the first place." I stopped talking for a second while that processed. "Which means all of this talk about Don helping Ronnie steal the gold is a diversionary tactic. And as long as the rest of the town believes in the existence of the gold, they'll believe the story and focus on that." I was halfway to the phone when Soot jumped down from the table and let out a howl. I looked down at the floor, where he stood on top of one of the pages that he'd knocked over. The page with the phone number and the red star.

"Don't tell me you're one of those cats who solves crimes," I said. He gave me the same glare he perfected when I once dressed him up in a pirate costume and then jumped on the windowsill and meowed. Apparently, his work here was done.

I called the number on the page. When I heard the phone pick up, I spoke. "Hey," I said. "It's Margo."

"Took you long enough. Meet me in the parking garage under the library behind the PCP. Eight o'clock. Come alone."

There was only one thing more troubling than the abrupt hang-up. The fact that the person on the other end of the phone wasn't Tak.

Chapter 25

I SPENT THE necessary ten minutes picking the pages up off the floor and getting them back in order, fed Soot, and poured a bowl of Fruity Pebbles for dinner. It was six thirty. I would finish that bowl of cereal in less than five minutes. And then what? I'd spend the next hour and a half worrying about what I was about to do. And already I knew that, regardless of the instructions that I'd been given, I wasn't going to just show up alone in a dark parking lot. I stopped myself from adding the milk to my bowl and poured the Fruity Pebbles back into the box. I called the person I'd thought I was calling the first time.

"Hey," I said. "It's Margo."

"Hey," Tak said.

"I was thinking about that 'proper celebration' I owe you. Want to join me for dinner at Catch-22?"

"As long as you're treating," he said.

"Deal. How's seven sound?"

"Good. I'll pick you up around ten till."

"Don't pick me up. I'll meet you there. See you soon."
I hung up before he could ask what was going on.

I changed from the blue scrubs to a white T-shirt, dark
jeans, and white sneakers, and then pulled on a red windbreaker from a series of costumes I'd made last year. The
letters *B.W.G.* were cross-stitched on the back. I'd been
hired to create twenty detective-themed costumes for a
rich guy's birthday party and had made seven of these
matching jackets in total, but because I'd had trouble with
the seams on the nylon, had only offered the customer
five. Two jackets had remained behind in stock. I'd all but
forgotten about them until Kirby accidentally filed them
with the 1950s display of letter jackets and poodle skirts.

Catch-22 was a local seafood restaurant. The joke
was: Who would eat in a seafood restaurant in the middle
of the desert? But somehow, the chef made it work. Every
day a shipment of fish was flown in and prepared twenty-
two different ways. The biggest expense, aside from the
ingredients, was the cost of printing up the menus.

Tak was in the parking lot leaning against his gray
RAV4. I parked the scooter next to him and hopped off.
My outfit—chosen more for my activities after dinner
than for the dinner itself—seemed awkwardly casual next
to his suit and tie.

"You're early," I said.

"You're late," he countered.

I looked at my watch and smiled sheepishly. The last
couple of times that Tak and I had been together had been
strained, and tonight was no different. His smile was
guarded. Impulsively, I stood on tiptoe and kissed him
on the cheek. "Come on. We don't want them to run out
of fish."

We were led to a booth next to a window. Tak ordered a beer and I ordered an unsweetened iced tea. A glass of wine might have calmed my nerves, but I wasn't much of a drinker and didn't think tonight was the night to change my habits. I ordered the tuna steak and Tak ordered the tuna tartare. I drained the first glass of tea quickly and started on the second before our entrées arrived. The caffeine, in addition to my nerves, made me jittery. I excused myself and went to the powder room to wash my hands, and then returned to our booth as the waitress was dropping off a basket of freshly baked sourdough rolls. I bit into one and chewed, and then followed it with another swig of tea.

"What's going on, Margo?" Tak asked.

"What? Nothing. It's the caffeine. And I haven't been sleeping well. And—"

"And you're downing those rolls like they're bonbons, and you've checked your watch four times since we sat down. And you wouldn't let me pick you up like we were going on a date. All of which tells me that you have other plans after dinner."

I set down my fork and folded my hands in my lap. "You're right. I'm meeting someone after dinner."

Tak pushed his plate away. I reached across the table and put my hand on his. "But it's not what you think. I'm not supposed to tell anybody, but I don't think it's a good idea not to tell anybody. So I was going to ask you if you'd come to the library with me when we're done. Only I can't tell you anything else, except park in the lot underneath and pretend you're not there, unless it looks like I need help."

"No," he said.

"What do you mean, 'no'? You won't help me?"

"I won't blindly agree to you heading into a potentially dangerous situation. And this sounds like a potentially dangerous situation."

"I just told you I'm going to the library. How dangerous can it be? When people say words are weapons, I don't think they're talking about throwing books at each other."

"Let's back up for a second. What time is this meeting?"

"Eight o'clock."

Tak looked at his watch. "That means you have twenty-seven minutes to eat dinner and get to the library. That's not a lot of time."

The waitress arrived with our entrées. She set Tak's in front of me and mine in front of him. We both waited until she was gone to swap plates. I picked up my fork and sliced through the corner of the tuna steak. I ate two bites and then set my fork down. Tak hadn't started on his meal yet.

"The clock is ticking," I said. "And I gave up a bowl of Fruity Pebbles for this dinner. It's not going to waste." I finished first and filled Tak in on what I'd learned from the package that had been delivered to Disguise DeLimit.

"The address on the return envelope was the mayor's office. I thought it was from you. I knew you started work there today, so I thought you found info, maybe made a copy, and had it delivered to me. You know, to help."

"Technically I'm working for the mayor, but not in the mayor's office. I thought you knew I was based out of the police station."

"I did. I do. I mean, yes, I might have blocked out that bit of information."

He smiled. "So you're meeting this guy in ten minutes."

"Yes."

"You'd better flag the waitress over. We don't have a lot of time." He pushed his plate away from him. "And for the record, this is not a proper celebration. You still owe me."

THE public library closed at eight o'clock. Only two cars were in the lot: a Prius parked in the space reserved for the librarian, and another car next to it. The second car was covered in a canvas tarp to protect it from the elements—an odd choice considering we were in the lower level of a parking garage. I drove in a circle through the columns, looking for something out of the ordinary. Except for the emptiness, it seemed like every other parking lot in town.

I left my scooter by the exit ramp and locked up my helmet. The plan was simple. Tak would park on the street up top and walk down, staying closest to the shadows. I was to stay as close to the ramp as possible.

"Are you Margo?" asked a man's voice. I squinted into the darkness and scanned the lot until I saw a young man in a baseball hat and buttoned-up raincoat standing by the elevator doors.

"Yes," I said.

"Come closer."

"No."

"I'm not going to hurt you," he said. "I have information."

"You already sent me information," I said. "Where did you get it?"

He was quiet for a moment. "Come closer," he said again. "I'm not going to hurt you."

"Who are you?" I asked.

"I have information."

The parking lot was silent, except for the sound of our two voices bouncing off the cavernous walls. I didn't want to go closer, but something about the man was familiar. I took two steps closer, reached into the pocket of my red windbreaker, and grasped a small flashlight. I switched it on with my thumb and pulled it out, aiming it at the man.

He was caught by surprise. A cell phone fell from his gloved hand to the ground. He threw his other arm in front of his face, knocking the baseball hat off his head. Long hair tumbled out.

And my source's identity was revealed.

Chapter 26

HE WAS A she. "Gina Cassavogli? What are you doing here?"

She cursed. The voice from the phone by her feet kept speaking, "Come closer. I won't hurt you. I have information. Come closer. I won't hurt you. I have information." It was a recording of a male voice on repeat.

Whatever anxiety I'd had over tonight's clandestine meeting vanished when faced with Gina. I went straight for the car with the tarp over it and pulled it off in the same manner that Magic Maynard used when performing one of his magic tricks. Under the tarp was Gina's sporty blue convertible.

"Don't you touch my car!" she yelled. I threw the tarp to the ground.

"Is this some kind of joke?" I asked.

"I told you I wanted answers about Ronnie's murder."

"So, what? You falsified documents and sent them to

me and then set up this meeting, for what purpose? What could you possibly get out of this?"

"I didn't falsify documents. Everything I sent you was real. All my life I thought she was the worst mother ever. What people said about her. But somebody murdered her. And then I found those papers and realized maybe it was all a lie, maybe the rumors weren't true. There wasn't any gold, so she couldn't have stolen it. Maybe she knew something and was trying to make it right and somebody didn't like that."

"Where did you find the documents?"

"Ronnie gave me a box of junk and the stuff I sent you was in the bottom under some old yearbooks."

We stood in the lot, face-to-face. Gina's hair was flat from being under the baseball hat. She wasn't wearing her usual full face of makeup, and a small red welt marked her right cheek. She caught me staring at it and put her fingertips to the flesh as if to hide it. Too late.

"*You* were the one at the final rehearsal. *You* dressed up like a Domino Diva to practice. *You're* the one Jayne slapped."

"That slap was the best thing that happened that day. No way anybody would question whether or not I was Ronnie after that."

"But where'd you get the costume? I only made enough for the divas and Ronnie had hers on when I found her."

"Like it's hard to make a domino costume. It's squares and circles, Margo. I'm not an idiot."

"But that was the day—"

"I know." She bent forward, put both hands up in front of her face, and started to cry.

The last thing I'd been prepared for was consoling Gina, but despite her ongoing attitude problem with me, tonight her grief was real. I put my hand on her shoulder to comfort her. She shrugged it off. I put it back. Behind me, a car pulled down the ramp of the garage and drove closer. I didn't need to look up to know it was Tak.

He parked in the space next to the discarded tarp and got out. "Gina, get into Tak's car. We need to talk." I guided her to the door and opened it. Tak put the tarp back over her convertible and then the three of us drove away.

TAK parked alongside the curb to the back entrance of the PCP. The sun had dropped below the horizon while we were at Catch-22. Twilight had vanished, leaving us in a cloak of darkness pierced by the occasional street-lamp. Gina looked at Tak then at me, then back at Tak. "What are we doing here?"

"We're talking. And when we're done talking," he said, moving his index finger back and forth from her, me, and him, "we're probably going to the police depart-ment to talk some more."

"I never agreed to that," Gina and I said at the same time.

Tak looked at me with an it's-the-right-thing look and then focused on Gina. "You agreed to talk to Margo," he said. "You all but summoned her. Why?"

She turned to me. "I told you to come alone."

"I'm not that stupid," I said.

She took a deep breath and then exhaled dramatically,

as if she were on stage and needed to be heard by the back row. Again, the resemblance between her and her mother shone through.

"Come on," I said. "The police station is only a couple of blocks away."

THE Proper City Police Department was housed in a sweet little building, white siding with light blue trim and a navy blue awning. If you relocated it to the woods and covered it with gumdrops, it would make a nice get-away for Hansel and Gretel. As I thought about how that story had ended for the children, I questioned the fact that I was going there voluntarily.

The word POLICE had been stenciled in white paint above the door and on the side wall that faced Main Line Road. A dark blue throw rug sat in front of the door. Since the last time I'd been here, a small cast-iron wiener-dog-shaped door stopper had been set to the right of the entrance.

Detective Nichols was waiting for us when we arrived. She held the door open and led us to a round table to the right side of the main desk. The lights by the main desk were off, making it difficult to see the interior. A fresh pot of coffee sat on the console. She poured two and handed one to Gina. I found a watercooler in the corner and filled a small paper cup for myself.

"Who's going first?" Detective Nichols asked.

Gina looked miserable. Her eyes were puffy and red and the welt on her cheek stood out like it had been drawn on with a marker, a small purplish oval of skin with a tail after it, like an apostrophe turned on its side. She reached up and pulled her hair back, and then twisted it around her finger several times until she achieved a thick mane that could hang over one shoulder.

"Six months ago Ronnie incorporated the divas. I don't know why," she started. "But once the paperwork went through, she approached the mayor about performing. After that, it was one big publicity thing after another. She made sure everybody who'd ever heard of the divas knew they were reuniting."

"Were you and Ronnie on speaking terms at that point?" I asked. Detective Nichols turned on me and glared, wordlessly indicating that this was her investigation, not mine. I looked back at Gina, expecting her to continue.

"Ronnie didn't want to be my mother any more than I wanted to be her daughter. I knew what people said about her, stealing the gold, running off to Vegas, leaving everybody and everything behind. I grew up in a trailer. When I turned eighteen, she gave me the keys, told me to have a good life, and left. The next day the trailer was repossessed. At least they gave me twenty-four hours. To this day, I think she knew it was going to happen that way. That's how life was to Ronnie. Always a game, always a gamble. You win some, you lose some."

"Why'd you go to see her on opening day?"

"Because she asked me to. She said something would happen when the divas had their comeback and it wouldn't all be good. She didn't trust anybody. She didn't even trust me, but she said I was blood and that meant something. She gave me a box of junk and asked me to keep it for a while and not tell anybody about it."

"The information that you sent to me," I said. "Why'd you bother?"

She glared at me. "You dig around in everybody else's lives, I figured you could do it for me too. Look where that got me."

I leaned forward. "You're giving me a whole lot of reasons why not to help you, but the funny thing is, you keep showing up in my life. Why don't you tell me the real reason you want my help?"

Gina glared at me. If we'd been the only ones in the room, I suspect she would have expressed her thoughts verbally, but having an audience of Tak and Nancy Nichols, she kept her behavior in check. Tears overflowed from her eyes. She swatted them away with the back of her hand and stared at the table in front of her.

"Ronnie couldn't dance anymore," she said in a quiet voice. "She needed me for that part of the act. When she first contacted me, I thought if I ignored her, she'd go away. But she didn't let it go. She called and sent letters. Newspaper clippings from the time she was gone. She begged me to come visit her, said I owed her at least a chance to talk face-to-face. So I went."

"When was this?" Detective Nichols asked.

"A couple of months ago. She said she wanted to catch up with me, make up for lost time. I got the feeling she was sick, but she wouldn't say that she was. One time I saw her medicine cabinet. It was filled with prescriptions, but I never saw her take any. She'd ask me about the store, about business, stuff like that."

"Sounds innocuous. Like she really wanted to reconnect with you as a mother and daughter."

"That's what I thought too, until she hijacked the bid for the festival out from under me. Candy Girls had the entire thing locked down. We were going to provide and sell costumes. It was going to put us out front as the best costume shop in Proper." She glared at me. "Whatever, okay? You think your shop is the best, but there's lots of stuff we do better. But we never had the chance to prove it because Ronnie stole the bid from us and convinced the mayor to do family game night and hire the divas. Next thing I know, Candy Girls is out. No cut of the box office, no publicity, no word of mouth."

"There is no box office cut," I said. "Every participant is donating their time and their products for the good of Proper City. It's a nonprofit event."

"Except for the Domino Divas," Gina said. "Good ol' Mom negotiated that she got a cut of ticket sales. That's right, *she*. The rest of the divas got nothing."

I already knew about the financial arrangements for Ronnie. The lack of response from Detective Nichols indicated that she knew it as well. Tak kept his poker face on, showing no indication of what he thought.

"But you said Ronnie couldn't perform, right? So how was this all going to happen?" I asked.

"That's where I came in. Whatever was wrong with her, it hit her hard. I don't think it ever occurred to her that she wouldn't be able to dance, but Ronnie isn't the type to set up a get-rich-quick scheme and then walk away from it. The only reason she wanted to reconcile with me is because I'm the only person who could literally fill her shoes. *And* her costume."

"So you agreed to perform as her. Did the other divas know?"

"Nobody knew. That's the reason I came to your store. I wanted to make sure you didn't know. The morning of the opening, I went to her trailer to get dressed. She wasn't there, and neither was her costume. I changed into the one I made but it tore. I found some thread and stitched it up, put on the wig and mask, and showed up at the rehearsal. Aside from the slap, everything went exactly as planned."

"What about the felt circle? Did one of them come off your costume?"

Gina scowled. "The fabric glue didn't work like I expected. I didn't notice the missing circle until later."

Everything Gina told me had a note of truth to it, but I couldn't shake the feeling that she was playing me.

"How'd you know not to show up after she was killed? When you came to Disguise DeLimit, you told me you were notified of her death on Sunday morning."

Gina's face turned a purplish-red shade. The mark on her cheek disappeared against her flushed skin. "I went to her trailer after rehearsal broke up. I still had on the mask so everybody thought I was her. I guess I wanted her approval—or to hear her say 'thank you.' Someone was already inside. A man. I heard sounds—noises. I hung the blue mask on the doorknob to the trailer and left. I thought she was—I thought they were—but they weren't. I know now that he was killing her. I heard someone killing her and I didn't get help." Fresh tears covered her face. She put her arms down on the table and her head on top of them. Her shoulders and back jumped erratically as she cried.

Detective Nichols leaned forward and put her hand on Gina's back. "Gina, do you have any idea who the man in the trailer was?"

Gina raised her head from the table. "I think it was my father," she said through her tears.

"Can you give me a name?" the detective asked.

Gina surprised us all with her answer. "It was Don Digby."

Chapter 27

"**DON CAN'T BE**—I mean, I heard that—why do you think—huh?" I asked. It was not my proudest moment of inquisition. I regrouped my thoughts and rephrased my question. "What makes you think Don is your father?"

"I don't know. I mean, I think so, now, after what I overheard," Gina said.

"Which was what?" Detective Nichols said. Her tone of voice suggested she was not about to accept anything Gina said without concrete proof.

"When I walked up to the trailer. I overheard their voices from inside. They were arguing. She said, 'She doesn't know. I never told her. It'll be our secret, I promise. Don't threaten me. For as long as I'm alive, nobody will know.'"

Detective Nichols, Tak, and I exchanged looks. As suspicious as that sounded, it wasn't an admission that Don and Ronnie Cass had reignited the flame of romance after she'd returned to Proper City.

"I'm the 'her,' don't you see? I'm the 'her.'" Her face twisted into a blotchy mess, streaked with mascara and tears. "I never knew who my dad was. She used me to get whatever it was she wanted, and then he killed her."

AFTER Gina's statement at the police station, Tak drove us back to the library. Gina balled up her tarp and stuffed it into the backseat, then pulled out in a squeal of rubber against asphalt.

I unlocked my helmet from the scooter. Tak held out the takeout bag from Catch-22. "Now that that's over, what do you say we resume our plans? Impromptu picnic in the park?" he asked.

"Nothing's over, Tak. Didn't you hear Gina? She just involved Don even more than he already was. In the past three days, he's gone from being a mild-mannered Hume Cronyn type to being a bank robber, a gold thief, a murderer, and a father. Next thing you know somebody's going to say he's Batman."

"Margo, Nancy has this under control. Let her do her job."

"You really expect me to just drop it and walk away?"

"It's the smart thing to do."

"You sound like a politician. It's the safe thing, not the smart thing. I thought you knew the difference."

We went our separate ways. I didn't comment on the fact that his loyalty had been toward Nancy, not to me. It might have been the safe thing, but it still felt like a violation of my trust.

* * *

I went to bed with questions and woke up with answers—well, not so much answers, but with a plan. Someone was going out of their way to make it look like the gold robbery was connected to Ronnie's murder. They were trying to create something out of nothing. I'd hit upon the idea yesterday while talking with Soot, but it hadn't really gelled until after hearing Gina's story. Someone was creating a diversion and putting Don in the middle of it. For all of the years he'd spent tracking conspiracy theories, here he was in the middle of one himself.

And I had a way to help him.

I showered and changed into a pair of jeans and the T-shirt Don gave my dad for Christmas last year. It was white with blue trim and had the words THERE WAS A SECOND GUNMAN printed across the front. I opened the top drawer in the bathroom and ran my hand over an assortment of fake eyelashes, glittery makeup, and pancake foundation—all left over from my time as a magician's assistant. It felt like years ago that I'd donned sequins and fishnets and paraded around onstage with a pair of doves. I shut the drawer, pulled a black knit cap over my wet hair, and went downstairs to the computer. It only took seven minutes for me to find the template for *Spicy Acorn*.

I pulled up the most recent file and then saved it as *Spicy Acorn Special Edition*. Lead story: "Gold Robbery a Hoax?" And then I started typing.

Fifty years ago, a robbery at the Proper City Savings and Loan resulted in the theft of a brick of gold that, in today's market, is worth close to $2 million. Rumors about the robbery have followed certain residents of Proper for years, but a source close to the mayor's office comes clean: the gold that had been on display in the S&L was just a cheap prop supplied by a movie company.

Documents from the archives of Proper City's early development corroborate these claims. The planning commission determined that residents would be more apt to trust this city-funded institution if it had a story behind it. A prop of gold was commissioned from Hollywood. One can surmise that confidentiality agreements were signed to keep the story under wraps.

The mayor's office has a long-standing reputation for putting the image of Proper City ahead of its residents. Are we seeing an example of that tradition played out in real time?

The last time I'd needed to write any kind of article for anything was a high school class in journalism, and that had been so long ago it was a distant memory. Besides, this was a conspiracy newspaper. Wasn't the point to get people asking questions? To stir the pot?

In keeping with the ground rules that Don and my dad had set up with *Spicy Acorn*, I searched the Web for an acorn recipe, copied it, and pasted it into the sidebar. Since this was a special edition, I didn't bother with any additional articles. I set the printer on low resolution, fed a stack of paper into the tray, and printed until I ran out of paper. I folded each one with the headline facing out, bundled them with rubber bands, and stuffed them into an old mailbag.

When Kirby arrived at the costume shop, he was peppier than I'd seen him since the Varla/Angus development.

"Guess what?" he said. "Angus failed trig. His dad took away his driving privileges."

"And this makes you happy why?"

"Because now he'll either have to ask Varla to drive on her own birthday or get a chaperone." He grinned. "Buzzkill."

"What about the school? Did you hear Principal Stanley said yes?"

"Ebony told me. She came up with a whole *Back to the Future* thing. It's Varla's favorite movie. I'm going to be George McFly and my science teacher is going to be Doc. Ebony's going to turn the gymnasium into the 'Enchantment Under the Sea' dance. It's going to be epic. Can you help with costumes and setup?"

"Sure. I think I can stop by the high school later today. What about the DeLorean?"

"Already got a call in to Dig."

I left Kirby with instructions to dress the mannequins in the windows in the new Rubik's Cube costumes and then headed out to the park.

Ebony stood by the entrance to Candy Land, surrounded by six women dressed as giant playing cards. Today Ebony was wearing a red tube dress and platform wedge-heeled sandals. A small red heart had been painted on the side of the wedge. Her hair was held back with red and white combs, and her lips were a shiny cherry red. A collection of red and white plastic bangle bracelets clinked against each other on her left wrist. She matched the Candy Land sign so well that I wondered which came first: the sign or the outfit.

"If I never see another board game, it'll be too soon," she said. "Last night, I actually called Elli Lisbon, that foundation director."

"The one you read about in *Southern Living*?"

"Yeah, that's the one. Do you know what she told me?"

"What?"

"She said if anything looked like it was potentially spiraling out of control, divert attention with food."

I looked up at the archway to Candy Land. "Is that why you're standing here?"

"You know it. I thought I could look to this board game for inspiration. 'Peanut Brittle House'? 'Lollipop Woods'? And get these character names: Grandma Nut and Queen Frostine. This is supposed to be a game for kids. It would take me a month to distill this into something usable."

I looked at the board game. "Why not just buy a whole bunch of little candy canes and stick them into cupcakes? People love cupcakes."

"Girl, you can't go jamming candy canes into cupcakes and calling it something special."

"I don't see why not."

She rolled her eyes. "You stick with the costumes. Let me handle the party planning."

Before I had a chance to talk to her about Kirby's surprise party for Varla, she stepped backward and surveyed my outfit. "You look like one of them singles from the Seattle scene circa 1992. That is not a costume, that is a big old advertisement that you are not interested in a relationship. Something happen with Tak?"

"Tak and I are currently on opposing sides of an editorial issue," I said. I reached into the duffel bag and pulled a wad of newspapers out. "Speaking of which, I'm taking over my dad's booth today. Send anybody who wants to know the truth." I peeled off a folded page and handed it to her.

Ebony had been friends with my dad and Don for a long time, but while he and Don claimed to help expose conspiracies behind much of what we believed, Ebony credited superstition and the will of the universe for what happened around us. She lived her life with karma as her copilot. I knew the only reason she didn't make a big deal out of the conspiracy theory booth was because of friendship, not because she had empty real estate at the festival. And I knew the only reason Don and my dad had tables set up to play Risk and Stratego was because they respected that Ebony had a theme and they didn't want to take advantage of her. But this—me using their newspaper to actively bring details of Ronnie's murder into her festival—might be too much. I held my breath as she scanned the article.

"This true?" she asked.

"According to my source."

"You trust your source?"

I didn't trust Gina as far as I could throw her. "I think somebody out there doesn't want us asking these questions," I said. "Besides, what's the point of having a conspiracy theory newspaper template on your dad's computer if you're not going to use it?"

She folded the paper in half and stuck it into the neckline of her strapless dress. "How many copies do you have?"

"Enough to rile up a whole bunch of people."

"You'd better get started," she said. "I'll tell the mayor I got a cupcake emergency on my hands, but that's only going to keep him detained for so long. Once he hears about this, you're on your own."

I kissed her on the cheek and took off.

A pack of people hovered around the *Spicy Acorn* tent, talking among themselves. I bypassed them and untied the flaps to the tent, and then tied each side back so the tent was open. Grady broke away from the group and followed me in. Today he'd left his suit jacket at home. The sleeves to his blue button-down shirt were folded back twice, exposing freckled forearms. A plastic press badge like the one my dad had worn yesterday was clipped to his belt.

"We weren't sure if you were showing up today," he said. "Heard the fuzz caught that cat, tossed him into the pokey."

"What is that? Underground newspaper lingo?"

"I think spending time with these conspiracy theorists is rubbing off on me." He grinned, the full thousand-watt smile that probably got him anything in life that his money couldn't. "I heard Detective Nichols arrested Don yesterday."

"You heard wrong. Don and Jerry are in Utah looking at golf clothes."

"Right. Dig that, sister." He winked and lowered his voice. "Do you have any more copies with you?"

"Sure." I reached into my bag and pulled out a stack. He grabbed the top half and stepped outside of the tent. I followed him.

"Hot of the press, dig it, man. Little sister came through for us." The crowd turned our way and Grady dealt the newspapers out like they were playing cards. In a matter of seconds, he depleted his stack and turned to face me. "See? It works. They think I'm one of them."

Behind the crowd of eager readers, Joel V. appeared. Today's ensemble was blue: floral shirt with a matching floral tie, blue striped pants, and blue and white saddle shoes. A straw hat with a blue and white grosgrain ribbon around the crown was perched on top of his head.

Joel grabbed my upper arm and steered me into the tent. He waved a copy of *Spicy Acorn* back and forth like he was a menopausal woman with a hot flash and it was his only source of a breeze.

"What do you think you're doing?" he demanded. His normal expression of happy-go-lucky spin doctor was gone, and in its place was anger.

"I'm putting the truth out there," I said.

He slapped the newspaper down on the table in front of me. "You're sabotaging the mayor's reputation."

"I thought your job was to get publicity? I'm handing you a story on a silver platter. The town scandal was built on a lie. You should be finding a way to distance the mayor from that, make him look like a stand-up guy. You should be advising him to forget the incorporation of Proper City for a moment and focus on what's going on here. You should make him publicly recognize that a woman—not just any woman, but a woman he was once married to—was murdered across the street from his precious festival."

Joel's shoulders tensed and his hands froze, as if he'd been doused with an invisible bucket of ice water. "Mayor Young can't be connected to the Ronnie Cass scandal. Her trailer was on public property."

"That's all you people can say, isn't it? 'The trailer wasn't on the festival grounds so we have no culpability here.' What about this? She was a resident of Proper. She was his ex-wife. Mayor Young needs to address that, now more than ever. When people learn of their relationship and see that he hasn't stopped once to acknowledge her death other than to point out that it didn't happen at the festival, he's going to lose a lot of votes."

"He's running unopposed," he said. "Besides, this city loves Mayor Young."

"They won't when they hear that he's more concerned with the profitability of his own festival than with the murder of one of the residents." I gestured toward the stack of newspapers. "And it wouldn't be all that hard to let them know."

Joel put his hands down on the table in front of me and leaned in so close I could smell the bitter coffee on his breath. "If you were smart, you wouldn't threaten the mayor's office," he said. "You never know what might happen." He swatted the stack of newspapers off the table. They fell to the ground in a cascade of paper, fluttering over the dirty and dead patches of yellow grass. Without another word, he turned around and left.

Chapter 28

I DROPPED DOWN to the ground and corralled the newspapers into a pile, and then scooped them up and set them on the table. Grady came inside and helped. "Is everything okay in here?" he asked, all traces of his new underground dialect gone.

"It's fine," I said.

He called to Finn outside the tent, and he came inside the booth too. Grady said something to him, and then patted him on the shoulder. Today Finn wore a white T-shirt with an oversized marijuana leaf printed on the front. Same big beard, same dirt-colored Birkenstocks. "Who was that guy?" he asked.

"Festival publicist. He works for the mayor."

Finn's eyes grew wide. "One of the mayor's minions came in here and trashed the booth?" He turned and looked outside at the group of people congregating by the tent flaps. "You have to follow this up with an article about that."

"Or not," I said. "I'm not the brains behind this operation. I'm just the daughter of the brains."

"Don't sell yourself short," Grady said.

Finn tapped the newspaper. "The acorn didn't fall far from the tree. Which one's your dad? Jerry or Don?"

"Jerry. You know them?"

"They're legendary in our circle. I've been pushing them to start up a newspaper for years but they could never find funding." He turned to Grady and put a hand on his shoulder. "And then this man came along and answered all of our prayers. Paying production costs and circulation. G-dog is making *Spicy Acorn* legit, man," he said. Grady had the decency to blush to the roots of his copper hair. Finn jutted his chin out at my outfit. "By the way, nice shirt."

"Yeah, um, you too," I said, pointing at his marijuana leaf.

He leaned back and grabbed the hem of his T-shirt and pulled it down so the image was stretched flat against his chest. "Forget kale, man. Okra, that's where it's at."

"Okra?"

"Yeah, I farm okra in my spare time. What did you think this was? Marijuana?"

I didn't want to appear that square. "Poison ivy?"

"Leaflets three, man, leaflets three." He shook his head at my feigned ignorance and left.

Okra farmers and underground circles in Proper City. The town never ceased to amaze me.

Now that Grady and I were alone, I turned to him. "What about you? Do you think there's something to what I wrote?"

"I wouldn't quit your day job, but it'll sell free papers."
He grinned.

"Can you do me a favor?" I asked. "I need to talk to
somebody about what just happened with Joel. Can you
get those people inside the tent so they stop drawing attention?"

"My job is to lend the paper an air of respectability
and pay the bills," he said.

I put my hands on my hips. "Fine. I'll get Finn to
do it."

Seconds later, I heard Finn's voice out front. "Got
questions? *Spicy Acorn* has the answers. Sometimes you
gotta get nuts to find out the truth. Wanna get nuts? Come
on, let's get nuts."

I snuck out of the booth while Finn and Grady ushered
people inside for a game of Conspiracy, ignoring whatever the code was for maximum number of people in a
festival booth. I had a feeling I'd created a monster.

I made my way to Bobbie's booth. Of everything that I'd
learned since Ronnie's murder, I couldn't shake the fact
that there was something big I was forgetting.

When I rounded the corner to Bobbie's booth, I saw
exactly what I'd forgotten. The giant teddy bear costume
that Don had promised to wear. It hung on a plastic
hanger in the back of Bobbie's booth. The teddy bear
head was on the ground behind one of the bookcases
filled with bears. Bobbie held a small teddy bear out in
front of a crying child. The parents were off to the side,
playing with the props on the back of the selfie table.

I snuck around the back of the booth and untied the swags. When nobody was looking, I removed the teddy bear costume from the hanger and raised the bottom of the tent so I could grab the teddy bear head. A teenage couple stood in the alley, watching me. I put my finger up to my lips, stepped into the bear costume, and set the head on my shoulders. Thankful for the relative comfort of the T-shirt and jeans that I'd worn, I took a second to adjust the head so I could see out the small mesh screens by the mouth, and then sauntered around the side of Bobbie's booth.

I wasn't sure who I surprised more, Bobbie or the parents. The crying child, however, was delighted by my sudden appearance.

I hopped from one foot to the other, holding my hands out to the sides. Most people don't consider that teddy bears often aren't equipped with elbows. I continued my jig until the little girl had forgotten all about her tantrum, and then I took her hand and led her to the table with the small festival bears. I tried to pick one up—unsuccessfully, thanks to my lack of experience with paws—which made the girl smile and clap even more. Finally, I scooped one and held it out. She took it, hugged it to her chest, and ran back to her parents.

Bobbie approached me slowly. As tended to be the case when people wore costumes, I forgot that I was dressed like a giant teddy bear and that she didn't know it was me.

"Don? Is that you?" she asked. She stood on her tip-toes and tried to look inside the bear's mouth. "Mitty! Where'd you come from?"

I put the paws on either side of the head and pulled it off. "Don's on a costume-scouting trip with my dad. It occurred to me that you were left out of that conversation."

"No he's not. I saw him at the grocery store earlier today."

"Are you sure?"

"Sure I'm sure." Her expression changed from cheerful to serious. "He said he needed some distance from what's been going on here. You think he's going to be okay?"

"Truth? That's the real reason I'm here." I set the teddy bear head on the table. "It wasn't like I set out to get involved, you know? But there's all of this information. Too much information, if you ask me. And none of it relates to anything but Ronnie."

"Like she's the wooden wheel at the center of a cluster of Tinkertoys and there are all kinds of radials sticking out from every side."

"Sure, that's one way to put it."

She ran her hand over the furry teddy bear head. "It's too bad he won't be here to wear the costume. This could have been a really great way to get exposure for the teddy bears."

"The teddy bears," I repeated. "*That's* what we forgot!"

"The teddy bears are right here," she said. She looked at me funny. "Are you okay?"

"Not these bears, the other bears. The bear that was in Ronnie's trailer—that Chet said he found out front. And the bears that had their heads torn off. Why so many bears? What do they have to do with anything?"

"You don't really think the bears took out Ronnie when nobody was looking, do you?"

"I'm serious."

She settled onto a white plastic folding chair. "Okay, let's talk teddy bears."

"First, there was the bear that I saw in Ronnie's trailer. Later on, Chet had it and he claimed he found it out front."

"You think Chet did it?"

"He's not above suspicion." I told her about my visit to the hospital and how he'd told the nurse to get rid of me. "He seems to have something to hide."

"Speaking of hiding, don't forget the bear in the sewer grate," she said. "What happened with that?"

"Detective Nichols still has it. She still has my phone too. Which I think she's keeping to spite me." I stood up. "Maybe a surprise visit will net me some information." I got about ten feet away from Bobbie's booth when she called my name.

"Don't you think you're forgetting something?" she asked.

"What?"

She pointed to her torso and I looked down. "Right," I said. I went back to her booth and stepped out of the teddy bear suit, hanging it back on the rear bookcase where I'd found it, and then left.

It was inevitable that I'd end up back at the police station. Before entering, I bent down and measured the wiener-dog door stopper with my hands, and then stood back up. *Resist the urge to make it a costume*, I told myself. Detective Nichols didn't deserve it.

I turned the knob and let myself in. A bowl of miniature candy bars sat on the raised counter in front of a woman in a yellow tank top and matching denim jacket.

Behind her, beige filing cabinets topped with white metal trays lined the wall. A plant, suspended by a macramé holder straight out of a '70s craft class, hung next to the ficus tree in the corner. Judging from the bright leaves on both plants, someone in the office had a green thumb.

"Can I help you?" the woman asked.

"I'm Margo Tamblyn. I'm here to pick up my phone."

"Margo," I heard behind me. I turned around. Tak and Detective Nichols stood in the doorway to a small office at the front left of the building. "You should have told me you were coming," Tak said.

"She's not here to see you. She's here to see me." Detective Nichols tipped her head to the side, raised her hand, and tucked a loose lock of blond hair behind her ear. She fingered her small gold earring with her thumb and forefinger for a moment, and then dropped her hand to a matching gold pendant. The entire display of body language—no more than two seconds' worth—held more feminine cues than I'd ever seen her show. She caught my eyes and held them for a second. A warning flare went up inside my brain: Tak must have told her about our argument last night and now she's trying to get him back. I knew with 100 percent certainty that it wasn't mere jealousy; it was a fact.

"Detective Nichols," I said. "You've had my cell phone since Sunday. I'm pretty sure you've ruled out any connection between me and Ronnie Cass's murder, so I'd like to get it back."

"It's not that easy. Your phone was taken in as evidence. I can't return it to you without a release from the district attorney. This is an ongoing investigation. I doubt your request will be granted, but you can pick up the necessary forms from the front desk."

Nancy Nichols and I had maintained a polite yet impersonal relationship when around Tak, and today was no different. She hadn't said anything that was untrue, even if her intent was to piss me off. I bit back my initial response and glanced at him to see whose side he was on. He crossed his arms over his chest and leaned back against the wall. His black hair fell to the side of his face. He crossed one foot over the other and winked at me. It was all the encouragement I needed.

"Sure, let me get the paperwork started. I know these things take time." I stepped back and let her pass in front of me. She went behind the counter to the file cabinet next to the hanging plant, opened the top drawer, and pulled out a sheet of paper. When she shut the cabinet, one of the long tendrils of the hanging plant got caught in the drawer. The woman behind the desk jumped up, opened the drawer, and freed it immediately. At least now I knew who tended to the plants.

I took the piece of paper. "I'll fill this out at home and bring it back tomorrow."

Tak stood away from the wall. "I'll walk you out," he said. Once we were on the other side of the door, he asked, "Tell me again how you lost your phone?"

"I dropped it in a sewer grate under Ronnie's trailer," I said.

"And why does Nancy think it's evidence?"

"Because it landed on top of a teddy bear."

"In the grate."

"Yes."

"How'd a teddy bear get into the grate?"

"Somebody put it there." At his expression, I held both hands up and stepped back. "Hey, don't look at me. I'm as curious as you."

"Come back inside," he said. He turned around and I followed him back into the station. "Hey, Nance. Can you show me this evidence?"

"Why?"

"You know as well as I do that the DA is going to release her phone the second that sheet of paper hits his desk unless you can prove that whatever was in that sewer grate had to do with Ronnie's murder. Now that Margo has told me what was in the grate, I'm not convinced it's related."

"You're not investigating the murder," she said.

"Humor me. For old time's sake."

I told myself that he said it for the greater good.

Nancy went to a door with a padlock on it. She pulled a ring of keys from her jacket pocket and flipped through them until she found the one she needed. She unlocked the door and disappeared inside. A few seconds later, she came back with a large clear plastic bag that held the teddy bear and my cell phone. She handed Tak the bag and he turned it over in his hands.

"I get how the phone got into the grate, but not the bear. How do you know it wasn't a geocache or a practical joke?"

"What's a geocache?" I asked.

"It's a game. The world's biggest treasure hunt. A cache is usually a container that holds a notepad and pencil. Coordinates are loaded onto a website and people have to find them. You can keep what you find, but you have to leave the container with the notepad and pencil for the next person who comes along. It's pretty cool. We should look for a cache sometime," he said to me.

I snuck a glance at the detective. She didn't look happy. "How would we know if the bear is a cache?" I asked. "He was right there in the grate. No container, no pencil or notepad."

"Look inside him. Maybe he *is* the container," Tak said.

We both looked up at Nancy. She pulled a pair of light blue rubber gloves—not unlike the ones I'd swiped from Chet Lemming's office—out of a box from the end of the front counter, pulled them over each hand, and grabbed the bag from Tak. She opened the bag carefully and reached inside for the bear.

"Looks like a regular teddy bear to me," I said.

She squeezed it a couple of times and then turned it over in her hands. She squeezed it again, and a hole along the seam on its back that ran down from head to bottom split open.

Detective Nichols poked her fingers inside the hole. "There's something in here," she said. She pulled a pair of scissors out of the cup holder on the desk and pressed the small bear facedown on the table.

"You can't just cut him open!" I said.

"He's a teddy bear," she said. "He won't feel a thing."

"Be nice, Nancy," Tak said.

The detective snipped a few stitches and plunged two fingers back into the bear. This time she wiggled her fingers around a few times. A few more stitches popped.

Slowly, she pulled out a small gold engagement ring. I felt sick to my stomach, like I'd eaten undercooked fish.

"Is it engraved?" I asked.

"Yes. 'To R, my favorite enigma. Love, D.'" She set the bear on the table and held the ring in her left hand. "Looks like I owe you a thank-you, Margo," she said.

No. No, no, no, no, no, no. I shook my head from side to side, knowing what she was going to say before she spoke.

"You weren't even going to look at that bear," I said.

"It was stuffed in a sewer grate underneath the trailer where Ronnie was found dead, and now I find out it's been holding solid evidence that connects back to Don Digby. That should be enough to get me a warrant." She smiled at me sweetly, and then turned to Tak. "I wouldn't waste your time calling in a favor from the DA's office now. Pretty sure they're going to side with me on this one."

Chapter 29

I GAVE A quick mental callout to St. Christopher, the patron saint of lost causes and bachelors. Considering Don was both, I figured it wouldn't hurt. "You still don't know how the teddy bear got into the grate," I said to the detective. "Don't you think that's suspicious? And why was the trailer moved from where it had been parked? You don't even know how long the bear was in the grate. You can't convict a man because of a teddy bear!" My voice rose to a near-hysterical level. Tak stepped closer from behind me and put his hands on my upper arms.

"Margo," he said, "Calm down." He leaned closer to my ear. "You won't do Don any favors by fighting her right now."

"Whose side are you on?"

"I'm not on anybody's side."

"But Don's innocent," I said. "You haven't heard his side of the story."

"He'll have plenty of chances to tell his story to his

lawyer," Detective Nichols said. "Sorry, Margo, that means I can't release your phone either."

It was a hard pill to swallow, especially coming from her. For appearance's sake, I kept my cool until I was outside in the parking lot. I hadn't expected Tak to follow me, but he did. The detective stayed inside.

"She didn't do that on purpose," Tak said.

"I know, I just, *grrrr!*" I said. I raised my arms and splayed my fingers out in an I-want-to-strangle-something gesture. If I'd been in the Frankenstein's monster costume, it would have made more sense. "Somebody's working really hard to implicate Don."

"Maybe he's hiding something," Tak said. He put his hand on my arm and I flung it off.

"He's not! Don Digby is not a murderer. He's not a bank robber either. The only thing he's guilty of is being in love with the victim a long time ago."

"Tell me something. How do you think that ring got into that teddy bear? How do you think the teddy bear got into the grate?"

"I don't know. I don't know any of it. Stop asking me questions that I don't have answers to."

Tak put his hands on both of my arms. "I have another question that has to be asked. Do you know where Don is right now?"

"He went on an out-of-state scouting trip with my dad," I said.

"Are you sure? I saw the Minnie Winnie parked by Eggcetera this morning."

"Must have been a different Minnie Winnie," I said. By now it was clear Don and my dad had lied to me about going out of town.

I drove back to Disguise DeLimit. The store was closed, but Kirby was still inside. He stood next to two buckets of water, one clear and one full of suds. In front of him was the wall of plastic clown shoes. The bottom shelf of shoes were shiny and wet. The top were dry and dusty.

"Hey, Margo, I was hoping you'd come back soon." He dunked a giant yellow, red, and blue plastic shoe into the clear bucket of water, pulled it out, and shook it a few times before putting it back on the shelf. "I asked Varla out for Saturday night," he said.

"That's great! Does she suspect anything?"

"I don't think so. Coach said you and Ebony can get in Saturday morning to set things up. Otherwise the secret will leak."

"I'll let Ebony know. Any luck with Dig?" I doubted Dig had a DeLorean on the lot, but with Dig, you never knew what to expect.

"Yeah, he said he'll see what he can do for me, but I'm not all that confident. He's a little backed up with the Zip lines."

"That's right. He was working on the Zip-Three the other day. Did another one break down?"

"Not sure. He said the mayor's on him to get them back into rotation as fast as possible." He laughed. "Mayor Young must have made it worth Dig's while, if you know what I mean." He held his hand up and ran his thumb back and forth over his fingertips. "Fat city budgets. I wish I could find a way to earn some of that bank."

I cringed. If there was a way for me to give Kirby a raise, I would, but sales had dropped off recently. Seeing an opportunity, I'd spent an unbudgeted amount of money on the supplies for the Domino costumes that I'd planned to sell at the festival, but now, nobody wanted them. In terms of publicity, our involvement in the festival had been a big fat bust and it was all my fault.

"Do you want me to finish up washing the shoes so you can leave?" I asked Kirby.

"I can finish. I'm almost done."

"Make sure you count this on your time sheet," I said. The least I could do was pay him for the additional effort of maintaining the inventory.

"Thanks," he said. "Any news on Don?"

"Nothing good, I'm afraid. Detective Nichols just found evidence that links him to the scene of the crime."

"Weird. Dig didn't mention anything new about the trailer."

I was confused. "What does Dig have to do with it? I'm talking about the Airstream trailer Ronnie had parked on Rapunzel Road. She was killed inside."

"I know. The mayor had it towed. He didn't want it sitting there on Rapunzel, reminding people what happened."

"How do you know that?"

"I was on the sidewalk when the tow truck showed up."

"So it's at Dig's tow yard? I thought he was busy working on the Zip line."

"The Airstream is parked around back."

I thought back to the night that I'd taken Bobbie back to the sewer grate to help me get my phone. The trailer that had been parked along the curb for days had been moved the day after the murder. When Dig had mentioned the tow job, I'd assumed it was the Zip. I'd been so distracted by the loss of my phone and the presence of the teddy bear in the grate that I hadn't stopped to wonder about where the trailer had gone.

I thanked Kirby for the info and ran upstairs. Soot was on the floor staring at his bowl. I emptied his water dish and refilled it, and then measured a cup of crunchy morsels and poured them on top of the fish skeleton that was painted on the bottom of his bowl. He meowed.

"You're looking a little chubby these days, so that's all you get." I scooped him up, planted a kiss between his ears, and set him back down. He buried his nose in the bowl while I called Dig. His machine picked up after four rings.

"Dig, it's Margo. Are you still there? I need to talk to you about the trailer the mayor had you tow. Call me back when you get this." I was in the middle of leaving my cell number out of habit when I remembered it was still at the police station. I hung up and called back. "Dig, it's Margo again. I gave you the wrong number. Call me back at the store—"

"Yo, Dig here. Whazzup?" he asked.

"Dig—hi—it's Margo."

"Yeah, I got that much. Whatcha need?"

"I, um, did you hear my message?"

"I was in the Zip, heard the phone keep ringing. When you called back, I figured it was some kind of emergency. You okay?"

"I'm fine. I wanted to ask you about the trailer you towed."

"Listen, I know you got all kinds of questions about how these things work, but I don't have time right now. Don't even have time to stop for dinner. Maybe next week, once I get these things back up and running. Got it?"

"Got it."

As soon as he hung up, I called Ebony.

"I need help," I said. "The kind of help only you can provide. I need you to pick up dinner for two."

"Sure. What are you hungry for?"

"It's not for me. It's for you and Dig. I need you to create a distraction while I snoop around his tow yard."

"Girl, one of these days you are going to max out my generous nature."

AN hour and a half later, Ebony and I pulled into the back lot of Dig's Towing. Kirby hadn't been exaggerating. Two large school buses were parked in front of the tow yard, and a silver trailer sat on the curb out front. I got out of Ebony's gas-guzzling Cadillac and slammed the door. She pointed her finger at me and pursed her lips. I held my hands up in surrender, and then led the way to Dig's office. Ebony grabbed a couple of takeout bags from Catch-22 and followed me.

"Dig?" I called out. "Are you in there?" I knocked on the side of the school bus. I heard a *clunk* and a curse.

"What did I tell you?" he asked. He appeared in one of the small windows toward the back of the bus. His expression changed when he realized I wasn't alone. "Ebony, what are you doing here?"

She held up the takeout bags. "Margo told me you didn't have time for dinner, and Ebony says that's unacceptable. It's shrimp day at Catch-22. I brought fried and Cajun." She dropped the bags to her side. "Unless you're too busy to join me, and then I'll have to go back home. Alone."

I was going to owe her big-time for this.

The light turned off inside the bus and Dig came out. He wiped his hands on his jeans and tucked a rag into his back pocket. "Dig always has time for his Ebony," he said. "Give me a sec to clean up." He went inside his office.

I turned to Ebony. "That was a little over the top, don't you think?"

"You want to help Don or what?" she asked. "Small miracle that today was shrimp day. Nothing speaks to Dig like the fried shrimp from Catch-22. It's his favorite."

"How do you know?"

"You're not the only one around Proper who notices things about people. Besides, it's good for a woman to pay attention to things like that. What's Tak Hoshiyama's favorite food?"

"I have no idea."

"You've got a lot to learn," she said, shaking her head. "Good thing I'm here to teach you." She unlocked the trunk and pulled out a large tiger-striped blanket and a couple of pillows.

"How far are you planning on taking this?" I asked.

"Ambiance, baby girl. I might be in a tow yard, but I'm not gonna eat my shrimp off the manifold of one of these cars."

When Dig returned, he was in a different shirt and smelled vaguely of Acqua di Gio. I hid my smile. One of these days, he was going to wear Ebony down.

"Must be nice collecting a check from the mayor's office," I said. "How do you negotiate a job like that?"

"Same as any other job. Cost of towing, cost of parts, and cost of labor. Once you compromise your standards and let the man know you're available to the highest bidder, things get complicated. People start to think they can buy you. Dig Allen doesn't have a price." He looked at Ebony and smiled. "How about we get at that shrimp before it gets cold? I got a bottle of champagne on ice in the office. Been saving it for a special occasion." He looked at me again, and I gave him points for keeping any possible disappointment from showing. "You coming with, Margo?"

"You two go ahead. I'd rather have a look inside the trailer by the curb," I said.

"Sorry, no can do."

Ebony put her hands on her hips. "How come?"

"That was part of the job. Get the trailer away from the festival and leave it locked. Somebody's supposed to come by in the morning and move it to the graveyard."

"You mean it's broken down? You can't fix it?"

"I could fix it if that's what they wanted, but it's not. No point wasting any time on that trailer now. It's getting compacted in the morning."

Chapter 30

"WHO'S GOING TO impound the trailer?" Ebony asked.

Dig shrugged. "Tow job came from that guy who wears the flowered shirts. What's the big deal? One of the Zips dies and it gets replaced. Happens all the time."

"Dig, that's not a Zip bus," I said. "That's the trailer that Ronnie Cass was in when she was murdered."

We all looked at each other. I didn't know what either one of them was thinking, but it seemed pretty significant to me that Joel V. had given instructions to tow the trailer the day after the murder, and even more significant that he'd made arrangements to destroy it. I wasn't sure how that fit into his job responsibilities as festival publicist. More likely than not, it didn't and he'd found a way to take advantage of the foot he had in the door of the mayor's office.

"Can I use your phone?" I asked.

Dig nodded. "Inside, on the counter. You okay?"

I looked back and forth between Ebony and Dig's faces. "Don't let that shrimp get cold on my account," I said. I left them standing by the Zip-Three and went inside. By the time I reached the phone, I knew there was only one person I could call.

TWENTY minutes later, the Minnie Winnie pulled up behind the trailer. Good thing there weren't any other cars on the road, because it appeared as though my dad still had some trouble with the concept of parallel parking the vehicle. The engine idled while I crossed the lot and climbed inside.

"Where's Don?" I asked. "I already know you didn't go on a trip scouting golf uniforms, so don't lie to me."

"Don't worry about Don. He's someplace where nobody's going to find him. Get in and buckle up. I'm taking you home," my dad said.

"That's as good a place as any for us to talk about what's going on."

"There will be no talking. This has gotten too dangerous. After what happened in October, I'm surprised you ever leave the store."

"I'm surprised anybody lets me." I pulled the seat belt across the SECOND GUNMAN T-shirt and clicked it into place. The black knit cap was no longer simply a part of my costume, but served the secondary purpose of keeping me warm now that the sun had dropped. My dad pulled the Winnie away from the curb and drove to Disguise DeLimit. It was one of the rare occasions when neither of us talked.

By the time he parked, I knew things couldn't continue the way they had. Ever since I'd been back in Proper, it was like I'd become five years old in a town full of babysitters, and enough was enough.

"You always said I could talk to you about anything. Well, this might not be what you had in mind, but I didn't set out to be involved in Ronnie's murder. But because of my involvement with the festival and the fact that I'm the one who found Ronnie, I am. And because I care about Don's safety, I asked questions. And I found things out—things that could help him. And I know you lied to me when you said you two were going to Utah for golf clothes. You probably never left Proper City, let alone Nevada. I don't know where Don's hiding, but there's going to be a warrant issued for his arrest by tomorrow morning, and the evidence is pretty strong."

He stared at me for a few seconds. His expression reminded me of how he'd looked the day he gifted me fifty thousand airline miles so I could leave Proper City and travel the world. He'd wanted me to know what was out there—what I was missing if I stayed—but I knew, I could tell, that he struggled with me leaving. Until that day, it had been him and me. We were the only family each other had. I saw that same expression tonight and, like so many years ago, it broke my heart.

"Dad, I'm not asking to do anything crazy. I just want to talk. Maybe between the two of us we can figure out what's going on."

"You might look like your mother, but you think like me. Maybe Don does need your help." He cut the engine and turned off the lights. "Go inside the store, feed Soot, and get something to eat. Turn on lights, act like you're going to bed. At five till ten, bring the trash out to the curb. I'll open the back door to the Winnie and you get inside. If the door doesn't open, then I changed my mind."

"Or you could get out of the Winnie and come upstairs like you have your whole life."

"Okay, fine, we'll do it your way." He unclicked his seat belt. "And I take it back. Sometimes you're entirely too pragmatic."

MINUTES later we were seated kitty-corner at the kitchen table. My dad had scored it on one of his local flea market trips. His focus was supposed to be costumes and other related merchandise, but he couldn't resist unique—and often free—furniture donations. The chairs had come to us when a local restaurant had closed. The real score had been for Disguise DeLimit in the form of twenty-seven red and white checkered hostess dresses with matching aprons and hats.

"First, what's this about an arrest warrant?" he asked.

"I was at the police station today." He glared at me. "Let me back up. I dropped my cell phone in a sewer grate on Sunday. Actually, let me back up before that. The day Ronnie was murdered, I saw a blue domino mask on the sidewalk. I know I saw it. Except I didn't think anything of it because I was going to see Ronnie. But then I found her dead inside the trailer, and when I told the detective about the mask, she said her officers looked around and didn't find it."

"How sure are you that what you saw was a domino mask?"

"It was a royal blue satin half mask. It's not like it could have been a leaf."

"Okay, so you saw it. We can safely assume someone realized they left it behind and took it."

"Not necessarily. I found out later that Ronnie didn't perform at the rehearsal at the festival. Gina stood in for her—in her costume and mask and wig."

"The Casserole?" my dad said, using the nickname he and Kirby used behind Gina's back. "What does she have to do with anything?"

"She's Ronnie's daughter and Ronnie was ill. She couldn't perform. She asked Gina to do it for her but to keep it to herself. It wasn't public knowledge. And another thing. Gina told the detective that Don was her father."

"That can't be true. Don's relationship with Ronnie ended when she took off for Vegas."

"Could they have reunited?"

"It's possible, but why keep it a secret? He would have told me, at least. You mentioned Chet Lemming the other day. It could be him too."

"But that would mean that he and Ronnie had an affair thirty-some years ago."

"That's when she was in her prime." We both thought about that for a couple of seconds. "Go back to the mask," he said.

"It could be that Gina dropped the mask, saw me coming to the trailer, hid until I went inside, and then picked up the mask and took off. Or it could be that the murderer didn't realize that the mask fell out of the trailer when he or she left and it blew under the trailer into the sewer grate."

"Which is what you suspected so you tried to see and dropped your phone into the grate."

"Yes," I said, surprised. "How'd you know?"

He shrugged. "It's what I would have done."

Maybe Finn was right. Maybe the acorn didn't fall far from the tree. "Here's the big problem for Don, though. My phone didn't fall on a blue domino mask. It fell on a teddy bear."

"In the grate?"

"Yep. And that grate was directly under Ronnie's trailer. So it's possible that she put it there."

"Ronnie Cass was not the type to wiggle under a trailer that was parked on the street," he said.

"She wouldn't have to. According to Dig, all trailers and buses have access panels in the floor. Ronnie could have opened the access panel from the inside and un-screwed the sewer grate from inside the trailer."

"You met Ronnie. Does that sound like something she'd do?"

"No, but if she had something inside the trailer that somebody wanted, and she needed a safe place to hide it, maybe she would."

"You said it was a teddy bear. What's so special about that?"

I leaned back against the chrome bars of the chair. "It wasn't the bear, it's what she hid inside the bear. It was an engagement ring that said, 'To R, my favorite enigma. Love, D.'"

My dad leaned forward. "How do you like that. She still had the ring."

"Yes, and probably nobody would have found it except that I went to the police station for my phone. And we got to talking about why a teddy bear would be in that grate, and one thing led to another, and now the detective thinks it's the piece of evidence she needs to link Don to Ronnie's murder, which is what she's using to get the arrest warrant. She thinks Ronnie left it there as a clue."

"No way. If she kept that ring all this time, it meant something to her. She wouldn't use it to incriminate him. More likely she hid it as a message—an apology." He stood up and opened the fridge, pulled a small gray plastic bag of old coffee grounds out and set it on the counter. I sat, silent, as he rinsed the coffeepot. He pulled out the used filter and set it on the counter while he fitted a new one in. Long ago the rest of the world had moved on to fancier coffeepots and premeasured pods, but not Dad. Once a week he divided the contents of the paper shredder into three plastic garbage bags and dumped soggy coffee grounds on top of each one. It was a tip he'd picked up from his conspiracy circles. Old habits die hard.

He finished prepping the coffeepot and clicked the on button. Soot jumped onto the windowsill. A small nut fell from the roof and landed on the outside sill. Soot raised a paw and swatted at the glass. I stepped closer to the window and looked outside.

"Dad, where's Don?"

"Don is someplace nobody would think to look."

I stood up and crossed the kitchen and raised the sash on the window. The round object that had landed on the sill was an acorn.

"Dad," I said. "Is there something you want to tell me?"

He stuck a finger inside the collar of his shirt and tugged it away from his neck. "I already told you. The pictures of the meteor shower in Moxie didn't turn out, so I set the telescope up on the roof."

I picked up the broom from where it was wedged between the refrigerator and the wall and banged the end of it against the ceiling. A few seconds later, the ladder alongside the house creaked and then Don appeared. He descended the rest of the rungs and let himself into the store. By the time he joined us in the kitchen, my dad had a hot cup of coffee waiting for him.

He was a little worse for wear than the day I'd paid him a visit at his house. His black long-sleeved T-shirt had picked up pieces of dried leaves and his charcoal gray pants looked like they'd been lived in. He adjusted his wire-framed glasses, though they seemed to be permanently twisted.

"What do you remember from the day you found Ronnie?" he asked as if he'd been part of the conversation all along.

"The door wasn't locked or even closed properly. I knocked a couple of times, and then I went inside. She was sitting in a chair, all dressed up for her performance. Costume, wig, the whole nine yards. I didn't even know which one she was—until I touched her and she fell over." I shuddered at the memory.

"What else do you remember?"

"Her wig fell off and there was blood on the side of her head."

"So whoever killed her put her wig on her head to hide the wound."

The ringing phone interrupted our conversation. I'd gotten better at ignoring it, but with Don and my dad in the chairs in front of me, I thought it best to face the music.

"Margo, this is Detective Nichols. Do you happen to know the whereabouts of Don Digby? I'm standing here with a warrant for his arrest."

Chapter 31

DETECTIVE NICHOLS ARRIVED seventeen minutes later. After hanging up, Don, my dad, and I spent the next seven and a half minutes trying to find a better suspect. When it became obvious that there was no easy answer, we changed course. The new number one order of business was to find a new place to hide Don, and on short notice, only one location sprung to mind.

I pulled Don down the stairs into the costume shop and handed him a long brown wig and a blue flowered overcoat. "Put these on and go to Landis House," I instructed him. "They'll help you. They have a no-questions-asked policy." I handed him the keys to Dig's Le Sabre and practically pushed him out the door.

I was waiting on the opposite side of the back door when the detective arrived. She rang the bell and I opened the door quickly. She was startled. "I was waiting for you," I said by way of explanation. "Come on in."

She followed me through the back door and down the

hallway that led to the stairs. I started up and then stopped and turned back around. She stood by the bottom step, staring into the store.

"Must have been fun, growing up here," she said. I was taken aback by the wistful tone of her voice. She cleared her throat and I led her up the stairs.

"Hi, Jerry," she said. She glanced around the kitchen. "What's this about evidence?"

"Have a seat." He gestured toward one of the vacant chairs at the table, and then picked up the pot of coffee and poured her a cup. He set it by the vacant seat. She picked it up and breathed in the scent, and then set the mug back down on the table in front of her without taking a sip. He topped off his own mug and held the pot up and looked at me. I shook my head no. Detective Nichols took one seat and he took another.

"I'll let you two talk," I said. I kissed the top of my dad's head. "See you later." I ran downstairs and pulled a black down-filled puffy vest from our *Deadliest Catch* costume over the SECOND GUNMAN T-shirt. I grabbed a backpack, put my wallet into the zippered pocket, and lingered for a few seconds by the bottom of the stairs to hear how things would play out.

"As you know, Don Digby and I have started a newspaper, the *Spicy Acorn*," my dad said. "We've been conducting research for an upcoming article about hospital negligence and uncovered some questionable activities that are taking place in Proper City."

"This relates to the open investigation of Ms. Cass?" she asked.

"It may. I'll let you be the judge. My source tells me—"

"Your 'source'?" she interjected. I leaned closer to the

bottom of the staircase so I could hear this part more clearly.

"I'm a reporter, Detective. I feel an obligation to you to disclose what I found out, but my information channel is protected by the Constitution of the United States." I imagined him smiling his charming smile, the one that got him extra breadsticks at Catch-22. "I thought it best to tell you what I could and let you follow up in the form of an official investigation."

WHILE my dad kept Detective Nichols occupied with stories about city-wide conspiracies, I snuck out the back door and rolled my scooter into the alleyway. I needed to go to Bobbie's booth at the festival and find the other bear from Ronnie's trailer. I didn't know why that bear was important, but when I connected the dots between Ronnie and Chet, the bear had been there all along. If teddy bears could talk, I had a feeling that one would make an even better informant than I had.

I drove to the PCP and parked my scooter next to a picnic table. The park was deserted. Where was the festival security? I set my helmet on the table next to the scooter and put my keys into the pocket of the puffy vest. We were less than a week into the festival, and it was normal for the staff to thin down to a skeleton crew after they knew how many people it would take to patrol, but with the recent murder, I'd expected the mayor to keep security staff on around the clock. Instead, the festival grounds felt like the backdrop for a fake ghost-town party minus the dry ice and fog machine. The tents, colorful and welcoming by day, shuddered with the nighttime breeze, creating flapping sounds as the heavy canvas snapped back and forth with the shifting wind.

I walked past Candy Land, through the temporary maze of festival booths. Ebony had used colorful snap-together foam tiles to create a path, painting instructions like "Advance two" and "Lose your turn" on alternating steps. It was the game within the game-themed park, the most minimal way to participate without patronizing any particular booth. My footsteps were quiet and cushioned, and I watched my sneakers move from red to blue to yellow to black, red to blue to yellow to black. I paid little attention to my surroundings, until I heard muffled sounds coming from a booth by the main stage.

I dropped to a crouch, and then advanced slowly on the path. When I reached the corner, I put my hands on the aluminum pole that anchored the last booth and peered around the side. A light was on inside Bobbie's booth and a large figure dressed in the teddy bear costume was moving around.

I held on to the pole for support. The whole reason I was here was to get to Bobbie's booth. Was that what someone else was doing too?

I was too far into the park to turn back now. If I left, there was a good chance the person in her booth would see me. I looked around again for security, and then it struck me: whoever was in the booth knew the park would be empty. I peeked from around the pole and watched the bear's paws reach up and undo the ties on the back of the bear costume. He bent forward and let the fur suit fall forward, exposing a floral shirt and striped pants. I didn't need to identify the face to know who was wearing it.

Joel V., the festival publicist.

The way we'd designed the costume was to put additional brown fur at the base of the head, like a dickie. When the rest of the costume was on, there would be no gap between the head and the body. Inside the head, there were mesh inserts by the bear's eyes to allow the wearer to see. The design had been specifically customized to put the eye holes near the costume eyes so the mannerisms and gestures of the bear would be that much more believable.

I stepped inside the tent and scanned the items I'd brought from Disguise DeLimit to sell at the festival. Colored hairspray, domino masks, short black wigs, and costumes. Under the cover of the booth, I pulled off the knit hat and tucked my own hair under one of the jet-black wigs, and then pulled on a blue domino mask. I grabbed a can of colored hairspray, popped the cap off, and stepped out from behind the bookcase.

Joel froze. He looked behind him, the bear head still on. The quick turn of his head had made the bear head shift, and it no longer appeared that his eyes were lined up with the vision holes. He reached up to the head. I raced up to him. The second the head was off his shoulders, I let loose with the hairspray.

He cried out in pain and threw his hands up in front of the spray. In the minimal light of Bobbie's booth, I could see that the color I'd grabbed was green. Joel's face, hair, and hands turned a chalky alien shade. He swatted at the air trying to hit me, but with his vision temporarily clouded, he couldn't see well enough to connect.

"Stop it, would you? You're going to ruin my shirt!"

He was worried about his shirt?

I stopped spraying and stepped backward. I kept the can in front of me. He wiped the green away from his eyes, leaving finger-width streaks on his cheeks and temples. When he opened his eyes, he looked startled. "What is it with you divas? If you ask me, you're all crazy. Didn't anybody tell you that you're not expected to perform anymore?"

I stood in front of him, not saying anything, not moving. After a few seconds, I slowly shook my head from side to side.

He looked at my face, at the can of hairspray, and then back at my face. "Don't tell me. Somebody changed their mind again. Was it Ebony? Or the mayor? When I took this job, my only requirement was that I was kept in the loop. And now what—you're back on the program and nobody told me. That's just great. How am I supposed to promote this thing when I don't even know what's going on?" He tossed the bear head on the table. It landed on its side and rolled off, falling onto the patchy brown grass. Neither one of us made a move to pick it up.

"Fine," he said. "You want to practice in the middle of the night? Go crazy. Like I told the other one, don't bother me and I won't bother you."

"What other one?" I asked.

"How should I know? In those wigs and masks, you all look the same to me."

"Why are *you* here?"

"I saw this costume earlier today and came tonight to try it on. A life-sized teddy bear is good publicity for this festival. The lady who runs this booth said the guy who was supposed to wear the costume skipped town and she needed a replacement."

"Bobbie told you that?"

"Is Bobbie the preppy one who makes the bears?" I nodded. "I asked her about the costume and she told me her original idea. I thought it would be a good diversionary tactic."

"But you're the festival publicist."

"Sometimes you do what you gotta do." He untucked his floral shirt and rubbed the tails over his face. "My dry cleaner is going to love me," he said. He picked the bear costume up off the patchy yellow grass and placed it on the empty padded hanger, and then hung it back on the bookcase where it had been earlier in the day. Next he picked up the bear head and put it on the shelf. He wasn't acting like a killer who was caught in the act of looking for evidence. He acted like a publicist who was looking forward to his current job being over.

"Practice your routine all you want, now. The place is all yours."

"Where's security?"

"Cut from the budget. This festival is bleeding money right now. Some new guy in the mayor's office red-lined any nonessential expenses. Better not blame me. I did *my* job." He turned to look at the empty stage. He rubbed the back of his hand across his eyes one more time and left.

I stood inside Bobbie's booth. Something Joel had said didn't add up. Bobbie had told him that Don had bailed on her? She wouldn't have done that, not after I told her what was going on. And the only new guy I knew of who worked in the mayor's office was Tak. He wouldn't have canceled overnight security. Businesses all over Proper—including his parents'—had brought expensive equipment and inventory here to fulfill the annual expectations of the residents.

Something else was going on. Why else would the divas be here to rehearse for a performance that was never going to take place? Alone, at night, with no witnesses.

But Joel hadn't said that he saw *all* of the divas. He'd only mentioned one. The wig and mask made him think I was another one. But what if I was accidentally walking into a trap? Something still didn't add up.

In the past, when things hadn't added up, I talked them over with Tak. But this time, it felt like Tak was on a different team. This was the exact reason why I avoided relationships. Getting close to someone made you vulnerable. Start to think someone is there for you, and it hurts more when they're not.

I bent down to pick up the head of the teddy bear costume and spotted a set of keys in the dirt. A brass *V* hung off of the chain. I picked them up and looked around for Joel. He wouldn't get far without them.

I grabbed my can of green hairspray and moved out of the booth toward the stage. If there were other divas in the park and there was a cloak-of-night rehearsal, that's where they'd be.

But they weren't. The stage, both front and back, was empty.

I walked around the setup of white plastic folding chairs and stared at the stage from the back. Less than a week ago, I'd stood here, watching the divas interact. For the rehearsals that Ronnie had shown up for, she'd been argumentative, nasty, inconvenient, late, hostile, and opinionated. Now I knew she was just trying to keep people from knowing she couldn't perform. She'd hijacked the value of the troupe, trademarked their name, and negotiated with the mayor for the profits to go directly to her.

But the Domino Divas wouldn't even be here if not for her. Ronnie had been the one to pull them out of retirement, to find each one of the other five women and convince them that the value of stepping back into the limelight outweighed their comfortable lives fifty years after they'd been stars. By reuniting them, pulling them back onto center stage, she'd made at least one person risk everything, and that one person had killed her.

I circled around the back of the stage and spotted someone in Bobbie's booth. Joel, most likely, back for his keys. I crossed the patchy grass and called out to him.

"Joel," I called, "I have your keys. I didn't want to leave them sitting out overnight."

I approached the booth with his keys in my hand. Only it wasn't Joel in the booth.

Chapter 32

THE DOMINO DIVA who stood inside Bobbie's booth was dressed in a wig and blue mask, just like me. She turned around slowly. For a few seconds, we faced each other in silence. The only sound was that of the nighttime breeze rustling the trees above the tents and the canvas snapping back and forth as the wind shifted.

Considering I was dressed like a diva, this woman should have been surprised to see me. But she wasn't. Aside from her wig and mask, her body was covered in black clothing and gloves. There wasn't an inch of recognizable anything. Whoever she was, she'd come here planning to go undetected.

With a scan, I took in the teddy bears in *Clue* costumes that had been thrown to the ground around her feet. It took half a second to realize that many of them had been destroyed, their heads torn from their bodies. The bookcase behind her was half empty. She was looking for something. Perhaps the same bear from Ronnie's trailer that I'd come for. The bear that Chet claimed to have found discarded on a table.

I went into the booth and picked up the teddy bear on the end of the shelf. The diva in front of me watched as I turned it over in my hands and then set it back down. I picked up the next one and did the same thing. My mind raced. What was I looking for? And then I saw it.

Red thread and a bit of gray stuffing jutted out from the neck seam of one of the bears that had been thrown to the ground. Gina had admitted to doing last-minute alterations on the diva costume in Ronnie's trailer. She'd used the red thread and left the threaded needle sitting on the countertop inside. I'd stabbed my hand on it when I was in the trailer. Someone must have opened his seam and hidden something inside of him, just like they'd done with the teddy bear in the sewer grate.

But the diva in front of me didn't know which bear had been tampered with.

Time to bluff. I tossed Ronnie's bear behind my feet and reached for the third bear from the second shelf from the ground and held him up. "Is this what you're looking for? The bear that was in Ronnie's trailer when you killed her?" It was a risky statement considering the bear I held wasn't any more special than the rest of them. It was a trick I'd learned while working as a magician's assistant. Confidence and misdirection. And until I knew the diva's identity, it was the only trick in my arsenal.

There were six original divas—one murdered left five—and one stood in front of me. So, which one did she think I was? Of everybody who'd been involved in the murder I could only think of two people who'd donned the costume: Jayne Lemming and Gina Cassavogli.

But I couldn't dismiss the possibility that someone had taken advantage of the matching costumes. Someone who wanted me to think that they were one of the six—now five—performers. Someone who'd had access to the divas' schedule and costumes back in the '60s and had robbed the savings and loan. Someone who had a reason to want to keep them from returning to the stage fifty years later.

Someone who had been on the fringes of their group in high school, who could have easily faked the documents that claimed the gold in the Proper City Savings and Loan wasn't real. My memory flashed to the trophy case at Proper City High School. *Young and ready to take on the world.* It wasn't a headline, it was a caption. Ronnie hadn't been alone in the picture even though she'd caught my attention. She'd been standing with Wharton Young. He was the "Young" in the picture. She was the "ready to take on the world."

My mind raced with pieces of trivia, testing shapes to fit into holes like a giant game of Concentration. Bank robbery in 1968—Wharton Young could have been there. He left Proper City shortly after the robbery, returning years later with Ronnie on his arm. Keep your friends close and your enemies closer. He'd romanced her in order to make sure she didn't know anything—and if she did, that she wouldn't tell.

But maybe, after all these years, after the diagnosis that told her she was sick, she'd changed her mind about keeping the secret. She'd been the one to negotiate the Domino Diva gig from his office. She'd wanted to let Mayor Young know that her time had come.

Mayor Young had been the one to demand that Ronnie's trailer not be on festival property. He approved a trailer for her—not the divas, but her—which allowed him to know where he could find her. And the picture in the trophy case at Proper City High School showed a very different Mayor Young than the one who paraded around the festival in his suspenders and belt over a spreading middle. Fifty years ago, he'd been a skinny guy. He could have donned Ronnie's wig and mask the day the savings and loan was robbed and nobody would have been the wiser.

And tonight, he could have hidden his spreading paunch under the black sweatshirt and pants of the person in front of me. The jet-black wig and the satin domino mask all but eradicated any hint of his identity. But the pieces all fit. Mayor Young had killed Ronnie Cass. And if I didn't stop him, he was going to kill me too.

I dropped the backpack from my shoulder and shoved the wrong bear inside. I put the backpack back on and glanced around for something—anything—that would confirm that I was right. There were no keys, handbags, or otherwise personal items in the booth. And worse—he was dressed in the most nondescript outfit imaginable. No identifying characteristics.

Except for the feet. Really giant feet in black leather rocker-bottom sneakers.

I took two more steps backward, moving past the booth into the open part of the park where Bobbie and I had done early morning yoga. "You won't get away with it, Mayor Young. I know you killed Ronnie Cass," I said.

He reached up and pulled the wig from his head with one hand and the mask from his face with the other.

"Well, well. If it isn't Proper City's resident girl sleuth. Looks like I'm not the only one who decided on a new look for tonight."

I'd forgotten that I was dressed in the diva costume too. I pulled off my own wig and mask and faced him. "It's not the first time you put on that costume, is it, Mayor? You dressed like that to rob the Proper City Savings and Loan fifty years ago."

"And why would I want to do a thing like that?"

"To steal the gold."

"I thought I read an exposé in today's issue of *Spicy Acorn* that says there was no gold." He pantomimed unfolding a newspaper and flipping through the pages. "Yep, right there. It says here it was a myth dreamed up by the city planners to instill trust in the town residents."

"You faked those documents that said the gold wasn't real. Why?"

"Diversion and publicity for Proper City. When people start to see us as the city with gold that wasn't gold, they'll forget about the robbery. I need them to forget so I can finally cash in."

"You've been sitting on the gold all this time? Where is it?"

"I've already said too much. Besides, you'd have a hard time proving any of these accusations this far after the fact," he said.

"Ronnie knew all along. She was part of it. That's why you killed her. After fifty years of silent agreement, she let you know that she could destroy you with one press conference."

"I killed Ronnie Cass. She won't be holding any press conferences now."

"She won't have to. She left enough evidence behind to lead the police to your office."

"That's why you have to give me the bear, Margo," he said. He reached under his sweatshirt and pulled out a pistol. "Give me the teddy bear and nobody gets hurt."

Movement to my right caught my attention. I turned and saw the giant teddy bear walking toward me.

"Joel!" I called out. "Can you come here and help me?" I yelled. I stepped further into the clearing.

"Joel?" Mayor Young said. "My Joel?" He stuffed the pistol back into the pocket of his sweatshirt and ran his hand over his thinning hair. The giant bear stalked toward us. As he grew closer, I saw his hands—paws—curling and uncurling. Joel V. worked for the mayor. Was he in on the mayor's illegal actions? Had I bought his innocent act earlier, and if so, was I alone in the park with not one but two killers?

As the bear approached, Mayor Young's face settled into an unnerving smile. "Joel, I need you to do me a favor. I caught this woman pillaging from the festival. Please escort her off the property."

No way was I walking away from Mayor Young—not if it meant taking a bullet in the back. "Don't do this," I said. "He's a killer! You don't have to be a part of this. Help me," I pleaded. "He killed Ronnie Cass!"

The mayor pulled the pistol out again. It fell from his gloved fingers. He reached down. The giant teddy bear pushed me out of the way. He tucked his head and charged like a bull seeing a red flag, knocking Mayor Young to the ground. The teddy bear straddled the mayor and pinned his arms to the ground.

"Call the police," he said. His voice was muffled by the teddy bear head.

"I can't. I don't have a phone."

"Reach into the back pocket of the costume."

I approached the teddy bear and pulled a cell phone out of his pocket, and then called 911. "This is Margo Tamblyn. This is an emergency. I'm at the PCP with Mayor Young. He has a gun. He killed Ronnie Cass. Send the police as soon as possible."

The emergency operator kept me on the line while she alerted the police. She asked me a series of questions: What happened, was I alone, was I in danger? I refrained from telling her that a giant teddy bear had overcome the mayor and was holding him until the police arrived. I suspected it would damage my credibility.

Sirens alerted us to the arrival of the police. Thick beams of light slicked through the darkness, moving up and down, back and forth, as if painting the festival with broad, temporary brushstrokes of illumination. "Over here," I called. The beams of light played on the three of us as the officers grew closer.

Detective Nichols led the group. She flashed her light over me first, and then the two men on the ground and the surrounding mess of decapitated stuffed bears. "What's going on here?" she asked.

"Mayor Young admitted to killing Ronnie Cass," I said. "He pulled a gun. Joel's been holding him since I called."

"Is this true?" Nichols asked the giant bear.

"She's telling the truth. I heard the whole thing."

Detective Nichols knelt down and secured cuffs on

Mayor Young and then tapped the bear on the shoulder. "I'll take it from here," she said.

The bear stood up and swung his head to the left and to the right. "One question," he asked. "Who's Joel?"

"I thought you were Joel," I said.

The bear reached up and pulled off the bear head, revealing bright, copper-colored hair.

"Grady? What are *you* doing here?"

Chapter 33

GRADY RAN THE back of his arm across his forehead, freeing a lock of red hair that had stuck thanks to perspiration. "I had to chaperone my little brother on a date tonight. I'm killing time until their movie is over. Bobbie recruited me to wear the costume at the festival tomorrow. I came over to try it on."

"But Joel said— Where is he?"

"Is Joel the skinny guy in the floral shirt?"

"Yes. Did you see him?"

"I caught him trashing the *Spicy Acorn* booth."

"Where's he now?" I asked.

He looked at me oddly. "I have a financial stake in the success of *Spicy Acorn*. That guy was trying to destroy what they'd worked for. You didn't think I was going to let him get away with that, did you?"

"Um, Detective Nichols? Before you leave you might want to check on the striped tent on the other side of Candy Land," I said.

She looked at Grady and at me. "I don't suppose either of you have any proof that what you're telling me is true?"

I stepped into the booth and picked up the teddy bear with the loose head. I looked him in the face. "I'm really sorry about this," I said, and then I put pressure on the red stitches that held his head to his body. After they popped, I reached inside the opening and felt around the fiberfill until my fingers closed on a small, hard item. I pulled out a miniature camera and held it toward the detective. "I'm pretty sure this is the proof you're looking for."

She took the camera, turned it over, and pressed a few buttons.

"The battery's probably dead," I said, "but I think when you charge it and check the recording, you'll find out who killed Ronnie Cass."

"This was hidden in the bear all this time?" she asked.

"Thanks to Bobbie Kay, everybody in Proper has a teddy bear. Who better to keep a secret?"

THE first publication to break the news was *Spicy Acorn*. In addition to what went public, Don added a first-person tribute to Ronnie Cass. Whatever fame and fortune she'd sought over the course of her life couldn't possibly compare to her newfound reputation as Proper City's darling. Don's reputation around town had gained a new sheen too. Twice when Don and my dad thought nobody else was around, I caught them discussing the order their names would appear when they won the Pulitzer.

A small group of those of us involved had been granted permission to view the footage at the police station. The recording device that had been hidden in the bear caught more than any of us had expected. First, a fight between Gina and Ronnie. My knock on the trailer door interrupted the argument, right after the crash and scream that I'd heard from the sidewalk. Others might have seen a typical mother-daughter tête-à-tête, but I didn't know what one of those was like. Ronnie told Gina to make sure she stayed in costume any time she was at the festival—that it would jeopardize Ronnie's reputation if anybody knew she wasn't the one performing. Gina, usually quick with a disparaging remark, had lashed out. The last words that Ronnie ever spoke to her daughter: "And don't forget: you're only the center of attention because everybody thinks you're me." No wonder Gina acted the way she did.

The next clip was Ronnie talking to the camera. "I've waited a long time for this," she said. "Fifty years. Don, you always said you wanted the scoop of the century, right? If all goes as planned, this should make up for what I did to us." She held up an engagement ring. "There are two things I've held on to for all these years. The truth about the Proper City robbery and this. It's time to let go of them both."

The third clip—the money shot—was what Wharton Young had been hoping to destroy. His visit to Ronnie's trailer. Her accusations. His denial and her proof. "I know the truth. I've kept your secret all these years—my insurance policy." She turned her head and coughed. "Turns out that's exactly what I need. Insurance. I'm sick, Wharton, and the only way I can afford treatment is for you to pay my medical bills. You want me to keep quiet about the gold theft and the way you faked documents in the mayor's office to make it look like the gold wasn't real? How you traded the real gold for campaign support? How the entire incorporation of Proper City is your way of paying back the people who got you elected and kept you in office all this time?"

"So what if I did? That gold bought me an introduction into the powerful circles that can make or break a political career. That gold put me on a rocket ship that's going to take me all the way to the White House. It's your word against mine, Ronnie. Nobody's going to believe an old dancer who couldn't make it in Vegas over the mayor of a city that's about to explode off the map."

"Maybe they won't believe me, but they'll believe you." She laughed. "And guess what? You just told them everything they needed to hear."

Wharton Young froze for a moment, his body very still while his eyes flicked around the interior of the trailer as if trying to find a camera. And then, swiftly, he grabbed a nearby frying pan. I didn't watch what I already knew had been caught on camera. Wharton killed Ronnie, and then took the black wig off the plastic stand and pulled it over her head to hide the impact wound.

He reached for Ronnie's hand and pulled away the engagement ring. A small teddy bear sat on the inside window ledge. Wharton picked up some scissors, cut a hole in the back seam of the bear, and shoved the ring inside. He dropped out of site. We couldn't see what he did, but we knew. He'd hid the bear with the ring inside the sewer grate under the trailer to implicate Don.

The last thing Mayor Wharton Young did before leaving Ronnie's trailer was to pause in front of her. "If I never see another domino costume, it'll be too soon."

Wharton Young had entered that trailer a thief. He left it a murderer. The very last thing on the recording device came about half an hour after Mayor Young had left. It was Ronnie, standing up and walking toward the bear. She picked it up and held it out.

"Take it," she said.

The voice of Chet Lemming answered. "You never could hold your liquor," he said. "You're lucky our daughter was willing to cover for you."

The last of my questions were answered. Ronnie had tried to give Chet the bear before she collapsed back in her chair and died. And Chet told us the one secret Ronnie had been willing to keep: that he was Gina's father.

WITHOUT a mayor to drive the attendance of the Sagebrush Festival, the vendors agreed to cut our losses and pack up. Even Ebony, who had done a bang-up job with the board game theme despite major obstacles, seemed happy to admit that it was time to move on. We were all looking forward to a new distraction, and Kirby's party for Varla was just the ticket.

I took one day to recover from my lack of sleep over the past week and then pitched in to help Ebony and Kirby. By Saturday morning, we were ready to roll. Kirby was on a special high. Grady had been held up at the festival because of what had gone down, putting Angus and Varla out past curfew. Even though they had a legitimate excuse for being late, her parents viewed Angus as trouble.

Saturday morning, Dig Allen delivered a package to Varla's house in his version of a DeLorean. It was the Le

Sabre that he'd loaned me. He'd removed the regular doors and welded on gull-wing doors that opened up and down instead of swinging out, and even added a make-shift flux capacitor to the interior. The package contained a powder blue strapless dress with several full crinolines underneath.

Kirby had borrowed an outfit from my dad's personal wardrobe: a vintage suit with narrow lapels and a skinny tie. And Ebony, who would be busy planning high school parties for the rest of her life if the reaction to what she'd accomplished was any indication, transitioned Proper City High School into the "Enchantment Under the Sea" set from *Back to the Future*. Even Principal Stanley had gotten in on the act, wearing a bald cap and strutting around, asking if anybody knew the whereabouts of Biff Tannen.

At the dance, Bobbie and I stood by the punch bowl acting as chaperones. "Do you think Proper City will ever be the same after this?" she asked.

I shrugged. "I don't know. A week ago we had a mayor, an annual festival, and a publicist. We had an unsolved bank robbery and two thousand residents who liked to dress in costumes. Today we're without a mayor, without a festival, and without a publicist. Nobody's pushing to incorporate Proper City. Probably nobody really cares what happens to us."

"What's going to happen to Tak?" Bobbie said. "Mayor Young wasn't exactly a good guy, but because of him, Tak had a job. Is he going to have to head back out there on a new job search?"

"I wouldn't worry too much about Tak Hoshiyama," said a familiar voice. Grady, looking James Bond handsome in a classic tuxedo, approached from behind us. He set a stack of *Spicy Acorn*s on the table in front of us and helped himself to a glass of punch. "I figured you'd want to join the cause."

The cause? I picked up a newspaper and flipped it over to see the headline: "Tak Hoshiyama—Proper City's Next Mayoral Candidate?"

I glanced up to the ceiling and wondered if there was a patron saint for this.

Recipes

SPICY ACORN TREATS

Wilton Chocolate Candy Melts
Chili powder
Unwrapped Hershey Kisses
Mini Nutter Butters
Mini semi-sweet chocolate chips

1. Put about 10–20 Wilton Chocolate Candy Melts in a microwavable dish

2. Microwave on 50 percent power for 30 seconds

3. Stir and repeat until discs are smooth consistency

4. Add 3 tsp. chili powder to melted chocolate, mix

5. Using chili powder/chocolate mixture as a paste, coat flat end of Hershey Kiss and attach to a mini Nutter Butter cookie

6. Swipe a small amount of chili powder/chocolate mixture on the flat end of a mini semi-sweet chocolate chip

7. Press the mini semi-sweet chocolate chip into the side of the Nutter Butter that is not connected to the Hershey Kiss

8. Set on tray

9. When you've made as many spicy acorns as you want, refrigerate for 10 minutes and then enjoy!

Tip: Serve with sprigs of mint to add to the appearance of acorn treats

———

SPICY ACORN SALSA

1 acorn squash
1 clove garlic
2–3 tbsp. olive oil
12 grape tomatoes cut in half
½ small red onion
1 jalapeño
1 bunch cilantro
1 lime
Salt to taste
Pepper to taste
Corn chips

1. Cut squash, scrape seeds and pulp. Peel. Discard seeds, peel, and pulp.

2. Dice squash

3. Mince garlic

4. Sauté diced squash and minced garlic in olive oil over medium heat for 10 minutes

5. Set aside and let cool

6. Dice onion

7. Mince jalapeño

8. Chop cilantro

9. Add juice from 1 lime

10. Add salt and pepper to taste

11. Combine all ingredients

12. Serve with corn chips

Costume Ideas for a
Conspiracy-Themed Party

Secret Service Agent
Alien
Man in Black
Grassy Knoll Shooter
D. B. Cooper
Fox Mulder
Dana Scully
Stanley Kubrick
Oliver Stone
The Knights Templar
The Masons
Elvis Presley
Lee Harvey Oswald
The Rothchilds
Count St. Germain

HOW TO MAKE A
SECRET SERVICE AGENT COSTUME

a. Black suit
b. White shirt
c. Black tie
d. Nondescript black shoes
e. Slick hair back with heavy hairspray or gel
f. Attach a curly white telephone cord behind one
   ear and tuck the other end into the collar of shirt
g. Aviator glasses
h. Clip on name badge that reads: "Secret Service"

Ready to find
your next great read?

Let us help.

Visit prh.com/nextread

Penguin
Random
House